# MASE

## STORM ENTERPRISES BOOK 5

**BJ ALPHA**

# AUTHOR NOTE

WARNING: This book contains sensitive and explicit storylines.
All content information can be found on my website. www. authorbjalpha.com
This book is recommended for readers ages eighteen and over.

# BLURB

**Mase**

It feels like I've waited a lifetime for this moment. A divorce. Freedom at last.

So, I downloaded the *Indulgence* app, at my best friends' insistence, and I intend on having the best night of my damn life.

A night of depravity.

Of sordid debauchery.

The darkness hidden inside me is about to be unleashed.

However, the girl stirs something inside me. An emotion I'm unprepared for.

I'm left wanting more after dreaming of freedom for so long.

Then my life takes an unexpected turn when my father's will is read and I discover I'm about to become the guardian of my younger stepsister.

My stepsister is the girl of my dreams.

My one indulgence.

**Summer**

I sold myself to the devil himself. A sinner. A handsome

stranger who unearths something inside me I never under-stood—until him.

One night to last me a lifetime. One night to enjoy my freedom.

When my guardian arrives, I realize one night will never be enough.

My secrets are about to be uncovered.

And Mase will do everything in his power to discover them.

# DEDICATION

If you've waited your entire life for that one person who makes you feel every emotion. The one who brings out the best in you, the worst too. When you find them, hold on to them with everything you have. Cherish them. Fuck them like it's the last time.

Make those memories and never let them go.

- Mase

# PROLOGUE

MASE

**TEN YEARS AGO ...**

MY PHONE BUZZES from beside me, and I groan as I roll over. It's too damn early for my alarm. Finally freeing myself from the tousled sheets, I hang over the edge of my bed and rummage around on the dresser until my fingers latch onto my phone.

Slowly bringing it to my ear, I press the button to answer the call. "Yeah?"

"Hello. Am I speaking to Mr. Mason Campbell?"

"Yeah," I grunt out while wiping the sleep from my eyes.

"Sir. This is Cheryl calling from New Jersey Hospital. I'm very sorry to inform you, but your wife has been involved in a traffic collision tonight."

My heart rate spikes as I peer at the empty space in the bed beside me. Tara was meeting with her friends for a girls' night—again, and knowing I was going to be up early in the morning for a meeting with the guys, she decided it was best if she just stayed over with them. Again.

"Is it possible for you to make your way over to us as soon as possible, please?"

I drag a hand over my head, trying to make sense of the call. Collision at 2:30 a.m.?

My throat becomes dry as anxiety rolls through me. "I-Is she okay?" I somehow manage to mumble, sliding off the bed, and start the process of getting dressed while the phone remains tucked at my neck.

The silence on the other end of the phone only adds to my fear. "It's best you come down as soon as possible and discuss her injuries with a doctor, I'm afraid."

My blood stills and a sickening feeling swells in the pit of my stomach. "She's going to be okay, though, right?" A lump gathers in my throat at the thought. I lost my mom in a traffic accident; I can't lose my wife too.

"I'm sorry, sir. I can't give you any more details."

Irritation takes over me, but I find myself nodding. "I'll be right there." I end the call.

After double-checking I have my keys, I check the time on the clock, and my nostrils flare. I want to demand more details. I want to know what the hell happened to my wife, and what the hell she was thinking. The girls were supposed to be watching a movie and ordering takeout while having a pamper session. None of that warrants being out so late.

I push my feet into my sneakers and head out of the door, my gut telling me something else has changed in our marriage. As the heavy ball of dread deepens, I head out of the door, hoping and praying my wife is okay, even if our marriage isn't.

———

My best friends and I are from affluent families; we met in boarding school and started our business, STORM Enterprises, five years ago. We already have a turnover in the billions, and it's only increasing. Growing and investing is our main goal right now, and with the connections, expertise, and money behind each of us, we're on course for creating the most successful enterprise in the United States. Something my father would be proud of … if I spoke to him—which I don't.

I never expected my life to take the turn it did, not in a million years.

Nobody tells you marriage is easy. Nope, not a damn soul. They all tell you it's hard work, a process of love and trust, something you build on as you grow old together. When I married Tara straight out of high school, it was because she was pregnant, and I've never shied away from that fact, nor has she.

I wanted to do the right thing by her, and I was determined to be the father I never had to our baby. I was going to be a better man; the man I wish my father had been to me and the husband my mom deserved.

Being the head cheerleader for the opposing school, Tara was the hot, forbidden chick everyone wanted to date, and I was the lucky bastard who snagged her.

She didn't come from money, but when I was dipping my dick, I didn't fucking care; I just didn't expect her to become pregnant a few weeks into us dating.

The moment Tara lost our baby, it felt like my world was coming to an end. I'd married the girl I barely had feelings for and promised her a future I could no longer see.

A family. A baby. That was what I signed up for, not the bullshit I later discovered about her.

Did I love her?

I don't really know what love is. I suppose I had at some point to have fought so long for us.

She has a way of sucking you in and keeping you. She's like a siren who lures you, making you feel like you're getting everything you ever wanted, when in reality, you never wanted it to begin with.

Now, as I sit next to the hospital bed with my leg bouncing, I know I can't take her secrets and manipulation any longer.

Something has changed in her recently; her lies and cold demeanor are destroying us. The way she's been avoiding spending time with me has stopped the arguments but created a distance between us I've only been too happy to have. But even I know, despite my traumatic childhood, this isn't normal, and this isn't good for either of us.

Of course, I'd never abandon her; I'd never leave her. I made her a promise, and my vows meant something, so I intend to follow through with them. But she's taken advantage of me for far too long now, and it has to stop.

Has to.

Her right arm is wrapped in bandages, her face marred with bruises, cuts litter her cheeks, and nausea coils in my stomach at the thought of how much pain she must be in. At least she isn't on oxygen or in a coma. That's what I keep telling myself.

She appears to be sleeping, and given her current state, that's probably best for her.

"Mr. Campbell?"

Slowly, I raise my head from staring at my clasped hands.

I clear my throat and meet the eyes of a doctor, one with sympathy oozing from him, and I swallow hard, knowing he's about to deliver some bad news.

"I'm Doctor Ford, and I've been caring for Mrs. Campbell. She was involved in a traffic collision tonight at approximately"—he checks his watch—"one-fifteen."

I nod, and he straightens his shoulders, releases a deep breath, then opens his mouth.

"I'm sorry to inform you, but the baby didn't survive."

A strange sound lodges in my throat, and confusion hits me.

My eyes bounce over his face before I look back at my

wife. Does he have the right woman? The right documentation?

"Baby?" I gulp out, in equal parts mortification and panic. There's no way in hell she was pregnant. None. She hasn't let me touch her in so damn long I've forgotten how she feels against me.

The doctor surveys me further and gives me a swift nod, clearly confident in his assessment. "Yes, sir. Your wife was five months pregnant."

Shock hits me right in the fucking chest, causing my lungs to burn. I throw my head back on a deep, sarcastic laugh that's so fucking loud it sounds maniacal.

The doctor flinches, and I can only guess I'm coming across as unhinged.

He stares at me with wide eyes, and I shake my head.

"My wife was not pregnant, never mind five fucking months. I'd have known if my wife was pregnant for five months!" Irritation infiltrates my bloodstream, and blood rushes in my ears. I grind my jaw from side to side, then lift my chin. "You're wrong," I declare.

There's no way Tara was pregnant. Hell, we haven't had sex in almost a year. She never wants it, tells me she hates me, and in those moments, I hate her too.

"I'm sorry, sir. I delivered the infant myself." He grimaces, and a flash of dread settles deep inside me. My heart squeezes tight, and I ball my hands into fists and continue shaking my head. I refuse to believe it. She wouldn't.

She cheated? My wife cheated on me. She was meant to be mine. We made vows, a promise to one another.

And worse, she got pregnant with another man's child, knowing how much I wanted that. Knowing how much it tore me up when she miscarried our baby. "There's been a mistake. There has to be," I whisper. Sure, she says she hates me, but this? She knows how much it would destroy me.

"I'm sorry, sir. There's no mistake." The solemn sound of his voice angers me. I don't need his pity.

Languorously, I push back in my chair, and the squeaking as it scrapes along the linoleum floor grates on my nerves. I stand to my full height, and the doctor takes a step back, with fear flashing in his eyes.

I'm tall—especially compared to his short ass—at six-three, so I must look like a giant next to him, but right now, I feel like the smallest man to ever live.

"Get me another fucking doctor and a second opinion. Now!" I bark, causing him to jump.

He nods frantically, like a fucking idiot, and heads toward the door. When he's about to go through it, he twists around to look behind him, and his eyes lock with mine. "Mr. Campbell. Just so that you're aware, the man Mrs. Campbell arrived with tonight passed away. His family is being informed now." He slips through the door, and my ass hits the chair, hard.

His words ring out in my ears like a warning siren. *"Mr. Campbell. Just so that you're aware, the man Mrs. Campbell arrived with tonight passed away."* She was with another man?

No, she was having a girls' night. A sleepover with friends. She told me she was.

My legs give way, and I slump against the chair as realization sets in. Unable to hide the hurt welling inside me, a pained gasp leaves my lips. "Please no, Tara." I hold the back of my neck with both hands and drop my head between my legs, trying to dispel the storm brewing inside me. Please no.

There's no way she'd betray me.

My lungs seize, and I struggle to suck in air. I can feel myself unraveling as my entire body shakes with a panic I can't contain.

She wouldn't. A sob catches in my throat, and I bite my lip to stifle its escape, trying desperately to remain in control.

No way.

She would never hurt me in that way. No, I refuse to fucking believe it.

Never.

We took vows; we promised one another a lifetime of commitment, love, and respect.

A lone tear trickles down my face, and an acute coldness takes over me while my mind races with the facts.

She was having another man's baby. The one thing I always wanted, and she knew it. I gave her everything, and she committed the ultimate betrayal, knowing how much it would hurt me.

"She told me she loves me," I whisper into the abyss.

Right?

Even as I tell myself all this, I feel it in the pit of my stomach, a sickening awareness coming over me. She lied to me.

I grip the arms of the chair as my world tilts on an axis.

She betrayed me, and there's no coming back from that.

In one night, our entire future is destroyed.

---

Another tear slips down my face, and I stare into the abyss, uncaring of how many hours have passed. She cheated and destroyed us after she promised us a future of happiness and loyalty.

I thought I'd escaped the path of deception when I left my father's home with her. I chose her; I promised her a lifetime of commitment, and I meant it. Jesus, I was prepared to fight for our relationship despite our flaws. Not once have I considered sleeping with someone else.

Losing our baby broke me; it's something I never want to experience again. Discovering she willingly chose to have a baby with someone else, knowing how much I wanted a family of our own, is what hurts the most. It twists my stomach at the thought of her doing this to me, to us.

"M-Mase?"

I slice my gaze to hers.

"I lost the baby, didn't I?" She reaches for my hand, but I keep them tightly balled at my side despite having a crazy urge to reassure her and protect her from the pain she's enduring. She's my wife, and she's in agony, the same pain we felt before, yet probably worse with how much she must have wanted this baby to carry it for so long in secret.

I clear my throat, but it's still scratchy. "Yeah. I'm sorry." My voice is monotone even though I feel sympathy for her. I want nothing more than to console her, but I'm broken, and I don't think there's any coming back from this.

"Mase, I need you." She sobs, and I squeeze my eyes closed as the harrowing tone of her voice has a flashback assaulting me.

*"Mase, I need you to promise me you're going to be a good man when you grow up." My mom pushes my hair off my face. She's kneeling before me with a bruised eye and a split lip. Her firm hand holds me in place with a harsh grip that is unlike her. The way her eyes bore into mine with desperation makes me nod, eager to comply and soothe her. "Say it. Say the words, Mase. Promise me you won't be like him," she says, giving me another swift shake.*

*I pull in a deep breath and broaden my shoulders. "I promise, Mom. I promise to be a good man." Her solemn face sparks with happiness, and a warm feeling spreads through me like a wildfire. I love making my mom happy, especially when my father makes her so sad.*

*"You're going to be a good man, Mason Campbell, I just know it. You won't let me down." She beams, and I replicate the expression, feeling it deep in my soul, and a determination sets in. I'll make my mom proud. My wife too. I'm going to have a family one day, one I will love and cherish, and they'll give me that very same feeling back.*

*Just like a family is meant to.*

"Mase, did you hear me? I said I need you." She sobs

louder as if feeling me slipping away. "It's happened all over again. My baby is gone; it's gone, Mase." Hearing her say that out loud causes a gut-curdling sensation to twist deep inside me. She's getting louder with each word she sobs, and I finally take her hand in mine and stroke her thumb. "Our baby is gone." My breath catches in my throat at the tortured sound of her wail.

"Shhh, it's okay. Everything is going to be okay." I stroke the hair from her face, and it seems to soothe her.

"Please. I need you. I need you more now than ever, Mason."

"I'm here," I whisper, but something has changed, something I can't acknowledge because I need to be here for her.

I need to follow through with my promise.

# ONE

**SUMMER**

I SWIPE my sweaty palms down my white linen dress and take a deep breath. This is it. This one night is going to change my entire life.

In only a few short months, I'll finally be free.

From the moment I was matched with this man on the *Indulgence* app, I felt a connection.

Of course, we've barely exchanged more than sexual preferences, but in his photo, I captured the longing in his green eyes that made them appear darker and found myself completely transfixed. The longer I looked into his orbs, the more I felt like I was seeing deep into his soul.

Something told me he'd been hurt, that this was more than sex for him, and I knew he would take good care of me just from the description on his profile. He was searching for something, and for tonight, I hoped that something was me.

If only for this one night, when I sold myself for someone else's pleasure.

My mind flips through some of our exchanges, and I'm quite possibly out of my depth.

Saintly Sinner: Are you as innocent as you're trying to portray?

Innocent Angel: Do you want me to be?

Saintly Sinner: Yes. Although, I'd love someone who is innocent but happy to feed into my darkest thoughts.

Innocent Angel: Like what? What dark thoughts?

Saintly Sinner: I want to take you roughly. Uncaring if I hurt you. But I want to know you're enjoying having me treat you like my fuck toy and using you.

Innocent Angel: I can be whatever you want me to be.

Saintly Sinner: I only want you to be one thing.

Innocent Angel: What's that?

Saintly Sinner: Completely innocent.

He asked for completely innocent, so that's exactly what he's going to get.

# MASE

The whiskey burns my throat as I knock back another glass. I contemplate using the little blue pill that Tate somehow managed to get a hold of for me, then decide against it. I've waited so fucking long for tonight—days, weeks, months, years, and the last thing I want is to fuck this up and to not feel everything after not feeling a damn thing for so long.

Besides, I pride myself on never doing drugs, especially after the shit that happened to Tara and the scumbag she got messed up with. When he and their baby died, I had a choice: to support my wife or walk away. She begged and pleaded with me, telling me she was addicted to prescription pills to help with her mental health, and I believed her. I shouldn't have, I should have walked the fuck away then and there and slammed the door behind me. Not spend nearly ten years trying to make us work, knowing damn well she was heartless.

I stood back and watched her fuck her way through the town. I listened with envy to my best friends' countless sexual encounters, and not once have I strayed.

But fuck, did I want to.

Until the guilt hit.

I promised to be a better man than the one I loathed, and I was, even if I didn't feel like it.

My body is ready for this, it's ready to be the person I so desperately want to be.

*Nope, don't need the little blue pill.*

My cock has been rock hard all day fucking long. So damn eager to slip inside Innocent Angel's pussy, it's painful.

Oscar O'Connell, a Mafia man with connections to Owen, provides an impeccable service to his clients who use his escort services. I bask in the elegance of the hotel penthouse, which is all part of the *Indulgence* experience, and my body fills with anticipation for the night ahead.

When my best friends talked me through using the app and making my selections, Tate encouraged me to select every fucking kink. However, Reed, who's become domesticated with his pre-made family, has given up using the app and suggested I start out with the basics of the services provided, including the penthouse that Tate described as "vanilla" as opposed to the sex dungeon he described as "dirty as fuck."

The room is nothing less than what you'd expect from a high-end service you pay over one million dollars for in order to receive the company of a woman matched to you for the night.

There's a bucket of the finest champagne, a bar, and the best and most-expensive view of Carbon Beach in Malibu.

A ginormous L-shaped white leather couch faces a huge flatscreen TV, one I already know has multiple hardcore porn films loaded at the ready, along with the possibility of camera functions that allow you to watch you and your partner on the screen. Something about that has adrenaline rushing through my veins.

I've never really considered myself a voyeur, not until that one time in Tate's office when he allowed me to watch him fuck Ava—his now wife—over his desk. I left there ashamed and embarrassed; I nearly came in my pants and told myself it was because it had been so long since I'd had any action at all. I'd previously been used to odd nights of spontaneous, mundane sex with my wife, who was only interested in my bank balance, and when even your own hand doesn't cut it anymore, anything out of the ordinary feels good.

The idea of someone watching me pleasure somebody else and using my body to bring them both to orgasm has my cock weeping with need. I was desperate for some excitement, and Tate gave me a glimpse into his passionate sex life, a stark contrast to the mundane sex I was used to. I'm not sure who he was doing it for, me or him. The man is obsessed with his woman, and who can blame him? Not only is she gorgeous and fiery, but she has a sensitive side reserved solely for her family, and she's slowly letting her walls down to allow us inside too.

A heavy sigh leaves me as anxiety makes a familiar appearance and ripples through my body. I check the time on my watch—another ten minutes.

Fuck.

I scrub a hand over my head, and my leg bounces. This better be worth it. This better be the best fuck of my goddamn life. I fucking deserve it.

Christ, do I deserve it.

Chewing on my bottom lip, I contemplate how this will go down. What the hell do I say to her? Reed ran me through it and told me to take charge, to be in control. That's something I've always wanted to do but have never been given the opportunity.

Tara always bounced from being celibate to wanting sex to appease me or to gain something for herself, and neither of those made me happy.

When my friends talk about their wild sexcapades, I sit back and watch the camaraderie with hope and, if I'm honest, jealousy.

I gave all that up multiple times over when I chose to

stand by my wife, to be the bigger person and trust in her when she betrayed me time and time again.

To be the husband my father never was.

To be the man I wanted to be.

But now, now I'm fucking free.

Free to be me.

# TWO

## MASE

THE SOFT KNOCK on the penthouse door jolts me from my thoughts, and I gasp like a lovesick teenager. My pulse races and my blood thickens with heightened expectation.

When we chose my first *Indulgence* woman, I didn't want someone with a multitude of experience despite Tate's encouragement to do so. I wanted someone who was as innocent as me and maybe only had minimal partners like me too. Not someone every fucker has been inside of for the right price, and Innocent Angel is that girl.

I clear my throat and broaden my shoulders. "Come in!" I say the words a little too loudly in an attempt to mask my nervousness.

My palms are sweaty, so I swipe them down my jeans, hoping she won't be able to tell I lack confidence. I'm on a mission to prove to her I'm everything she needs, if only for tonight.

The door opens, and I snap my gaze in her direction. The moment my eyes land on her, I suck in a sharp breath, and all ability to speak, to move, is stolen from me.

She's smaller than I imagined, fresh-faced with not a lick of makeup on, just as I asked. My mouth becomes dry as we hold one another's stare. Her long blonde hair is in a braid resting over her shoulder, glowing under the hallway light, and I fucking love it. She's like an innocent siren, calling to me and willing me to protect her. She reminds me of a librarian or something.

A good girl.

The blonde hair is not what I asked *Indulgence* for, but fuck me, do I like it.

Her pale skin is begging me to mark it, and my cock twitches at the thought.

Fuck me, where the hell did that come from?

Her cheeks pinken as she watches me with bright-blue eyes, causing my chest to restrict at the intensity behind them. She's stripping me bare, just as I am her. It's like I am looking into her soul, seeing her own anxiety and nervousness, her innocence. She's natural, with an edge of girl next door about her, she wrings her hands in front of her, giving away her discomfort.

When I said I didn't want someone like my wife, I wasn't quite prepared for this. The girl standing in the hallway is the complete opposite, and my cock is well and truly on board with the prospect.

She's in a white sundress, and her tits are on display beneath the fabric. They're on the smaller side, but not tiny; they fit her small frame perfectly. The thought of feeling the naturalness of them has my cock weeping. I can just make out her panties beneath the fabric of the virtually see-through dress, and I'm happy to see they're plain and not the skimpy lace, just as I requested. Innocence personified.

My hand trembles as I reach for my bottle of whiskey, and if I even attempt to pour myself another glass, it's going to end up all over me, so I take a swig of the bottle, hoping I look cooler than I feel.

"Do you want a drink?" I grunt out. "If you do, there's a bar over there." I tilt my head toward said bar, mainly because I'm so damn nervous I don't have it in me to walk, let alone make her a fucking drink.

She shakes her head, and it only emphasizes the blonde locks as the silky braid sways against her shoulder. "No, thank you." She rolls her hands in front of her, and I want to do something to comfort her, but I can't help but wonder if this is all part of the innocent act, what I'm paying for. My teeth grind together, another fucking manipulative woman.

Jesus, I'm such a fucking hopeless idiot. I scrub a hand over my head, hating the way my demons consume me. Then, with a heavy sigh, I lock gazes with her again.

"Are you going to come and service me? Or do I need a fucking refund already?"

She jolts, and I imagine my sharp tone and harsh words have hit her hard, but it's the truth, a deep-seated hatred of truth burning deep inside me. She's essentially a prostitute, an actress; this isn't a fucking date. It's a fuck I've paid for.

And I intend to treat it as such.

I will not get drawn into another woman's web of lies.

Nope. I'll use them—like they use me.

# SUMMER

"Are you going to come and service me? Or do I need a fucking refund already?"

His words hit me like a truck. My stomach tightens, and I try to contain the hurt lancing through my chest. After all, this is my own choosing. I'm selling myself, my virginity, to be precise, and as much as I'd have liked to save it for someone who means something to me, at least this way, I'm choosing who I'm losing it to. So, with that thought in mind, I lift my chin, straighten my shoulders, kick off my ballerina flats, and walk toward the handsome bastard wearing a smug grin on his face.

Saintly Sinner is his username, and my god, he has sinner written all over him. Broad shoulders are housed in a white T-shirt that stretches over his muscles. Tattooed skin can be seen beneath the fabric, and I long to explore it. His cropped hair is longer on top, a light shade of brown, maybe you could even class it as dark blond, and I can't help but smile when I imagine what beautiful blond babies we would create. The thought brings me to an abrupt stop, and I shake my head. *Summer, you idiot, don't be so childish.*

He takes another drink from the whiskey bottle, then swipes his hand over his mouth and studies me.

Ignoring the pounding of my heart, I saunter toward him, hoping the swing of my hips looks seductive and not as hideous as I feel.

His thick thighs are parted wide, and his green eyes dance with mirth as I look him up and down.

There's an obvious bulge in his jeans, and excitement rushes through me at imagining sitting in his lap and rocking myself over his hard length.

I'm not sure where the hell that thought came from, but my god, do I like the prospect of it.

"Fuck," he grunts and shuffles from left to right, then takes another drink, and my mouth falls open at the thought of him realizing I was daydreaming about his cock.

I tilt my head. I've heard stories about men not being able to keep erections due to alcohol intake. I wonder if he'll have this problem. Judging by the copious amount missing from the bottle, he's drunk a lot already.

"Get over here and put that mouth to work, sweetheart," he growls, popping open his jeans, his gaze never wavering from mine.

I plant my feet in the space between his legs, and before I know what I'm doing, my knees hit the plush carpet. Taking a deep breath, I steel my shoulders, and the scent of his bergamot cologne is so intoxicating I sway beneath his scrutiny, so my hand lands on his thigh to steady me.

*Jesus, I want to lick him.*

Saintly Sinner tangles his fingers in my hair, tugging my head closer, and with his other hand, he frees his thick, angry cock. I've never seen one so close before, so I swallow back the trepidation building inside me. It's girthy, rock hard, and long with a stream of pre-cum sliding down his shaft.

I barely have time to register what's happening before he's pushing his thumb into my mouth, forcing my jaw to widen, and shoving the thick head of his cock between my lip. He groans, then lifts his hips, sliding the bulbous head farther down my throat and causing me to gag until he eases himself back out enough to stop me from choking.

"Ah, fuck, you feel good," he grunts, and I glimpse up at him through my thick lashes to witness the most incredible sight.

His head is tipped back, his lips are parted, and the expression on his handsome face is one of clear euphoria. The fact that I've never done this before but have somehow drawn this reaction from him has my confidence soaring.

My body comes alive, and every atom inside me sparks to life at the look of pure ecstasy on his face. I want to witness it all night long and am determined to make that possibility a reality.

# THREE

## MASE

HER EYES FILL with tears as I thrust into her mouth again and again with powerful snaps of my hips. Watching her struggle to take me, her lips stretched to capacity and spittle somehow escaping her mouth, has a sick sense of satisfaction shooting up my spine.

When she moans, I almost come on the spot. "Oh, fuck, sweetheart," I mumble.

I've never felt anything like this before. Sure, Tara has given me head over the years, and I had the occasional blowjob before her in high school, but what I'm feeling right now is nothing short of sensational.

I yank her hair, encouraging her mouth back and forth as I fuck her face. She chokes and splutters but doesn't attempt to stop me from using her as I see fit.

*Jesus, she's incredible.*

"That's it." *Thrust.* "Take all that thick cock, little girl." *Thrust.* "Ah fuck, that's good." I pull her off for a few seconds, but her mouth follows my cock like a magnet, and my lip twitches. "You're hungry for it, you want this." I slap her cheek with my cock. "You want my thick cum to fill your hole, don't you?"

Her hooded eyes plead with me to deliver, so I guide myself back to her waiting mouth. When her tongue swipes over the swollen head, pre-cum streams from the slit.

"Fuck, you're a desperate whore." I slam back inside her mouth, unable to hold off any longer. "Take it all. Let me feed you my cum."

A choked moan escapes her lips, and I take pleasure in it. The sound is so erotic it sends a current of electricity through me. Like she's spurring me on, encouraging the filth.

After hearing my friends talk about their sex lives and never encountering anything of the sort, I'm starting to let my walls down. Embracing my demons, I let them show for the first time in my life.

My orgasm is fast approaching, and truth be told, I'm surprised I haven't come already. It must be the alcohol. "You're a filthy little cock sucker begging for my cum. Isn't that, right?" I pull my cock from her mouth, and her dazed eyes meet mine. *Jesus, she's stunning.* My parted lips release a whoosh of air as I take in her perfect features. Her beauty holds me captive while I wait for her to respond. A few freckles sprinkle her button nose, her hair is mussed, and her cheeks are reddened, with tears streaking down her flush.

She licks her lips, and my balls draw up with eagerness to spill inside her, pissing me off that a simple action can cause such an intense reaction from me. Anger combines with self-loathing, and it simmers through me, creating a toxicity of hatred I've no place feeling toward her.

"Answer me!" I demand. My words are as hostile as I feel.

She whimpers, and that only annoys me more, especially when all I'm asking of her is to want me, to receive what I paid for.

Am I really getting screwed over by a hooker now too?

My fist tightens around my cock, and I slap her cheek with

it, then drag the sticky head down her face, coating her in pre-cum and spittle. She startles at the action, causing me to chuckle. Then I lean forward and take hold of her chin. "Beg for my cum, little slut."

Her eyes widen, and she squeezes her thighs together, giving away her arousal at my words. It delights me, igniting a fire inside of me so strong, I threaten to combust here and now.

"Beg to taste my cum," I hiss through gritted teeth.

"Pl-please."

"Good girl." I smooth her tussled hair almost tenderly. Then, much more controlled this time, I push the head of my cock into her mouth, and she sucks me like a lollipop, almost making my eyes roll to the back of my head, but I'm determined to watch this, to see my sordid dreams become a reality. "You're to lick only the tip. Do you understand me?"

She nods frantically, her pupils blown wide as I jerk my cock with the tip in her mouth. When my slit widens, I withdraw from her wet mouth on a pop and watch in pure bliss as my warm, thick cum pumps out of me. I clench my teeth and lean over her face, with rope after rope coating her and that tongue. Fuck me, she laps at my slit like a starved animal, one greedy swipe after the other.

"Fuck, sweet girl," I groan into the room. "You're worth every damn cent."

# SUMMER

Every muscle in his body coils as he peaks. His orgasm rips from him in a roar of euphoria, causing his cock to jerk, and in its wake, he leaves thick white ropes of cum. I quickly swipe at it with my tongue while waiting eagerly for the next command.

I lap at his cock like a hungry animal. Watching the cum spill from the tip has my panties drenched. The saltiness hits the back of my throat when I swallow, and I welcome it. The masculinity radiates off him in heated waves of pleasure, causing my body to mirror his feral need.

"Fuck, sweet girl," he groans loudly. "You're worth every damn cent," he rasps, and like the desperate girl I am, I delight in his words.

As soon as he's finished coming, he drops back against the couch with a heavy sigh, and his chest continues to rise, leaving him breathless and gasping. Then he rolls his head forward slowly as if dazed. His green eyes lock with mine, and a smile curves his lips. "Fuck, that was everything I hoped for and more."

The contentment in his words has me preening, and I lick my lips, waiting for his next instruction.

He leans forward and traces my swollen lips with the tip of his slippery cock, and like the perfect submissive, I lick him clean.

"Are you wet?" There's hope in his tone, and any nervousness surrounding his intentions toward me is eradicated by that simple giveaway; he wants me to be aroused too. He's not a brute; he isn't going to fuck me, uncaring if I'm wet or not. No, this man wants my arousal as much as I do, even more so, judging by the promising gleam in his eyes.

Dominance radiates from him as he leans forward, and my cheeks heat further under his scrutiny. His attention latches onto my peaked nipples, then he quickly diverts it to my face, and the red hue now coats his cheeks too. I tilt my head to the side to survey his face. Embarrassment? Surely not.

This man is far too experienced to be feeling that. Anger, maybe?

His handsome face darkens. "Stand up and take your clothes off. I want to see what the fuck I'm paying for." Not giving me time to answer, he barks, "Now!"

Definitely anger. I just wish I understood why.

# FOUR

MASE

"STAND up and take your clothes off. I want to see what the fuck I'm paying for," I snap when I realize she's watching me a little too closely. "Now!" I don't want someone as experienced as her to know I've no clue what the fuck I'm doing, not really. I'm done with being the underdog, never feeling good enough.

It's my time now.

My time to be exactly who I want to be. Me.

Her face contorts into hurt, but she wastes no time masking her feelings. She rises to her bare feet, lifts the dress over her head, and drops it to the floor, then she shocks the hell out of me by locking eyes with me in a dare for me to command her. A potent blend of arousal and submissiveness swims in her eyes as she drags her panties down her legs to the floor.

Those glorious tits of hers are begging to be held, squeezed, licked, and kissed. Every inch of her is calling for me to explore and caress, and I intend to do just that.

My cock lengthens once again, and I chuckle, recalling

that Tate suggested I use enhancers to sustain a sexual appetite all night. There's no need for that, no need at fucking all. My cock is acting like it's on steroids, throbbing with a dull ache that begs to sink inside her tight pussy.

Jesus, she better be tight.

I brush a hand over my head and laugh. This night is turning out to be everything I wanted and so, so much more.

Please be tight.

If she is, *Indulgence* will be getting a full fucking five stars from me and a bonus.

Her cheeks flame, and she ducks her head, probably thinking my chuckle comes from her nakedness. If only she realized.

"You never answered me before." Her attention lands back on me, and I crook an eyebrow at her. "Is your pussy wet?"

She nods coyly, playing into the whole innocent act perfectly. I refuse to listen to the nagging voice in my head telling me this is all lies, a ploy to fulfill her role, to gain those five stars that will help her receive a bonus. Nope, instead, I'm opting to enjoy the million-dollar woman who is mine for only twelve hours. So, I'm playing along with her.

"Y-Yes."

"Good. Turn around and bend over. Touch your toes. I want to see that slick pussy."

She sucks in a sharp gasp, then slowly turns on the pads of her feet. My eyes lap up the sight as her perfectly toned ass comes into view. Fuck me, she's sensational. I almost swallow my tongue, my palms twitching to touch her, and my mind whirls with sexual possibilities.

Fucking her from behind while I watch my cock drive into her. Having her straddle me while I play with her tits. Her pussy on my face while I devour her. So much I want to do to that little body; I already know one night will not be enough.

A sound leaves her lips, something akin to a whimper as

she bends over, putting her small holes on display for me. Her asshole is bare and looks untouched, and my hand grips one of her cheeks, causing a startled yelp to leave her lips. I squeeze her ass while drinking in the spectacular view before me. "Did you leave some hair on that pussy for me?" I push two fingers between her legs, and elation floods me at how wet she is. Her arousal coats the tips of my fingers, and I rub them against my thumb in awe.

"Y-Yes."

"Good girl." Again, I stroke over her soft curls, relishing the feel of her soaked slit with each movement.

After knowing my ex-wife was continuously lasering off every hair on her body, I was determined to make this experience something completely different, so I requested for my *Indulgence* girl to have a small tuft of neatly trimmed pubic hair. Something the guys were shocked by. Bare pussy is the in thing right now, but I've no intention of feeling that again. Not when I can have the feel of this in the palm of my hand. I want a natural girl. "You're all nice and soft for me. All wet for me to slide my cock inside," I rasp, watching my fingers toy with the slick folds between her legs. "I'm going to fuck this pussy so good, my sweet girl." She mewls at my words.

Unable to help myself, I spit at the top of her crack, causing her to jolt, then stare in rapture as my spittle trails slowly down the crack of her ass and gathers at her asshole.

Fuck, yes.

My cock leaps with anticipation. Of course, the fucker wants in there. That's something I've never done before; Tara wasn't keen on trying it either. Apart from when I was determined to see our divorce proceedings through and she attempted to seduce me with filthy promises she'd no intentions of fulfilling. In the end, it was her tears and despair that broke me down. As it always did.

I remove my fingers from between her legs, and her body

sags a little, and I can't help the smirk that graces my face. She wants me.

This young, innocent-looking chick, who's hot as fuck, wants *my* cock buried deep inside her. "I wonder if I fuck you hard enough, if I can make it hurt, huh?" I muse to myself, fisting my aching cock to fullness. "I wonder if I can make you forget all others." I shake my head. "I'm sure as fuck gonna try."

She fidgets a little, and I lift my hips, imagining just that, gripping onto her slender hips and forcing her onto my cock. But I want to look into her eyes the first time I slam inside her. I want to witness the look on her face when I stretch her wide, when I use her like the whore I paid for.

"Ask me to lick your pussy, sweetheart," I groan, pumping up and down my length. "Ask me to lick your pussy juices away."

"Oh god," she pants.

The slapping of me fisting my cock fills the room. "Beg me to taste your wet pussy."

"Please."

"Please what, sweet girl?" I groan.

Her body rises on each breath, and I love the effect I'm having on her. "Pl-please taste my pussy."

My cock leaks streams of pre-cum over my fist, but I shake my head. "Not good enough, sweetheart. Beg!" I chide, with a sharp smack to her ass cheek that's bound to leave a mark.

"Holy shit. Please." She swallows audibly. "Please lick me. Taste me, Saintly Sinner." The sound of my username on her tongue sends electricity shooting through me like a live wire to my inner thoughts, and the darkness I've kept hidden sparks alive.

"Back your ass up and let me lick your little hole."

"Oh, Jesus," she moans wantonly.

Then she shuffles back until her legs align with the edge of the couch. I only have to lean forward slightly for my tongue to be within reach of her ass, and I push my head into her spread cheeks and bury my face between her thighs. My tongue darts out, and I flatten it to sweep through her slick folds. She sways on her feet, and I'm left with no choice but to reach out and hold her steady. "Good girl," I croon, and her taste bursts onto my tongue. "Fuck, you taste good."

Again and again, I groan into her wet heat while my cock throbs, willing me to let him get in on the action. I lick her deeper, and with each stroke of my tongue, my balls fill and my mind wanders with possibilities.

Her pregnant, swollen with my child as I lick her sweet pussy clean of her arousal.

She arches her back, pushing her cunt into my face, and I smile on a sharp inhale of her scent.

"Sinner, I-I think I'm …" Her small body becomes rigid, so I pull back, breaking the connection between us.

"You only come on my cock!" I smack her ass hard, and she whines at the contact. Then I dive back in, lavishing her pussy with calculated strokes of my tongue, burrowing inside her hole to bring her closer and closer to her orgasm.

The taste of her pussy is addicting. My cock is ready to burst, and I can't help but pump my hips and delight in the thought of her choking on my length while I lick her.

Lap after lap, my tongue devours her, then retreats each time her body tightens, determined to keep her on edge. "Fuck, yes," I groan into the room when an unexpected burst of pre-cum pours from my tip. "Fuck!" I grunt, struggling to stifle my impending orgasm.

Releasing her, I sink back into the couch, breathless and lightheaded, and when she straightens and turns to face me, I rake my gaze up and down her body. She wobbles, and I realize she's lightheaded too, but she didn't get to come yet, and I love having that control over her.

I flick my chin toward the bedroom door. "Go get on the bed and spread your legs. I want inside that cunt."

# SUMMER

"Go get on the bed and spread your legs. I want inside that cunt."

My eyes widen. His crude words are so abrupt, so filthy I don't know whether to slap him or climb him like a tree. My feelings and body are at war with one another. Never in a million years did I expect to like a man talking to me like this, especially after my upbringing, but with Sinner, I revel in it, but above all, I want that orgasm. I want it, like yesterday. Each stroke of his tongue filled me with desperation and had a rush of heat sweeping through me. The fire became so strong, I felt I was going to combust, but the ultimate pleasure was withheld, and with that, a feeling of need consumes every cell in my body, forcing me to submit to his demands.

When I push open the bedroom door, I'm not surprised by the elegance of the room. White satin sheets cover the gigantic bed centered in the room. Crystal vases adorn the elaborate furniture, and there's a huge oil painting of soft blues above the bed, giving the only splash of color in the room; everything else is white and silver.

My nerves hit me once again, and a ball of anxiety gathers in my throat, so I take deep breaths, then walk over the fluffy white carpet and climb onto the bed. The luxury sheets and plush mattress make it easy to sink into, and I close my eyes, listening to the sound of him moving through the penthouse. My heart thuds with each step that he takes, and when the bedroom door opens, I squeeze my eyes closed tighter at the anticipation thrumming through my body like electricity.

"You look so innocent laid out for me," he rasps, and I snap my eyes open and lift my head to see him.

He's leaning against the doorjamb, and the intensity behind his eyes has deepened into a glare. When he takes another swig from the bottle in his hand, a wave of uncertainty washes over me.

I'm actually doing this; I'm going to fuck a stranger for money. I'm going to lose my virginity to a man for money. One who has drunk a lot of alcohol.

*What the hell am I doing?*

*At least he's good-looking.* My heart thuds under his scrutiny. Not just good-looking, he's insanely hot, and my body quakes to touch him, lick him, devour him, like he has me.

"You're absolutely beautiful, yet I don't think you know it." He speaks so low I almost don't hear, like he's talking to himself. Then he pushes off the door, takes another gulp of the liquor, and places it down on the glass dresser, causing it to clink against the top.

"Are you ready for my cock, sweetheart?" He lifts his T-shirt over his head and drops it to the floor, and I choke on thin air.

Oh, sweet Jesus, the man is built, crafted to perfection.

Tattoos adorn his skin, painted on him so beautifully it's almost heartbreaking how gorgeous he is. The look in his eyes is one of uncertainty, and he swallows thickly before darting his eyes away, but they're just as quickly back on me, filled with heat and a newfound confidence that makes my hands curl into the sheets. The insecurity that was there only moments ago has dissolved, disappearing in the blink of an eye, yet I can't help but want to see it again, see all of him like he's seeing me—open, exposed, and vulnerable. There's a necklace hanging around his neck with a ring attached to it, and I hate the thought of it meaning something to him. Did he have a loved one who meant something special?

"Hold your pussy lips open. I want to see your hands stretching you wide open for me to take you while I slide into your tiny cunt," he snaps, as if annoyed with me.

I swallow hard when he pushes his jeans and boxers to the floor, then steps out of them and kicks them to the side. His solid thighs are covered in tattoos, and I practically drool at the prospect of tracing them, all the way up to the one that appears to be curling around the back of his neck.

He climbs onto the foot of the bed, and his stomach muscles contract as he crawls over me like a wild animal. I follow the trail of trimmed hair down to his solid length. My body responds to the desire on his face, all the way down to where his thick, heavy cock hangs tall and proud, leaking a bead of pre-cum at the very tip.

My throat is husky from his rough thrusts. "I don't think it's going to fit," I admit on a nervous swallow.

His lips tip up into a cunning smile, and he chuckles, his emerald eyes gleaming down at me as he holds himself off my body with his elbows.

"I'll make it fit." He smirks. "And you'll thank me for it."

That does nothing to ease my anxiety. If anything, it's only heightened, and fear clutches my throat, causing me to blanch. When he nuzzles his nose into my hair and breathes me in, as if committing my scent to memory, I melt, widening my legs to accommodate him. I'm so unbelievably needy for his touch I forget all about my apprehensions.

"I'm going to come deep inside your pussy, sweetheart, so fucking deep, you won't be innocent anymore. I'm going to dirty your innocent pussy up."

*Holy shit.* Why does that sound like a promise, and why the hell does my clit throb on his words?

"Then I'm going to taste myself from inside you."

My eyes widen further; he's going to …

"Lick my cum from inside your slick hole." He peppers feathery kisses down my neck and over my chest. "Then you're going to open your mouth nice and wide." He trails the pad of his thumb over my bottom lip, and his tongue darts out over my nipple. "I'm going to spit my cum into your greedy little mouth." As his thumb surges past my lips, I suck on it and lift my hips.

"Pl-please."

His chuckle vibrates through me, and he removes his hand and wraps it around his cock. When he slaps at my clit, a wave of pleasure sweeps through me. "Please!" I beg, louder this time.

"That's a good girl," he croons, delighting me further. "Let me slip inside your perfect cunt."

He directs the head of his cock to my opening, and I wrap my legs around his solid waist, anchoring him to me while my hands move between us to open my slick folds for him.

He inches inside, his muscles bunched, and he's stretching me to the point of pain. I bite my lip to stop myself from crying out while spreading myself wider. Eating up the scene before him, he watches with hooded eyes. His locked gaze so profound it's bordering on feral.

When he attempts to push further inside, I grimace at the head of his cock nudging at my hymen. He freezes, and his head snaps up toward me, his eyes asking a thousand questions, but I answer none. I don't have to. He knows.

He knows I'm a virgin.

As if burned, he rears back, leaning onto his heels, the tip of his cock still at my entrance as he scans over me. "You're a virgin?"

My mouth won't work; my brain doesn't compute to speak.

"You sold your cunt to be a whore?" he spits out, and his jaw falls slack, but his eyes are a contrast. They spark with intrigue before his Adam's apple slowly slides down his throat, and he gives his head a swift shake.

"Fuck. You're mine." He drags his eyes back up to mine. "Tell me you want this before I rip you open. Tell me you want me as much as I want you."

Those words do something to me; they give me the confidence to admit my truth, albeit a slightly skewed version. The truth is, as much as I need the money to do this, I need him more. A thrill chases up my spine. "I want this. I want your cock deep inside me." I chew on my lip. "I want you to punish me for taking your money."

He chokes on a laugh, but it lacks humor. No, it's patronizing, taunting with a cruel edge, and I wonder how much of this is the alcohol and how much is him, the real sinner. I stiffen on his sneer, my eyes holding his as we face-off.

He glances down to where we're joined. "I'm not sure this is a good idea."

I wonder if he's backing out. He can't.

"Maybe I need a real man to fuck me, then," I snipe back.

# FIVE

## MASE

"MAYBE I NEED a real man to fuck me, then." Her words cut through me so brutally, I feel like my heart is being torn out all over again; throw in the salt too. It's a damn good thing she doesn't realize how much those taunts affect me; otherwise, I'd have made her pay all the more for it.

Her ignorance is her savior, but that doesn't mean I'm not about to destroy her, leaving her a soppy mess of my making. She'll be lucky if she can walk out of here unaided.

I'll make her pay.

For the women who came before her, and all the ones after.

She will be the catalyst to my future.

I lean over her, gripping her chin between my fingers so tight she flinches. "I'm about to brutalize every hole you own." Then I release her, and she sags onto the mattress. Her eyes dart from my cock to my face, flashing in fear.

Rearing back, I slam inside her, breaking through her innocence so hard she slides up the bed and her cry echoes off the walls. I pin her shoulder to the mattress with one hand while clamping the other around her thigh to hold her in place.

I stare down at her, and a reel of her pregnant plays out in my mind, causing my cock to jerk inside her. The idea of me forcing a baby into her small innocent body has me clenching my teeth to ward off my orgasm.

Once I'm controlled enough to move, I start sliding out of her, but it's difficult with how her walls clench around me, holding me in like a vise. Once I'm almost all the way out of her, I slam back inside with ruthlessness. She cries out as the tip of my cock hits her cervix, and a satisfied grin spreads over my face.

"That's it, sweetheart. Take this thick cock in your virgin pussy." *Slam.* "Take every"—*thrust*—"fucking"—*slam*—"inch"—*thrust*—"of me." The bed rocks, banging against the wall, and my balls ache as I pound into her. "Cry for me. Beg for my cock, little whore."

Each beautiful thrust is solidified with a moan of twisted pleasure, the pain in her expression is coupled with the need consuming her as much as it is me.

My body works to fill her, but only one result will suffice: marking her as mine and diving so deep inside her she's no choice but to remember me. *Every fucking inch of me.*

Pleasure zips up my spine, igniting embers I never knew existed, bringing every cell to life along the way. Knowing I'm the only man to have been inside her, unlike my fucking wife, has a sense of ownership thrashing through me. *Mine!*

My balls draw up, and I clench my teeth as I give myself over to pure euphoria. This is it; this is the experience I've been waiting for.

This is everything.

"Fuckkkk!" I growl into the room, and my cock pumps a torrent of thick cum deep inside her.

# SUMMER

Watching him come undone is the most incredible sight I've ever witnessed; his facial expression holds so much passion it's hard to describe. Exhilaration, euphoria, awe … and finally relief.

If I could bottle up the look of pure wonderment on his face as he comes down from his orgasm, I would. I'd never sell it, though. Not how I've sold my body. Never.

No, this look deserves to be treasured.

He pulls out of my pussy, and I wince while he smirks down at his cum and my juices blended together.

"You dirtied my cock up, little girl." His gaze drifts up to mine, but he doesn't look the least bit annoyed. If anything, he looks thrilled. "Feel it, feel your ruined pussy." He guides my hand to my swollen pussy. It's wet and tender to the touch. "Can you feel how wet you are?"

I nod frantically and stroke over my aching clit, still waiting for the orgasm that seems to have edged away with his brutal fucking.

"Paint my lips with your blood, sweetheart. Paint them and make me yours too."

*Oh, sweet Jesus.* Does he mean? My eyes widen, and my

hand trembles as he lowers himself toward me. When my fingers touch his lips, the sight of my blood combined with his cum has my pussy clenching in desperation. "Please," I beg. His tongue darts out over his lip, and I swear something inside me gushes at the action. *Holy shit, he's tasting us.* He closes his eyes and rolls his lips, dragging the sticky, bloody substance into his mouth and savoring our taste.

*Holy hell.*

He groans, then snaps his eyes open.

"Fuck, we taste good. Your innocence on my tongue has truly released the sinner inside me." His smile turns into a salacious grin, then, without warning, he pulls back and flips me over. "I suggest you rub your little cunt, sweetheart. I'm about to take your ass, and if breaking your pussy in made you cry, this is going to make you scream."

I'm stunned to silence, but he positions me onto my knees, and I move my hand quickly, rubbing over my aching bud with vigor, determined to get the feeling back he drew out of me with the swipe of his filthy tongue. He chuckles as if knowing my thoughts, then grabs hold of my braid and wraps it around his fist like a rein. The swipe of his wet cock up and down the crack of my ass has me rubbing my clit faster and faster.

"I'm going to fuck your ass so hard, sweetheart." His words send a shiver of expectation through me. This is going to hurt, but I welcome it. After all, I agreed to being someone's whore on my application form; this is what's expected of me. What I never considered was being so attracted to the man who would take my innocence and pour gasoline on it, burning it to the ground, and the flames roar with an overwhelming fireball of indulgence.

# MASE

My cock breaches her tight little asshole, and the tender skin stretches around my tip. I force myself inside her, only using our blended juices from her pussy as lubrication, and I adore the fact. "Fuck, yes," I groan, holding back the hungry need to slam viciously inside her like a feral animal.

One hand grips her hip while I yank her hair harder to hold her in place, giving her no option but to remain on all fours while I break her ass in.

"That's it, let me in," I grunt as I inch farther inside.

"I don't think I can. It burns so bad," she whines, and I slap her ass hard. She's my whore to control.

My guttural groan vibrates in my chest. Fuck, yes. "You're mine to use."

She tenses and releases a low whimper. "Oh god."

Her hand moves faster between her legs as she thrums at her clit, no doubt trying to capture that pleasure point to subside her pain.

Despite the gnawing voice at the back of my mind, telling me to go easy on her, her earlier words scream at me louder than before, bringing with them a reminder of my past. A past that still haunts my present.

———

"You're not even man enough to give me a fucking child, Mason!" Tara screams like a banshee. "I want a man!"

"You don't even let me near you to fucking try!" I bellow.

It's been two years since she lost the baby, a baby that wasn't mine to begin with. Two years since she destroyed my trust, crumbling it into a thousand pieces until it was nothing but ash. Then it blew away, never again returning.

She later told me she kept the baby for us. For us? Did she really expect me to raise another man's child? When I told the guys, Owen was quick to point out that the guy she just so happened to be impregnated by was a billionaire too.

I'm not stupid; she doesn't love me. Not in the way a wife should love a husband, at least. "That's because I like normal sex, Mase! You want more. You make me feel like I'm not enough for you!" she screams, and I roll my eyes.

I've never said she's not enough for me. Not once.

"When it's you that's not enough for me." She continues on her tirade. "Why can't you just be normal? Be happy with what we've got."

I snort at her analogy. Me not happy? She's the one who fucks around, not me.

"I don't want sex as much as you!" she screams, and guilt invades my veins, then I shake my head, refusing to acknowledge it. It's another one of her tactics to manipulate me. I've never once pressured her into sex, and if she didn't want it, she wouldn't have it with other men.

The deep realization that my wife enjoys sex with other men and not me makes me want to whimper pathetically. I clear my throat to disguise the hurt.

"I just want a normal sex life," she snipes, snapping me out of my thoughts.

"So do I!" I bite back.

Sure, I've suggested spicing things up over the years, but each and every time, she's shot me down like I'm some sort of predator. I even suggested couples counseling. Any-fucking-thing.

She stomps her foot. "You're not man enough for me!" Those words slice through my chest, rendering me speechless. Each time she says it, a little part of me dies inside. The part of me that thought I looked good today, with the tattoos I added that helped me release the anger and pain inside me, the way I try not to wear my shirt unbuttoned at the top because it makes me look too casual for her when she likes me to remain professional looking around her friends. All the attempts to satisfy her and make her happy while trying and failing miserably to make me happy in the process.

Obliterated.

Rage builds up inside me.

"You go to the gym all the fucking time. It's all you do! It's like you don't care what I think of your appearance."

"To get away from you!" I clip back, ignoring her snide comments about how I look. She's made it blatantly obvious, multiple times, she prefers someone with a smaller frame, someone who wears slacks and a button-down shirt. She wants one of the men who visit the country club her friends hang around at.

"I don't like meatheads in jeans," she sneers with a curled lip. I want to tell her she doesn't like me either, but, in all honesty, I don't want her to admit that to me. That would hurt more—all the trying, the changes, all for nothing. She scoffs. "What? Nothing to say?"

I shake my head solemnly, looking down at the floor, toeing it with my sneaker. If I say something now, I'll regret it because not one damn word will be a kind one, and I refuse to be like my father.

"God. You're pathetic," she grumbles, snatching her purse off the counter. All of this over me not wanting to go on vacation with her country club friends.

"Did you hear me? I said, you're pathetic!" She screams it louder this time. Yeah, I heard, but this time, her words slide off me. They don't hurt as much as they used to.

"You're useless."

I bite back a retort, knowing how my mom felt when my father *belittled her. I itch to defend not only myself but every other person who has endured a partner demeaning them. Jesus, did my mom feel every word. I shake my head, unprepared to go there. "It's a fucking vacation, Tara," I snap, instead of saying all the things I want to say. Like, you're being childish, acting spoiled, grow the fuck up, you're my wife, act like it. "I have meetings; I can't just go on vacation at the drop of a hat." Even though it's not my scene, I'd take her if I could. Evenings of black-tie nights and wine tastings are not on my agenda, but if it would stop her bitching, I would.*

*She draws in a deep, sharp breath. It's calculated and full of raging fury, so I quickly glance around at my surroundings, making sure there isn't a damn vase within her reach like the last time.*

*"Maybe we can fly out for the weekend." I shrug, hoping it appeases her.*

*"I don't see why I can't go alone for the week. Scared I'm going to fuck someone better than you again?" Her words cut me deep. I try so hard to get past her indiscretions, but she brings them up, taunting me and recreating the feeling of being worthless, being nothing. Not good enough, never enough, a letdown. We agreed after our last therapy session that we'd only go on vacation together, and her throwing that back in my face is just another reminder of how she isn't as committed as she says.*

*My head drops as the weight of devastation makes it difficult to hold it upright. "Do what the hell you want, Tara," I whisper, then turn on my heel toward the door, hating the fact I said those words, yet praying she won't act on them.*

Resentment flows through my bloodstream, boiling it along the way, and I bare my teeth.

Each cruel taunt that taints my soul is being obliterated as I ravish the woman in my control.

I push my hips forward, surging inside her, and she releases a scream that rattles off the walls, turning me on further. My eyes roll with the satisfaction of finally fucking a woman's ass. Me. I'm in control. "You belong to me!" I roar, pounding into her, my hips bouncing off the globes of her ass.

I watch in sick fascination as my cock continues to push in and out of her tight hole, now stretched wide to accommodate me. "Fuck. Oh, fuck, that looks good, sweetheart. So good."

She claws at the sheets with one hand while the other continues to play.

"Fuck, sweet girl."

Her body writhes, as if my words turn her on. So unlike my ex-wife, who despised them.

"Do you like me talking dirty to you?" I groan, sliding in and out of her ass. "Do you like me fucking your virgin ass? Having all your holes taken in one night like a good little slut."

She moans, then releases the most beautiful sound of sheer, choked pleasure, causing my orgasm to slam into me. It's so profound, so powerful, it's like a tsunami of emotions —exhilaration, anger, awe, rage. My mouth falls open and my head drops back, all while continuing to pump what feels like an endless supply of cum into her ass.

My head spins with intoxication and gratification after experiencing so much pent-up sexual frustration and finally being able to be me while releasing inside her. Inside this beautiful creature, who has endured my worst to allow me to become my best.

"You've changed my life, sweetheart. I just wish I hadn't had to pay for it," I whisper into the room, collapsing onto the bed beside her.

# SIX



THE ROOM SPINS when I open my eyes, and I wince at the morning sun shining through the parted curtains, making my head throb from the intensity of its brightness. "Fuck. That hurts," I mumble. Taking a deep breath, I sit up and clench my teeth at my brain pounding against my skull.

Definitely shouldn't have grabbed another bottle of liquid courage before I entered the bedroom last night.

I throw my legs over the bed and sit on the edge, leaning forward to drop my head in my hands while I slowly come around.

"Hey, are you okay?" a silky voice asks, and her soft fingers graze my back, causing me to flinch at the realization.

Oh, shit.

I did it. I actually fucking did it.

Memories flood back to me from last night.

The way I pinned her to the bed and mounted her, slamming my cock inside her over and over again. My disappointment at not using protection to fuck her ass so I could slide inside her pussy again straight after, coupled with my plan to shower and fuck her in there too, which failed epically after we fell asleep with her wrapped around me like a koala.

I've never slept with another woman before, in every sense of the word, and that realization has me batting her hand away as I struggle to stand.

Clinging onto the dresser for support, I bend over and grab two bottles of water from the fridge, then throw one onto the bed for Innocent Angel while I twist the cap off the other and down it as if I've been abandoned in a desert for days on end.

She stretches to grab her bottle, so I take her in again. She's young. Holy fuck, she's young.

I blink several times.

She didn't appear this young last night.

I slowly lower the bottle from my lips, with shock rendering me speechless. Oh shit, what the hell did I do? My stomach rolls as I assess her.

Her hair is mussed, giving her the roughly fucked look, and after I see the blood staining her inner thighs, I turn my focus to my rock-hard cock—there's blood on me too. My cock flexes, and I grimace. I should not get excited about the sight of her blood. Her virginity, for Christ's sake.

I asked *Indulgence* for innocent, and they fucking delivered.

The sooner I get her out of here, the better. I need some time to collect myself, to come to terms with what the fuck I did, and worse, how much I enjoyed doing it. The thought of her leaving has my heart hammering against my chest. Maybe I should ask her for another night? No. She's young. An escort, for Christ's sake. Besides, she might say no.

I clear my throat. "Do you want me to order you breakfast?"

She nibbles on her bottom lip, her cheeks heating under my scrutiny of the mark on her neck, and her nipples pucker the more I stare at her. Then she darts her eyes toward the crystal clock mounted on the wall, and when she shakes her head, it sends a welcome rush of relief through me.

"No, thank you. I need to get going. I'm already going to be late for school." She rolls her eyes.

*School?*

My heart stops beating, I swear it. I know she worded it wrong, but still, something inside me tells me to query it.

"You mean college?"

She tilts her head to the side, scanning me up and down, then toys with the label on the water bottle.

The sound of blood rushing around my body can be heard in my ears, and I wince at the sensation.

"You mean college?" I ask, sterner this time, and even I can admit I sound like an ass. "Hey. Fucking look at me and answer!" I demand, harsher than before.

She looks up at me from beneath her lashes, those beautiful fucking long lashes that make me want to press delicate kisses on her pretty little face. When her stare collides with mine, my lungs deflate; the air is being sucked from them as I wait for her response.

"No. I'm still in school."

A disgruntled sound erupts in my throat, and I shake my head. "No. Your application said you wanted the money for college," I sneer, pointing my finger at her.

"I do!" she snaps back. "I want it so I'm able to go to college. Besides"—she lifts her shoulder—"it's no big deal."

A loud scoff erupts from me. "No big deal?" My voice gets louder with each syllable. "No. Big. Fucking. Deal?" Just how old is she? My eyes widen with the realization. "How old are you?" She's twenty-one. She has to be; her application said as much. *Indulgence* carries out all relevant security checks. Thorough checks.

Oscar O'Connell wouldn't run a business without those checks.

"Eighteen."

The moment she says it, my legs buckle from beneath me, and I reach out to cling onto the dresser in order to keep me upright.

"Eighteen?!"

She nods coyly, then slides off the bed, causing me to stumble back, away from her. Hell no, I don't need her near me despite my cock having other ideas.

Simply rolling her eyes, she grabs her dress, ignoring my meltdown, and I watch on in horror as the teenager I fucked into oblivion last night gets dressed.

The innocent teenager.

The virgin.

Oh, shit. I fucked her ass. Hard.

Oh, my fucking god, no.

My quest to achieve my dream night has resulted in my worst nightmare. "Holy shit." I swallow hard, and my eyes burn through her as she smooths her dress over her bloodied thighs. "You're in school."

"I did it for college money," she reiterates.

For college money?

The girl needs financial support. She sold herself to a bastard like me, whored herself out, in order to pay for her education. What fucked-up world do we live in?

I shake my head, pissed at myself, pissed at *Indulgence*. Hell, I'm pissed at the world right now.

Her gaze bounces around the room as she looks everywhere but at me. Shit, she might have some fucking trauma or something after what I did to her last night … for her first time. I squeeze my eyes closed. "I need to leave." The softness in her tone has me opening my eyes, and I spin to face the dresser. I open the top drawer and take out the wads of extra bills I brought with me. "There's about five and a half thousand there. Take it." I shove it into her chest, and it's only now that her blue eyes meet mine.

Uncertainty wavers beneath them, shrouded in reluctance

but bathed in excitement. She chews on her lip. "Take it. You were great." I wince at my words, then push the tip money at her again.

Her shoulders sag, and she takes it from my hand, sending a spark of electricity through me when our fingers touch. Her, too, judging by the way our gazes collide and her lips part.

Hmm, they part just enough to allow me to slip my tongue inside and taste her properly.

Jesus, she's beautiful. Beautiful and dangerously forbidden.

But instead, I tilt my head toward the door in encouragement.

She needs to leave right fucking now, before I do something I regret, like throw her on the damn bed and fuck her again, age be damned.

Anger contorts her features as her mouth snaps shut, her lips pucker, and she becomes redder as she glares at me. Then she spins on the balls of her bare feet and heads toward the door.

Every cell inside me tells me to go after her, to ask her name, take her number, something. Just to check if she's okay, nothing more. Nope, not a damn thing more.

But like hell do I want another lawsuit on my ass, not after taking years to get my divorce over with. So instead of listening to my heart, I listen to my head and ignore the pain stabbing at my chest. It's a one-night stand, a transaction.

I stride toward the bathroom with a purpose.

To wash away every part of Innocent Angel. It's just a shame I can't wash my mind of all the filthy images of her too.

She's branded me without realizing it. I thought my wife was my biggest downfall, but I already know it's not. Letting her go will be.

# SEVEN

## MASE

IT'S BEEN weeks since I saw her and felt her in my arms, but I can't think of anything else. I'm barely functioning. The number of times I've considered asking Owen to track her down is ridiculous, and I've given myself a constant barrage of reasons why that is not a good idea.

The top one being all hell has broken loose lately; my four best friends' lives are as hectic as my own.

When I asked Reed to travel with me to my father's office to listen to his will being read, I expected him to accompany me with no issue. What I didn't expect was a tirade of poor excuses and to ultimately be left with no lawyer when there're three of my father's best legal team staring me down like I have no right to be here.

I have every fucking right!

This company was funded on my mother's dime. My dead mother, to be precise. The same mother who barely reached thirty-three years old before she was killed in a car accident while trying to leave her abusive husband, with seven-year-old me in the back seat witnessing the horrors of it all.

"You don't have legal representation?" Gareth Barnes goads. He was my father's favorite attorney, the one who gets him out of the assault-and-battery charges of the women he falls into bed with.

I glare down the scumbag and sit forward, forcing the piece of trash to slink back into his seat away from me.

"I don't need representation. This is simply a reading of his Last Will and Testament." The darkness in my tone is full of feigned confidence.

His thick, caterpillar-like eyebrows rise, and he shoves his glasses up his nose as he fidgets from side to side.

Reed reassured me my mother made sure there were no loopholes in the legalities of the business—her father had insisted on it before my parents' marriage.

Every cent of the financial business should belong to me now, along with the relevant shares, but something tells me my father won't have made it that easy for me. He hated me almost as much as I hated him. When I left and never returned, I didn't just walk out on him as a parent, I walked out on the business, and in his eyes, it was the ultimate betrayal.

Oliver clears his throat. He's a decent enough man and knew my mother when she was alive. Shame he didn't help her when she needed it. I might have actually liked him if he had.

"This is all standard, Mason. You're already aware of your father's Last Will and Testament. Here's your copy." He slides the paperwork over to me, and I don't even spare them a glance. Had it not been for my mother's money being invested in this business, I would burn it to the ground with a smile on my face, and the hatred rolling off these men in waves tells me they know it.

"Anything else?" I can't wait to get the fuck out of here.

Oliver shifts in his chair. "Actually, there is one clause he was able to ascertain."

"Of course there is," I grit out through clenched teeth, wishing Reed had drowned in the damn lake he went to with his newfound family. Leaving me here exposed to these damn vultures has irritation thrumming through my veins.

Since the moment he rediscovered his one-night stand is pregnant with his child, the man has done everything in his power to ensure his place in her already made family. The issue with that comes when he's deceiving her, working with her father behind her back to take control of the shares she owns within her father's business. Still, he's my fucking attorney, which our company pays him well for, so he should've been here.

Even Shaw offered to accompany me, mainly to get out of a scheduled family meal he has to attend at his brother-in-law's estate. Unfortunately for him, his wife is a Mafia princess and her brother is the Capo of the Mafia. He holds Shaw's balls in a firm vise so fucking tight it's a wonder he can still get an erection, let alone have kids.

Lucky bastard might have it tough, but in my eyes, he has it all—a family. Something I can't see happening for me anytime in the future despite how much I wish for it.

"It's nothing to worry about, just a small clause to protect an asset."

My spine bolts straight, and my forehead creases as I lean forward with intrigue. "What asset?"

Just what the fuck has my father gotten himself into? Correction, what the hell has he gotten me into?

Oliver chuckles awkwardly, then raises his hand. "Nothing to worry about. Don't worry," he says as if hearing my inner thoughts. "He has insisted on you becoming guardian of your sister until she finishes school, then all this" —he taps the sheets in front of me—"will be yours."

I rear back, stunned.

What fucking sister?

Guardian?

He's moved the fucking goal posts is what he's done.

"Your stepsister," Gareth offers, and I only now realize I spoke aloud.

I shake my head, my mind whirling. "What the fuck?" Fury strikes through me, and I want nothing more than to launch my chair through the office window. Instead, I practice the same techniques I have on Tara all these years, breathing in through my nose and out my mouth in small, sharp bursts.

"She gets impeccable grades," Gareth tacks on with a snakelike smile, making him appear deranged. The sight causes something to twist inside me.

"He left me a kid?" I blurt out bitterly.

"Only until she finishes school," Oliver offers, as if it makes everything better. It doesn't. It absolutely doesn't.

"She won't be any trouble." All three nod in unison, and it's only now I acknowledge the third man in the room, Lenard Strong, chief executive of the company. I sneer in his direction; the man is a weasel. He's probably trying to keep me on his side so I don't sell up. No chance of that now, not yet anyway.

"You could get her a nanny?" he suggests. "Someone to watch over her while you go back to New Jersey." He smiles, then looks toward Gareth, whose eyes dance with glee. They're enjoying this.

A sharp pain hits my chest when the enormity of my situation sinks in. I now have a child to take care of, and I live in fucking New Jersey. We're in Los Angeles. Shit, the poor kid's world is about to be turned upside down. Surely, she has her own family, right? "Where's the mother?" I ask Gareth, and he shakes his head solemnly. "Her biological father?" I ask Oliver. He shakes his head. Great, the kid's practically an orphan, which means she'll have issues I don't have time for. "Her family?" I ask Lenard with hope, but of course the fucker shakes his head grimly, like someone killed his latest mistress.

"Your father kept custody of her when her mother died," Oliver adds.

Part of me resents this kid already, the unwelcome responsibility being forced on me and creating a stumbling block in my quest to regain control of my mother's assets and reinvent her legacy. But to be left with my father as her only parent, how fucking shit her life must have been.

A heavy ball of responsibility to be better for her sinks to the bottom of my stomach. This was meant to be a quick visit, to retrieve access to my mom's legacy and move on, not be lumbered with what is bound to be a traumatized child.

"Here are her files pertaining to her welfare. Her name is Summer Campbell." Of course he married her mother, another wife. Oliver pulls a manila folder out of his briefcase and slides it across the table toward me with a guilty expression. My heart pounds against my rib cage with the weight of the responsibility.

A fucking kid.

I drag a hand over my head.

My mind whirls, thinking about how I can shirk this responsibility. Maybe she can go to a similar boarding school I went to. That would solve things. For now, she's going to have to have a nanny. I'll speak to my father's butler, Hugh, first, then ask the guys for advice.

"Here're the keys to the property. You know the access codes to all the others," Oliver drones on while I'm left stunned, almost too overwhelmed to take it all in. "I'll touch base with you next week." I nod and scoop up the files along with my phone and keys, then head toward the door, ignoring the shared looks of concern.

"Mase?" Reluctantly giving Oliver my attention, I lock eyes with him. "This might be the best thing to ever happen to you." He looks at me with hope in his eyes, and a knot gathers in my throat.

"Doubtful," I respond.

The only time I ever came close to feeling that way was when I had her in my arms, and she walked away from me. *Because you paid her, you idiot. You were a transaction, nothing more.*

I chastise myself for the hundredth time.

She came in the form of an innocent blonde girl, too pure to taint with my demons.

# EIGHT

## MASE

AFTER LEAVING my father's office building, I went straight into town, found the nearest bar, and began drowning my sorrows while ignoring the foreboding feeling of dread creeping up my spine. The bastard is even fucking with me from beyond the grave.

The bar I'm in is busy but gives me the perfect opportunity to wallow in self-pity, and thankfully, the server has the good sense to continue delivering me a bottle of beer each time I finish the last.

My phone has been buzzing in my pocket on and off all evening, and I know it's Owen checking in on me, so with a heavy sigh, I pull it from my pants.

Owen: You good?

Owen: Brother?

Owen: Can see you're at a bar.

Owen: You need me. Call me, yeah?

Owen: Gonna leave ya to it. Just find a fuck
toy and lose yourself in them. You deserve it.
Call me tomorrow and tell me what
happened.

Reluctantly, I text him back, knowing how worried he is about me lately. Maybe he can sense the change in me from that night. I feel like I'm being torn in two, my head and my heart vying for opposing sides.

Me: Speak tomorrow.

Sure, there're plenty of women in here, and judging by their hungry stares, it wouldn't be difficult to get lost in one of them. But not a single one of them appeals to me. Nope, the only one who appeals to me is the girl with the username that is perfectly apt—Innocent Angel. I scoff at the irony. The girl might have been a virgin, but she was anything but innocent. She did look it, though. She certainly delivered on that. God, did she deliver.

I'm still contemplating searching for her. But how fucked up would that be? A man of thirty-four paying for sex from an eighteen-year-old, then tracking her down. Essentially, that would be stalking. My cock throbs at the thought, and thoughts of taking her roughly from behind in an alleyway of a crowded street begin to take hold.

"Another beer?" The server with the big tits smiles broadly at me.

They're probably fake; everything else about her appears to be, and when she pushes her tits out farther, I slide out of the booth and throw a wad of money onto the table.

"No, thanks. I have a kid to get home to."

She licks her lips like my words excite her. Great, she

probably has a whole bunch of kids herself and thinks I'm about to play daddy. With that thought in mind, I hightail it out of there and grab the nearest cab, making a mental note to have my truck delivered to the mansion tomorrow.

———

Staring out the window, I don't even take in my surroundings. My mind whirls from the day's events.

Why the fuck couldn't Reed have been there? He might have gotten me out of this shit. All of it.

The cab comes to a standstill, and my stomach sinks. Blowing out a deep breath, I look up at the mansion, the one I used to call home. My personal hell.

"That'll be fifty bucks, man," the taxi driver prompts when I fail to move.

I pull my wallet from my back pocket and fumble to get the money out, then shove the cash at him and throw open the door.

This is it.

At least the kid will be in bed now.

Coldness hits me, causing a dark foreboding sensation to skitter down my spine. A shadow of doom lingers over me, filling me with trepidation. Just being back here is like a nightmare come true. "Come on, Mase, pull yourself together. At least the bastard is dead now." I bounce on the balls of my feet like I'm about to go to battle.

Pulling my shoulders back, I stride up the stone steps toward the mansion doors.

Music penetrates the walls as my hand rests on the door handle, and the vibrations cause the hairs on my neck to stand. Shouts and screams of joy filter through the thick wood.

*What the actual fuck?*

Are my father's staff celebrating his demise? I wouldn't

blame them; he treated them like shit. There's only ever been one to stick around for long—Hugh. The man must have been paid well to endure my father. Though, I do know he has a kid out there somewhere, maybe he funds them.

It sounds like the partygoers are destroying the damn property. My fucking property.

Throwing open the door, I step inside, and my eyes widen. Holy. Fucking. Shit.

It looks like hundreds of teenagers partying. The foyer is crammed with near-naked bodies, and two women are grappling on the floor, their tits out, money being thrown at them from a crowd of young men. I glance around the room, trying to figure out what the hell is happening. Did someone sell this place already?

It looks like a damn frat house.

I push through the crowd of drunken partygoers, using my broad shoulders to barge them out of the way. The confusion coupled with the alcohol makes it difficult for me to grasp what is happening. Am I in the *Twilight Zone*?

The scent of alcohol in the air rolls my stomach. I've had too much of my own already, so the smell hits me like a Mack truck.

A DJ booth is set up in what was the dining room, with speakers blasting in each corner of the room and laser lights slicing through the air, and my temples pulsate with the impact.

Jesus, this is insane.

The throb of the bass reverberates through the floorboards, and I head into the living room. I come to a standstill when I see a full-bodied ice sculpture of a naked man standing in the corner of the living space. A girl on her knees takes shots from what appears to be an ice dick, and I can't help but stare dumbstruck.

I blink.

What in the ever-loving fuck?

As I take in the carnage of the room, I can't help but wonder if I walked into the right house. What the hell is happening?

My father would never allow parties. Ever.

A hand wraps around my T-shirt and tugs me toward a hazy-eyed brunette, a very young-looking brunette, who I quickly push away like she has the plague. When she stumbles, I grab her arm to steady her, then release her just as quickly. "Do you work here?" I ask above the music, and she gapes back at me as if I'm a lunatic before spinning and throwing her arm onto another guy's chest, who she proceeds to grind on.

Great. Nobody knows what the hell is going on. I have at least a hundred horny young adults in my house, drinking alcohol and fucking, and God only knows if some of these fuckers are underage.

The latter thought makes me sober up really quick and turns the alcohol in my bloodstream to fury.

Not on my fucking watch.

Someone is going to pay for this.

My nostrils flare when I see one of my mother's favorite paintings tipped on its side. Sure, the thing is ugly as fuck, but that's not the point.

Moving through the crowd, I head for Hugh's quarters. The man is my father's head butler who runs this house, and he would normally not allow this to happen. The kitchen is just as wild as the rest of the house, and when I turn down Hugh's corridor, I breathe a sigh of relief from being away from the rambunctious bodies.

Before I get to the entrance of Hugh's live-in apartment, his door flies open and the man himself steps out. "I told you to keep it contained!" he sneers in a tone I've never heard him use. His face falls, almost as if his mask has slipped, and he straightens. "Oh, Mason. Sir, how wonderful to see you." He holds his hand out for me to shake, and I don't miss the tremble behind it.

I eye his hand, and when he realizes I'm not about to shake it, he quickly withdraws it. He's aged a lot since the last time I saw him, but that's what being away for decades will do, I guess. A lot has changed, clearly.

"What the hell's happening?" I spit out.

His mouth works, but nothing comes out, aggravating me further. Then he sighs and opens his mouth again. "I'm sorry, but she's out of control."

My eyes bounce over his face. What the hell is he talking about? "Who?"

"Summer."

I rear back. "Summer?"

He nods frantically. "Your stepsister."

Confusion takes over me. "She did this?"

He continues to nod, and I want to smack the man upside his head. Who lets a young girl control him like this?

"Where the hell is she?" I bite out.

"Oh, she's probably in her bedroom." He tilts his head toward the corridor. "The old guest room on the third floor."

I nod and take off in that direction, marching through the house like a man on a mission.

This party is about to be shut the fuck down, and what the hell does this kid think she's doing opening the house up to all ages.

Fuck, she clearly needs some guidance, or a damn boarding school. Otherwise, before she reaches adulthood, she will have fucked up her entire life.

Does she not realize how dangerous it is to open the house up to strangers? Of all ages, no less? She could have been kidnapped. Abused. Oh, fuck no. My legs move quicker as I surge through the bodies of people and rush up the stairs. She's probably cowering in a damn closet realizing her mistake, poor kid. She's clearly acting out.

My chest heaves when I reach the third floor, then I dart right and head for what was the guest bedroom.

Throwing open the door, I burst into the room, and it takes a moment for my eyes to adjust in the low lighting. "Summer?"

"Yeah?" A soft voice moves from beneath the bedsheets, and when her head springs up, my eyes widen.

Her mouth falls open.

My jaw drops.

Her cheeks redden.

My body pales.

She drops the sheet, exposing her bra-clad tits.

Holy.

Fucking.

Shit.

I close my eyes, then snap them open just as quickly.

Her eyes bulge.

I shake my head.

*No. Oh, God, no.*

She looks seconds away from passing out.

Please, no.

*What the hell?* I mouth.

Another head springs up from below the sheets, and all the disappointment that was there moments ago dissipates into unadulterated fury.

The guy's eyes dart from me to Summer.

My hands ball into tight fists.

"What the fuck is happening?" I snarl out, asking no one in particular.

"You're here," she squeaks, still wearing a stunned expression. "You're here. In my bedroom."

"You're in my fucking house!" I fume, jabbing my finger in her direction. "What the fuck are you doing here?"

Those baby blues of hers become wider somehow. "Your house?"

"Mine!" I snap. Every muscle in my body contracts to the point of pain.

"Oh, shit," the prick replies. Her eyes jump from the dumbass in the bed to me. "Y-You're Mason?"

"Damn fucking right I am!" I fume.

"You're Mase. Jeff's son?" she asks, but it's clear she's only confirming what she already knows. "Oh my God! You're my stepbrother!"

"Are you going to tell me what's happening?" the punk beneath her asks, and it's only now I register he's without a shirt. I'm seconds away from tearing him apart, and judging by the way he blanches, he realizes it too.

I've never been a jealous man, not at all, but the idea of her in bed with this asshole has me wanting to slaughter him, slowly, and something tells me he can see exactly what I'm thinking because the little punk springs up out of sheets.

"Maybe I should go." He scrambles out of the bed, and I'm grateful for his sake he at least has jeans on. He trips as he shoves his feet into sneakers and pulls a hoodie over his head while my eyes remain glued on the piece of shit.

"Go on, frat boy, get the fuck out," I sneer in his direction. "And tell all those fuckers downstairs to get out too before I call the police on their asses for trespassing."

He looks like he's about to puke as he inches toward the door with nervousness, realizing he's going to have to ask me to move to walk through it.

"Erm, sir, can you please move?"

"You're being a dick!" Summer screeches, jumping up, then I realize she's only wearing panties beneath the sheets too. Oh, hell no.

"Get some fucking clothes on, right now!" I stride toward her while the kid makes a run for it. Summer darts across the bed, her eyes wide like a deer caught in the headlights. Then she crosses her arms over her chest, enhancing her tits. My eyes flit to the little white lace bra that under normal circumstances wouldn't be classed as anything sexy, but the innocence behind it, the fact it's on the most beautiful girl I've ever set eyes on, the one I haven't been able to get off my mind from the moment I laid eyes on her … Yeah, it's sexy as hell.

I freeze and swallow thickly as my arm stills midair to grab her, and she remains on the other side of the bed, staring back at me. Those fierce blue eyes of hers have softened under my scrutiny, and a flash of vulnerability shimmers in them. I want to take her hesitation, her purity, and demolish it. When she licks her lips, my cock thickens, remembering what it looked like to have her on her knees struggling to take me, her lips stretched wide over my girth as I slid in and out of her wet hole, with tears streaming down her pretty face.

Holy fuck, I want that.

A whimper leaves her, and somehow, it pulls me out of my thoughts.

"Party's over," I whisper, then retreat from the room, preparing to shut this hellhole down.

All the while, my heart thumps rapidly and my cock twitches with excitement.

The moment I slam the door behind me, my feet come to a halt, and I try to regain some control, some clarity.

She's my fucking sister—and I want her.

# NINE



MY BLOOD PUMPS WILDLY AS he retreats from the room, his feet dragging, and my body sags the moment the door slams shut.

Holy shit.

I rub at my temple. *Did that just happen?*

He's here.

He's actually freaking here, and worse, he's my step-brother.

I've spent weeks trying to block the memories from my mind of our one night together, but they whirl around constantly, taunting me with the way he marked me.

The memories are burned into my mind, engrained so deep it's like they've become a part of my everyday life.

Do all girls feel this way after losing their virginity?

I chastise myself again, hating how attached I've become to someone I ultimately don't know.

But I do know him now; now he has a name other than a username. He's no longer Saintly Sinner, he's Mason, or Mase, as Jeff would refer to him as during his hate-filled tirades. And he's my stepbrother. He's going to be in the same house as me. But for how long? I want to know his plan. Will he live here? Will he make me homeless?

I shake my head, unwilling to go there, and slowly lower myself back down to the bed, chewing on my bottom lip as I go over the night's events that led him back to me. Back to us.

*Two hours ago …*

*"Summer, this party is insane!" Travis bumps my shoulder and takes another shot.*

*I grin back up at him, and he pulls me into his solid chest. My best friend is the epitome of hotness, and I love the fact that he doesn't even care. He doesn't lack confidence per se, it's just misdirected, but I promised him we would figure shit out together, just like he promised me.*

*He's the only person I've ever had in my corner, the only person I've ever loved, and even though he knows all about my one-night stand, he hasn't judged me or my decision, and I know he'll take it to the grave.*

*"Don't look now, but Levi is checking you out," he breathes into my ear, and I stiffen.*

*Levi Williamson is hot, sure, but he knows it, and the guy is also a major douche. In fact, he's a womanizing pig. He treats girls like they're disposable, then he moves onto the next before he's barely kicked the other to the curb, and what do the girls do? They throw themselves all over him, like he's the last man on earth.*

*"Oh, God, he's coming over," I whisper, tugging my dress down.*

*When Travis told me I looked incredible as I slipped on the little red number, I actually believed him. He's the only person besides Sinner who's ever made me feel beautiful.*

*"You don't need to pull it down any more, Summer. How about you just take it off?" Levi smirks and takes another sip from his red cup.*

*"How about you leave her the fuck alone?" Travis spits back, stepping in front of me.*

*"Jealous?" Levi mocks, staring Travis down.*

*I step up behind Travis and rest my hand on his back. "It's okay, Trav." I step to the side. "There's no way in hell you'd be able to make me take it off," I sneer in the arrogant asshole's direction.*

*A crowd is gathering around us, and my cheeks heat. "Really?" He chuckles. "I think this might do it."*

*Before I know what's happening, he's thrown the contents of his cup at my dress, the liquid drenching the material, and chills sweep through me.*

*"You fucking asshole," Travis roars before driving his fist into Levi's nose, causing blood to spray through the air.*

*"Holy shit," I gasp, tugging on Travis's T-shirt. My instant reaction is to get him out of here before Levi's minions arrive as backup. "Trav, come on. Let's go."*

*Always my protector, Travis reluctantly allows me to pull him out of the kitchen, spitting and snarling in Levi's direction as we go. "Come on. I need to go change," I coax.*

*The moment my bedroom door is shut, I relax. The throbbing in my temple has been there all day again, along with a wave of dizziness, nausea, and fatigue.*

*"You look like shit," Travis remarks, heading toward my bathroom.*

*"Gee, thanks!"*

*I lift the dress over my head and drop it to the floor, then step in front of the mirror and grimace. Turning from side to side, I rest a hand on my lower stomach.*

*"What the hell am I going to do?" I whisper.*

*"Bed. Relax for a bit, then we'll go back out there and kick them all out," Travis says, coming back into the room, shirtless, his six-pack gleaming under the light. "And stop staring at me like that. You look like you want to eat me alive." He throws the comforter back on my bed. "Come on. In you get," he rumbles. "I'm going to hold you and my bubba for a little while." Anxiety coupled with guilt eats away at me as I slide into the sheets and let him do just that.*

That same heaviness I've been feeling for weeks now comes over me, and I rest my head on my pillow and close my eyes. Then I allow myself to succumb to the darkness, where he waits for me. Those green eyes shimmer back at me with intensity, holding me captive with his possessive dominance.

# TEN

## SUMMER

THE SUN BEAMS into my room, and the birds chirp, but I'm miserable. I'm hiding away in my bedroom until I have to leave for school, hoping and praying I don't see Mase this morning. After falling asleep last night, I managed to stay in ignorant bliss. Today, however, is going to be worse than yesterday; I can feel it. The tension in the house literally radiates through the walls, and the feeling of being watched burns through my skin. I burrow deeper into the sheets, trying to stave off the inevitable fallout.

Ignorance is bliss if you allow it to be, and that's something I've become very accustomed to, it seems.

My phone buzzes beside my bed, and I reach my hand out of the sheets to grab it.

Travis: Are you okay?

Me: No.

Travis: Feel sick?

Travis: Have you seen your brother yet?

Me: No and No.

Travis: Do you want me to come over so we can talk to him together?

After seeing Mason so crazed last night, I know him coming over isn't a good idea.

Me: Can you just collect me from the gate. I'll be fine.

Travis: You NEED to talk to him Summer.

Me: I will.

Suddenly, as if on cue, nausea floods me, and I throw the sheet off the bed and rush toward the bathroom. My knees hit the cold floor as I retch into the toilet, wishing someone was here, anyone.

Loneliness consumes me, but the fear of what's to come is stronger.

"Jesus, Summer. What a mess of your life you've made," I mumble, and wipe my mouth with toilet paper before standing and flushing away my sins.

Sleeping with a stranger for money was supposed to be the end of all my problems, not the start of more.

Still, at least the memories of that night are something I can cling to. The best night of my life, with a hot guy who just so happens to be my stepbrother.

———

After applying another coat of lip gloss, I assess my hair, finger-combing my blonde locks, and give myself the mental pep talk I need to open my bedroom door and walk out of it.

"Come on, Summer. You got this." I blow out a deep breath, grab my backpack, and head for the door.

As I slowly step down each stair, there's nothing but silence. Thank God. Hopefully, I can grab some food and make it out to school before he wakes.

Making my way down the marble stairs, the first thing I notice is that the foyer's clean, tidy, devoid of any trash, not a streamer or empty bottle in sight. You wouldn't think that only a few hours ago a house party was in full swing.

My shoes squeak as I walk across the floor and into the kitchen, and I consider removing them so as not to disturb anyone. Anyone being Mase.

I push open the kitchen door and slip inside, determined to remain undetected, then I head for the refrigerator. Grabbing the orange juice, I make quick work of pouring myself a glass, then I close the door and head for the fruit bowl.

There's not much I can stomach in the morning, but a banana is one thing I can manage.

"What the hell are you wearing?" a dark voice growls, penetrating my soul. It sends a shock wave through me, causing goose bumps to break out as I take a deep breath, then turn to face him.

Irritation rushes up my spine at the hate in his tone. It's not like this was done on purpose—none of it was done on purpose.

I lift my head, and my eyes clash with his, where I see the venom in his stare, so I take a step back.

*Great, he hates me.*

He's just as guilty as I am in all this, yet I don't hate him, not a single part of him.

"It's called a school uniform," I snark back with feigned confidence while peeling the banana.

Heat travels over me as he looks me up and down at a leisurely pace that sends excitement rushing through me, and it gathers in my core. And now my panties are wet.

"That skirt doesn't fit you right." He gestures toward my skirt, and I peer down at it. It absolutely does fit me right. There's no way in hell I'd be allowed to wear one any shorter; our school is the best in the area, most expensive too. All their students are dressed accordingly, with not a bit of wiggle room. Trust me, I've tried.

"Take it up with the principal." I slowly eat the banana, loving his attention on me much more than I should.

There's silence between us while we eat, and I can't help but wonder what he's thinking. I use this time to study him, drinking him in like he is me. He's just as handsome as I remember; more so if that's even possible. How I'd love to explore his tattoos fully, giving each of them the attention they deserve, and to be able to touch him properly, to trace them with the tip of my finger while I kiss his bronzed skin. Those gray joggers he's wearing showcase his thick cock, and I long to release it. Wow, that monster fit inside me. I smile internally when it jumps as if knowing where my attention is focused.

"How long will you be staying for?" I ask nonchalantly.

"I went to the will reading yesterday."

"But you didn't come to your father's funeral?" I interject with venom. Nope, the bastard never showed his face; I had to do that alone.

"Not that it's any of your business, but we didn't have a relationship. I wasn't about to pay my respects to a man I had none for."

"Lucky you," I snipe back.

His eyebrows fly into his hairline, but he continues on as if I didn't just call him out. "His attorneys informed me that I'm your guardian until you finish school."

The banana falls from my hand onto the counter, and my mouth drops open. "What?"

Mase looks smug, his eyes glimmering with retribution. "That's right. I'm essentially your daddy."

"M-my ..." My words fail me.

He chuckles, but it's patronizing, lacking humor. "I'm in charge of your ass, Summer. So, no more whoring yourself out until you finish school, at least. Then you can do whatever the hell you want." He shrugs, wearing a calculating smile.

His words are like a dagger to my heart, slicing through it and crippling me. Tears spring to my eyes, but I refuse to let them fall. Instead, I straighten my spine and blink them away.

"It's okay. I learned a hard lesson that day. Some men don't know how to please you at all." Then I lift my chin, scoop up the banana, and drop it into the bin. Pasting a smile on my face, I sway my hips as I walk out the door and head to school.

Mason Campbell can go fuck himself because I wouldn't go near him if he paid me. Again.

# ELEVEN

## MASE

"IT'S OKAY. I learned a hard lesson that day. Some men don't know how to please you at all." Her sexy ass sashays out of the room while her words ricochet around my mind like a drum beating repetitively.

I clench my teeth so hard they hurt.

Why the fuck do those words bother me so damn much anyway? Tara's taunts come to mind. After years of her throwing insults at me, I shouldn't be surprised Summer's words cut so deep.

"Morning, sir, would you like me to make you a coffee?"

My eyes snap up toward Hugh's. "Huh?"

"Coffee?" He nods toward the espresso machine with a supercilious smile.

"Yeah, thanks."

"It was a late night for you, wasn't it?"

"Yeah," I grunt, replaying her words again. One after the fucking other.

My focus remains on the doors she walked through over

an hour ago, and I realize I didn't hear the garage door when she left.

"Does she drive to school?"

"I'm afraid Miss Summer doesn't have a car. Your father liked to keep control over her. She can be quite the handful," Hugh states, and my attention is back on him. "You did well to get the house straight for this morning."

I ignore his comment. He knows damn well I had a team come in and take care of things. Instead, I ask what's been eating away at me all night long. "How long does she have left at school?"

After leaving her room and organizing for a team of cleaners to come in, I was torn between slipping back into her bedroom and holding her hostage, convinced she was going to run after the punk who left her half-naked ass in bed, or spend the rest of the night jerking off to memories of her trying to take my cock while simultaneously not giving her a choice in the matter. The latter won out, and now, when I thought I'd emptied my balls completely, they're proving me otherwise. I'm like a damn horny teenager all over again. Only, this time, I'm more determined than ever not to get screwed over by a woman.

"Only a few months," Hugh replies. "She turned eighteen just after your father passed away."

I nod and breathe a sigh of relief. At least she was eighteen when I fucked her, just like she said. That's good; I can work with that. And do what? I'm not sure. Fuck her again? Pack her bags? Something along those lines. I drag a hand down my face. *Ugh. As. Fucking. If.* I want the girl, so what's the point in denying it.

"My father made me her fucking guardian until she finishes school."

"I heard." He grimaces, and I narrow my eyes. The walls have fucking eyes in this place. It was the same when I was a child. I never could take a step out of line without my father knowing about it, and I can't help but wonder just how much input Hugh had in that. How much does he know? Everything, no doubt.

"Who was her mother?"

"Miss Angie."

"And she passed away?"

"Yes …" He ponders for a moment. "Possibly seven or eight years ago now. Or maybe more like ten."

I sit there, stunned. Ten fucking years ago. I've seen my father in that time, and there was never a mention of a kid. Although, there was that one time when he introduced me to some woman in his office; she had a kid. I shudder at the thought of Summer as a child, one I could have previously met and have now fucked. Shifting on the kitchen stool, I scrub a hand over my head. *Jesus, that's fucked up.*

"He married two more women after that," he says, making his way around the kitchen to start breakfast. "Both of them didn't last long." His words come out laced with boredom.

"Sounds about right. But he kept Summer around?" That surprises me.

"He had a soft spot for her," he confirms. I'll bet he did. The dirty bastard had a thing for younger women. Thank fuck, she never came of age when he was around. My knuckles are pained, and I glance down to stare at the tight ball I hold them in without even realizing.

Hugh pushes a cup of coffee into my hand, and I give him a guarded smile while scanning him. His hair is definitely silver now, and his shoulders are hunched. Age has served him well, though, I'll give him that. He still wears the black suit my father provided and the white shirt with the cufflinks my father gifted to him for his fiftieth birthday a very long time ago.

*Shouldn't this dude be retiring soon?*

"If I were you, I'd keep her away from that Travis."

My muscles stiffen, and I cock an eyebrow. "Travis?"

"The boy she had in her bedroom. The one who left shortly after you went inside."

The hairs on the back of my neck stand on end.

"He's not to be trusted," he adds on, staring at me pointedly. This fucker knows all my movements, of course he does. He's one of my father's minions, after all, and while I'm living here, that's something I need to sort ASAP. I need to call Owen and have someone come in and check the house for cameras. I wouldn't put anything past these fuckers. There's no way in hell I would leave Summer here, knowing how vulnerable a position she could be in. My body calls to her, even though it shouldn't.

The thought of leaving her at all sends a ripple of dread through me.

Of all the women to have this effect on me, it had to be her.

The one woman I shouldn't want.

# TWELVE

## MASE

I HATE the fact that she's been gone all day. I hate that she's gone to school in a short-as-fuck skirt, and more so, I hate that the little prick Travis is the one seeing her in it.

Did she fuck him?

Of course she has; she was in bed with him, half-naked. If only I could have moved on as easily. Did her pussy convulse around him like it did me, holding me deep while I filled her full of my cum.

Anger surges through me as my emotions turn to hatred, and I'm grateful when my phone cuts through my spiraling thoughts.

"Hey, you good?" Owen grunts.

"Yeah," I lie, dragging a hand down my face, and Owen chuckles knowingly. I've known him since I was a small boy. He knows me just as well as my other best friends and business owners, Tate, Shaw, and Reed. So he knows when I'm full of shit. My friends have been with me through thick and thin, the good times and the bad, and there isn't anything I wouldn't do for them, and them me. They're the family I never had. "No. I'm not good. The bastard put a clause in the will."

"What?" he bellows. "Did you speak to Reed yet?"

I pace the lawn of the back garden because there's no fucking way I'm having conversations in the house. "No. I have other shit to figure out first."

"Like what?"

A lump forms in my throat, and I contemplate my next words.

Do I tell him about Summer?

Do I admit she's the girl from *Indulgence*?

Will he think badly of me?

I decide against it, choosing to keep it vague.

"He left me as a guardian of my stepsister."

"What?" He chuckles. "I didn't know you had one."

"Me neither," I grunt.

Before he can ask further questions, I change the subject.

"I think he has cameras in the house, and I want them all found and taken down."

"Cameras?" Disbelief is evident in his tone.

My gut tells me there's so much more to this, and the familiar heavy lead ball settles in my stomach, rising by the second. "Yeah. I just want the house secure." I omit the part about wanting Summer safe, because something doesn't feel right, or maybe it's just being back here that's making me angsty.

"I'll make contact with some guys in the area and message you back shortly. If there're cameras in the house, they'll find them. If that's the case, I'd also consider some new staff, Mase."

This won't go down well with Hugh, but you know what? Fuck him. He can stay on as my gratitude to his service, but everyone else can leave. They haven't done a very good job of securing the property so far, since Summer managed to throw a party and end up in bed with someone while I just walked inside like a stranger off the street.

My fists flex as I consider how much she could've been taken advantage of; did that little prick force her into bed?

No, she whored her tight little ass to me. She isn't a prude, clearly, and now he's reaping the benefits of me breaking her in. I was used by her, just like Tara used me.

Fury has my vision turning hazy.

"I got you, Brother." Owen ends the call, and I turn to stare back at the mansion. An ominous feeling creeps up my spine, and a shiver washes over me.

Something tells me I'm not going to like whatever the fuck happens next.

# THIRTEEN



I'VE AVOIDED HER AGAIN. She came home from school and made herself scarce while I hid away, looking at prospective properties on the laptop for our next business endeavor. Though my mind wasn't in it at all.

Nope, all I could think about all day was my gorgeous little stepsister, the one I shouldn't want but crave with my entirety.

She's here in the same house as me, sleeping just down the hall from me. I could take her, make her mine.

My mind flickers back to this Travis. Is he her boyfriend? Has he been touching her like I want to touch her? Fury has my blood boiling, causing a deep-seated cavern of vengeance to grow, and I fucking hate the feeling. It's like I'm losing control.

Throwing the sheets off me, I check the time—11:56 p.m. The house is silent as I head down the stairs to grab a bottle of water, and when I step into the kitchen, my blood stills and my tongue thickens. Hell, I almost choke on it.

Jesus. Fucking. Christ.

Not being able to sleep because I'm back in this hellhole has its advantages, and one of those advantages is, it appears, my sweet little stepsister can't sleep either.

She's bent over with her head inside the refrigerator, her slinky sleep shorts exposing the globes of her ass to me and begging for me to slap them and leave a mark behind.

I adjust my cock in my joggers—the head still peeking out of the waistband, eager to get in on the action—while watching Summer in fascination as she makes a sweet little sound that tells me she's drinking something.

Fuck, she'd sound hot with my hand wrapped around her throat while she chokes on my cock and tries to guzzle down my cum.

A glistening bead of pre-cum oozes at the slit of my cock, begging to be licked away by the innocent bombshell currently releasing the cool air into the kitchen. I bet her little nipples are all pointed.

Unable to help myself, a hungry growl rattles in my throat, startling her. She spins to face me, spewing what looks like the entire carton of milk from her mouth, down her camisole, and onto the floor at her feet.

She's stunned to the spot, wide-eyed and dripping and, fuck me, did she ever look so perfect.

"Aren't you a messy girl?" I croon, stepping around the counter, uncaring if she sees my solid cock, and judging by the way her cheeks heat, I'm betting she has.

"I was looking for dark chocolate," she says, and my lip twitches at her explanation.

Unable to help myself, I wrap my hand around the back of her neck and pull her closer to me to trail my tongue down the column of her neck and over her chest.

"I think I'd rather taste your milk," I growl.

Her breath hitches at the contact, and her toes curl. So fucking beautiful. My mouth waters for a taste of the forbidden. Just a taste.

For one night.

She bats her lashes, her stunned reaction an aphrodisiac, and before I can stop myself, I admit my thoughts.

"You look fucking beautiful covered in milk, sweetheart." I relish the whimper leaving her lips. I can't help myself as I deliver a long, slow lick over the spilled milk dripping down her chest and disappearing into the low neckline of her camisole. "Let me lick you clean, precious girl."

She tilts her head, as if giving me approval, but I wasn't asking for it. Moving a strap off her shoulder, one after the other, her top falls to her waist, giving me access to her pert little tits. Her nipples are pulled tight for the taking. My mouth waters and my cock throbs. "Fuck, look at you." I blow over her nipples, loving the way goosebumps break out over her exposed skin.

"Please," she pants, and her hand finds the back of my neck, her fingernails digging in to hold me in place.

"Who do you want, little Innocent Angel? Saintly or Sinner?" I smirk against her silky skin.

"Oh god." She moans when my tongue laps at her nipple. "Sinner. I want Sinner. I want you, Mase."

My chest expands with pride. She wants me.

"Do you want me to lick at your sweet little tits, sister?" I rasp. "Do you want me to clean up your mess?"

"Ye-yes."

I hold one of her tits in the palm of my hand and squeeze, stroking over the tip of her nipple while my tongue works over the other. "Fuck, you'd look so damn beautiful feeding me." My tongue ravishes her with each stroke. The thought of her full of my baby and her gifting me milk has me feeling feral. "So damn pretty producing milk for me."

"Ahh ..." Her body tightens when I tug her nipple into my mouth and suck. Then I release it and gently lick over the tip.

"I'd fucking bathe in your milk, Summer." She pushes my head against her harder.

"I want that."

"Are you going to make milk for me, sweetheart?" I deliver smoothly, my cock weeping in appreciation.

"Ye-yes."

I love the fact that she's embracing my kink, having never realized I had this one until now. Now all I see is my girl pumping her milk from her heavy tit while I open my mouth and wait for a stream of her warmth to splash against my tongue.

"Fuck, Summer, you're so damn perfect." I grunt, my cock leaking ropes of pre-cum against the waistband of my sweatpants, leaving a sticky patch on my abs.

"Mase, I think, I think I'm going to ..." Her mouth falls open as she stares down at me, her nails biting harder, and my lips suckle while I give myself over to the dream of her being the one to provide the milk for me.

Hot. As. Fuck.

The moment her body relaxes, she steps back, and I miss the feel of her tit. Annoyance rumbles inside me, but when she lowers to the floor, for the second time tonight, I almost choke on my tongue.

Kneeling in a puddle of spilled milk is my sweet girl.

My sister.

"I want some too."

Holy fucking shitballs.

I scramble to lower my sweatpants, my cock springing out and bounces back hitting my abs in the process. "You need fed too, beautiful?"

She licks her lips and nods.

"Open that mouth. Let me fill your mouth with my milk, Summer."

"Oh god," she whines, but proceeds to part her lips.

"You need a drink? Let me stuff those sweet lips for you."

Her hair sways as she nods her agreement, and I have a deep-seated desire that needs to be sated. I want to mess my little sister up.

With her mouth open, I loom above her, fisting my cock as I pump it up and down ferociously. A wave of heat licks up my spine, pure, unadulterated bliss filling my bloodstream.

"Such a good girl for her stepbrother."

Her pupils flare as her tongue stretches out of her mouth, giving me no choice but to swipe the tip along it, delivering her with a stream of pre-cum, which drips off her tongue and down her chin. Such a beautiful sight. Such a beautiful mess.

My hand works quicker, and my balls draw up. "Oh, fuck." I grunt at the sound of my skin slapping against my thick length. "Let me give you your milk now, sweetheart. Be a good girl for me and open wide." Faster and faster my fist pumps. "Let me feed those little pouty lips."

The first spurt of my cum hits her tongue; it's thick and white, hot and heavy. The next splashes over her face, then I aim for her blonde locks, over her chin, and finally over her beautiful tits.

Jesus, how the hell have I come so much?

"Do you like it?" I ask, pulling back, and use my knuckles to trace down her perfect face. She ducks her head submissively. "You're so fucking beautiful, Summer."

She closes her eyes, and her chest rises with short, shallow intakes of air. I use this moment to take a step back, unwilling to be drawn in by the way she makes me feel, and worse, the way she makes me unravel like never before.

# FOURTEEN



**SUMMER**

MY MIND CONTINUES to wander to a few nights ago. It's almost like it was a dream. I mean, did that really happen? Did I really spill milk? Did Mase lick it from me while whispering dirty promises into the night before I sucked him off?

Surely, I dreamed it.

We've spent the last few days avoiding one another, and at some point, we need to have a conversation; I know we do. It would be the mature, adult thing to do, but I can't bring myself to make the first move.

Although he stared at me with such hatred, I clearly cause a sexual reaction in him. It was impossible for him to hide his arousal, and that has me biting into my lip as I contemplate that the man I gave my virginity to is also the same man who is now not only my guardian, but my stepbrother.

Travis launches a piece of bread at me, and it hits my forehead. "You're staring into space."

"What the fuck, Trav?"

"Hey, I finally grabbed your attention." He shrugs and continues eating his lunch with a shit-eating grin on his face.

"Funny. I'm having an internal meltdown here," I whine.

"Right, you've gone from having a psychopathic father to psycho brother."

I wince at his words. "Please don't call him my brother."

"Well, I hate—" A cold liquid spills over my head, and I jump up from my chair with a shriek.

Travis pushes his chair, sending it screeching across the floor and cutting through the noise of the cafeteria. It goes silent, and all eyes are on us. On me.

I stand frozen to the spot, drenched in an ice-cold drink. Again, for the second time in less than a week.

"Oops." Levi smirks.

"Oops?" Travis's voice sounds deadly.

"Yeah, oops." Levi shrugs. "At least she's wet for you." He chuckles, and the cafeteria breaks in to fits of giggles while my eyes fill with tears. Just what the hell is his problem? It's like he hates me.

Travis moves quickly, roaring as he charges toward Levi, and I step back just in time to witness him slam him to the ground, where he delivers blow after blow to Levi's face. The sound of bones breaking finally snaps me out of my stunned state.

"Oh, shit, Trav." I pull on his shirt while darting my gaze around the room, hoping there's no staff around to see it. "Stop, please." I try again, but he's too consumed with anger. "Come on, Trav. Stop," I plead helplessly.

When a whistle is blown, my heart sinks, and I release my grip on his shirt.

This is it; this is the end for Travis. He's already retaking his final year after what went down last year, and now he won't be able to graduate. All because of Levi fucking Williamson and his weird obsession with me.

# FIFTEEN

## MASE

I'VE SPENT the morning reviewing Summer's file I was given at the will reading, and although it's filled with meaningless shit, it has given me an insight into her personality. My father kept close tabs on her, noting where she spent her free time and with who, and while I hate that information, I like the fact I have something to judge what kind of person she is, and it only makes me like her all the more.

She enjoys the outdoors, eating out, and has few friends. Her grades are good, excelling in literature, where she wrote an essay on how losing a parent affects your health. In social studies, she won a prestigious award for essay on 'Family structures and the effects on children,' and that caused sparks to fly in my chest when I read it. It gave me a deeper understanding of her pain. It's something someone as innocent and sweet as her shouldn't have had to endure, and I hate that she has.

While I was reading up on the girl who consumes my every thought, Owen had a team of security experts sent into the mansion, and what they discovered made my stomach turn.

My father was a sadistic, controlling son of a bitch, and the thought of Summer growing up in his care terrifies me. Just what the hell has she witnessed and experienced under his care? I know firsthand how callous and cold he is, and only now do I wish I'd been around to protect her from his torment.

I'm not sure why I feel an incredible sense of protective possession toward her. Maybe it's because she gave me her virginity, maybe it's because I'm her guardian, her only family. I don't fucking know. All I know is I want to keep her safe. I want to shout from the rooftop she's mine to protect while meaning every damn word of it.

I twirl the small camera lens, the size of a dime, between my fingers, trying to figure out what my old man's objective was. Yet, at the same time, I'm terrified to find out.

There's a knock on my father's office door, and before I open my mouth, Hugh has pushed it open. The fact he didn't wait for me to call him has my jaw grinding from side to side. The fucker has overstayed his welcome in this house, and when I voiced my concerns to Owen, he suggested keeping him on until he's accessed the footage from the cameras.

Oscar O'Connell has stepped in to help; a tech genius who also happens to be a part of a Mafia family, therefore, has some incredibly productive connections we've used once or twice ourselves when needed. Luca Varros, a Capo for the Varros family, being one of those connections. He's also a notoriously sick bastard who has a basement for torturing the life out of those deserving such punishment. Shame my father never made it down the concrete steps to Luca's playroom. I hear he has someone who loves to torment their victims with a cattle prod, of all things.

In between time, Owen has diverted all calls to the mansion to my phone and has placed all new firewalls on the internet, as well as instructed our own security teams to oversee the property.

"Mason, I have to say, I'm concerned about the welfare of your father's estate," he says in a disgruntled tone that has my eyebrows raising. Prick has most definitely overstayed. "The cameras"—he gestures toward the camera between my fingertips—"were placed in the mansion for Miss Summer's protection."

"Protection against what?" I lift my head, meeting his eyes, and he slowly swallows.

"She can be a handful."

I nod. "But what does she need protecting from?" I query, locking my gaze on him with a challenging glare. Not only does the fucker make no sense, but I also think he's full of shit. He knows something. Hell, he probably knows everything.

"Your father wanted to be sure she was safe."

"From what?" I counter, getting pissed that he's averting my questions.

He shifts from foot to foot and scratches the back of his neck.

"What did my father want to keep her safe from?"

"I've no idea, sir."

Hmm, back to referring to me as sir now since the pressure is on and he's not as comfortable as when he first burst into the room.

"Don't worry, I have her handled," I reply. His eyes bounce over my face, searching for something. "That all?" I lift an eyebrow.

Again, he swallows harshly, and I calculate each and every move. "I don't want to overstep"—he shifts from side to side—"but have you made your father's associates aware of your relationship with your stepsister?"

I remain stunned. The old bastard doesn't miss a damn trick, that's for sure, and I don't fucking like it.

"That's nobody's damn business but mine and Summer's," I grind out, holding his stare with an intensity that forces him to glance away.

"Very well, sir." He gives a firm nod, then turns on his heel and opens the door.

"Actually, Hugh. Could you help me with something?"

He looks over his shoulder. "If I can," he replies.

"Where does the footage from the cameras go?"

He blinks, then gawks back at me, and my eyes zero in on the bead of sweat gathering on his forehead. "I'm guessing to your father's computer." He glances at a spot on my father's desk, an empty spot. "His laptop, I mean."

I cross my arms over my thick chest and relax into the chair. "And where might I find the laptop?"

His jaw sharpens and his focus intensifies. That's right, fucker, I know you know something. "I don't know. I'm too old for anything like that. I know nothing about technology; I'm almost seventy, Mason." He chuckles, but I just stare at him. Is he deliberately trying to piss me off by evading my questions?

"I didn't ask if you knew about technology. I asked you if you knew where his laptop was."

His face falls, and his eyes sharpen. "No. I don't know where it is." There's a dark edge to his tone I don't like, and I'm not even sure he knows he revealed it.

"That'll be all." I force a smile; one I drop as soon as the door closes behind him.

I'm going to discover your secrets, motherfucker. If Summer is in jeopardy in any way, I'll happily take him to the Varros residence. I need to let off some steam, and Hugh is looking like the perfect candidate.

My phone buzzes, and I fumble with it as I accept the call. I'm expecting one from Owen with some answers, but it's too soon for that.

"Hello?"

"Is this Mr. Campbell?"

"It is."

"This is Preston Academy. I'm sorry to tell you, but we've had an incident with Summer Campbell"—my pulse rushes and my head feels light—"and you're down as her next of kin. Is it possible for you to come into school to discuss the situation, please?"

"Y-yes, sure." Holy fuck. What the hell happened? "Is she okay?"

"She's perfectly fine, Mr. Campbell. We just need to discuss the situation with you."

"Okay. I'll be right over."

I end the call, push back in the chair, and grab my truck keys, mentally preparing myself.

I'm about to go into a fucking school to collect the girl I want to fuck. Hell, *have* fucked already. How screwed up is that?

# SIXTEEN



I THROW open the school door and march toward the reception, and my feet come to a halt when my eyes are drawn to Summer as if magnetized toward her. She's sitting outside the school office in a row with three students, but the others don't exist to me.

She appears wet, really fucking wet, and not in the good way.

Her blue eyes shimmer, on the verge of tears, and I want to wrap her in my embrace and protect her. She quickly averts her gaze while I remain rooted to the spot, heart hammering like a love-struck teenager, and time stands still.

Why the hell does my body crave hers like no other? Why do I feel so alive and finally like myself when I'm in her proximity?

Why did it have to be her?

When she lifts her head to face me, my confusion is replaced with fury pumping through my bloodstream. Someone has hurt her. Someone has purposely put that vulnerable look in her eyes, the one that calls for me to protect her, to control her. She gets up from the chair and looks to me with hope, and when I hold out my hand, relief floods her features. Her lip wobbles, and I want nothing more than to slam my mouth against hers.

The moment her hand slips into mine, the anger diminishes but doesn't vanish. I tug her until she collides with my chest, then take her face in my thick palms and hold her there, staring down into her blue eyes, eyes as deep as the ocean and as bright as a clear sky. I fall into her orbit, where there's only me and her.

She searches my gaze, and I hope she can see every unspoken thought in my mind, especially the loudest one—she's mine.

A throat clears, making me drop my hands to my side, and I instantly miss the feel of her warmth. "Mr. Campbell, I'm Mr. Franklin, the principal." He shakes my hand. "It's unfortunate that Summer was the victim of a disagreement between two of our students."

My attention skips to the other students in the chairs, and I jolt when I realize one is the kid from her bed. Travis. My nostrils flare, but I quickly look away, unwilling to become more jealous of a kid than I already am.

"A disagreement?" I snipe back.

"It appears so." The principal nods. "They will be punished accordingly; you have my word on that."

"I want a full report tomorrow," I bite out, and his jaw falls lax. Fuck him, nobody messes with what's mine. "My sister doesn't come to school to be the victim of mindless bullies." Summer flinches beside me, then steps forward and opens her mouth, but the glare I send her has it snapping shut just as quick. "Let's go." I wave a hand toward the door, and without giving her time to consider her next move, I grab her arm and tug her along with me. "Tomorrow; otherwise, I'll have the police involved," I throw over my shoulder toward the stunned principal.

# SUMMER

His grip on my arm tightens, and my feet rush to keep up with him as he strides toward his truck.

"Mase? Mase? Will you slow down?"

He releases me when he reaches the passenger door, then swings it open and nods toward the seat. "In."

I roll my eyes at his gruff tone and slip inside. Then he shocks the hell out of me and leans in, and I almost combust as his deep-bergamot cologne fills my nostrils, sending a rush of nostalgia through me.

His muscular weight presses in on me, pinning me down, but the click of the seatbelt diverts my attention, and my cheeks heat at realizing he strapped me in.

When he slides inside the truck and starts the engine, I chew on the corner of my nail.

"What happened?" he asks, reversing out of the spot a little too fast. The vein on his neck is pulsating, and I want to trace it with my tongue.

I shake my head as lunchtime plays out in my mind. "Levi poured a drink over me."

His eyebrows furrow, and he steals a peek toward me. "Levi?"

"The douche. The other guy back there." I throw a thumb in the direction of the school.

He nods, but he can't understand, not based on a small incident in school. Nope, the prick has had it in for me all year. Travis said it's because he wants to fuck me, but I think he gets a sick kick out of fucking with me.

He glances at me, then back at the road, gripping the steering wheel. "I don't want him anywhere near you." I'm about to tell him me too, but he continues on. "The other guy. You're to stay away from him too."

My spine snaps straight, and a disgruntled noise leaves my lips, drawing his attention. "No."

"No?" I can practically feel the steam pumping out of his ears, and his face turns redder. His T-shirt pulls tight as he adjusts himself in his seat; he looks seconds away from exploding.

I cross my arms over my chest, grimacing at the way my wet shirt clings to me.

"He's my best friend."

An obnoxious scoff leaves him, and outrage surges through me.

He turns toward me, the vein on his temple twitching. The muscles on his forearms are tightly strung with the grasp he has on the steering wheel now turning his knuckles white. "You fuck all your best friends?"

My mouth gapes open, and I delight in the fact his eyes zero in on my lips before he darts his focus back to the road.

"I haven't fucked him," I grit out, pissed I'm explaining myself.

"Yeah, right," he mumbles under his breath, causing irritation to prickle my skin. Just who the hell does he think he is?

"I'm not a liar, Mase." I flick my wet hair over my shoulder and straighten my spine. "And you can go to hell if you think I'm listening to you and your demands."

I swear I hear his teeth grind. "Didn't have a problem

listening to my demands when you had my cock in your mouth." My mouth falls open; he did not just say that. "Besides, I'm your guardian," he spits out like it's killing him. "You'll do as I fucking say."

"Make me," I taunt, with a condescending smile I feel down to my bones. If he thinks he can walk into my life and change my carefully crafted plans, then he can think again. Mason Campbell might be a walking wet dream, but I can be his worst nightmare.

# MASE

"Make me." She smiles with taunting glee.

I've had a short fuse from the moment I stepped foot in my father's office. Hell, from the moment I discovered I had to enter the will reading without one of my best friends beside me. I knew, I just knew something would go wrong and my life would change.

What I did not expect was Summer Campbell, and that fuse? That fuse is about to short circuit and ultimately combust.

Red-hot fury fills every cell in my body. The fact that she's unwilling to comply causes a wave of anger to overtake my entire being.

The Mase I try to tamper down, the one I refuse to be—the darker, meaner, controlling version of myself I never let show —is about to take over.

I swerve onto the dirt at the side of the road so fast Summer squeals and clings to the oh-shit bar like her life depends on it.

As soon as I put the truck into park, I'm out and moving around to her side. Her startled gaze greets me, and I don't allow myself to glimpse down at her wet shirt as I unbuckle her and grasp her arm.

"Oh my God, you're insane. You can't leave me here!" she screeches, and my mind barely registers her words, too intent on one thing. Making her comply.

She drags her feet in the dirt as I maneuver her and open up the back passenger door. "Get in!"

She spins to face me, and the scent of the strawberry drink in her hair wafts in the breeze, only pissing me off further. "What?"

I tilt my head toward the car. "In. On your knees."

Arousal sparks in her baby blues, and when she swallows hard, my cock rubs against the waistband of my jeans from imagining her swallowing me down. It's barely been soft all day. Thoughts of her have consumed me so much I need a release. Then she submits to me, tamping my fury just enough for me not to want to make my mark on her permanent.

Not yet anyway.

She clambers into the back, then kneels on the seat, and excitement thrums through me, stealing my breath.

Holy shit, I'm going to do this.

Me and Summer Campbell. My stepsister.

Never in my wildest dreams did I imagine punishing a brat. But with my palm twitching and my cock throbbing, I know I've no choice but to give myself over to the dominant side of me battling to get out.

"You're being a brat. Now you get spanked like one."

She peeks over her shoulder, and her bright-blue eyes clash with mine. They're full of need, full of want, and my heart pounds against my chest like a drum as she silently pleads with me to give her what we both want.

Unable to wait any longer, I flip her skirt over her ass and delight in her innocent white panties exposed to me. Jesus, why the fuck are they so hot?

*Because they're not the fancy lace shit Tara always wore.*

She's not trying to be anything she isn't.

Pushing her panties into the crack of her ass, I step forward and raise my hand. The impact of my palm sends a resounding smack through the air. A sound that makes my balls draw up and causes my cock to leak.

"You're being a brat," I announce again, louder this time.

*Smack.*

"You've got to be a good girl."

She gasps, and my eyes roll. Holy fuck, I could come from that sound alone.

*Smack.*

"Gotta learn, Summer."

*Smack.*

"Gonna be a good girl for me?"

She moans, actually fucking moans. "Oh, god, please."

*Smack.*

"Say sorry, Sum." I smooth my palm over her reddened cheek. "Say it."

Her panting breaths fill the space between us, and it's clear she's struggling to remain in control and not give in to me.

*Smack.*

"Ahh! S-Sorry," she whispers, sending a rush of euphoria through me.

"Good girl."

My fingers fumble with my belt, then I pop open my jeans and pull out my leaking cock. Snatching her by the hips, I yank her toward the edge of the seat. When I push her panties to the side, I delight in the way they're wet, soaked in her arousal.

"You like me punishing you, sweetheart?" I rasp, lining my cock up to her dripping hole.

"Y-yes."

I slam inside her, and her body stiffens as I plunge all the way in, then draw back and slam inside harder, faster, deeper with each punishing thrust. My hips bounce off her ass as I take what I want from her. "That's it, give it up for me. Give me your tight cunt, Summer."

She somehow manages to grip me tighter, and the slapping of our skin is an aphrodisiac to my pent-up, tension-filled soul.

"Fuck. Fuck," I chant, pleasure zipping up my spine.

With a hand between us, I press the pad of my thumb on her already-swollen clit, circling it as I do. "Come," I command, and she lets out a scream that bounces off the trees. I stumble forward, pumping her small body with thick, hot ropes of my cum before falling against her and causing us both to collapse onto the seat. Our heavy breaths fill the truck, and the smell of sex permeates the air, bringing with it a sense of solace, and I know in this moment, I found my person. She's it for me, the one who sees all of me and doesn't want to change a damn thing. No, she embraces me for who I am.

She sets my body ablaze, weathers the onset, then becomes my calm after the storm.

We're about to walk into the darkness together and bask in it.

# SEVENTEEN

## SUMMER

I CONTINUE BITING my nails as Mase drives. He's quiet, deep in thought, and staring ahead like I don't exist, and I hate it. He did, after all, just come inside me. Again.

He spanked my ass, and I loved it, submitting whole-heartedly.

My body came alive beneath him, and in that moment, I would have given him whatever he wanted because I wanted it even more.

But the silence isn't something I can take; it feels like a rejection, almost as if he's shutting down and blocking out what we did.

His hands are still clutching the steering wheel like he's angry. Is he angry with himself for giving in?

There's an odd tension between us, similar to the night I gave myself to him. I'm waiting for something to happen, but I have no clue what. I only hope this isn't rejection; not when I crave his touch so much.

"Do you regret it?" I whisper.

He turns toward me, scanning my face, then looks back toward the road. "Fucking you?"

I nod, but I know he can't see.

"Of course not."

His knuckles are white where he clings to the steering wheel like it's his lifeline. "Then why are you still hyped up?"

"Hyped up?"

"Your hands are tight on the steering wheel; your jaw keeps twitching as if you're angry. Are you angry with me or you?"

He chuckles, but it lacks humor. "You take note of everything, huh?"

I chew on my lip. "The anxiety is rolling off you in waves."

He drags a hand down his face. "Ugh. Yeah, I'm still wound up."

I hate that for him, but love the fact he's admitting his vulnerability, like he's trusting me with a part of himself he maybe doesn't share with many.

"What can I do to help?"

His green eyes are heated but full of angst as if he's toying with himself and unsure of letting me in and seeing this part of him. He drags his tongue over his top lip, and, coupled with the hunger in his eyes, it has me squirming against my wet panties.

When his attention goes back to the road, my shoulders sag.

"I guess I just like to feel you close to me, and that's fucked up." He lifts his shoulder, side-eyeing me.

Hope builds inside me, making my confidence soar. "I like feeling you close too." My voice comes out breathy.

Mase shifts in his seat, and I delight in it. "How close, exactly?"

I can't help but smile. "What do you have in mind?"

His tongue darts out again. "Your lips around my cock."

My eyebrows shoot up; he's hard again already? "You want me to give you head?"

His eyebrows knit together, and his hands shift on the steering wheel. "I just want to feel you there. In my lap with me inside you."

Holy shit. He wants me to suck on him to bring him comfort.

"That sounds hot," I rasp.

He side-eyes me. "Yeah?" Skepticism laces his tone.

"Yes. Really hot, Mase."

His eyes dance with jubilation. "If you're a good girl, I'll fill your mouth with cum after." His lips curl into a satisfied grin.

Unadulterated passion spurs through me, and I want nothing more than to bring Mase comfort that ultimately will allow him pleasure. "I'll be a good girl. I promise."

# MASE

"I'll be a good girl. I promise." Her words swirl in my mind as I try not to harden in her wet, warm mouth.

I'm not fully hard, but it's becoming more and more difficult to withstand the feel of her encompassing me so graciously.

"Such a good girl," I say, her bright-blue eyes pleading with me for praise.

When she leaned over the bench and rested her head in my lap, it took me a minute to register she was actually following through with my orders. But when she began unbuckling my belt, I gave her a helping hand and quickly stuffed her pouty lips with my cock.

"You're doing so good," I croon, stroking her damp hair. "I'm going to bathe you when we get home and make my sweet girl all nice and clean for me. Would you like that?"

She gurgles around my thick length and, fuck me, do I love seeing her pouty lips stretched to accommodate my semihard cock filling her mouth.

"You look so beautiful, Summer." I hiss when she sweeps her tongue over my tender tip. "Can you taste your pussy on me?"

She moans, and I delight in the vibrations of her confirmation.

"I want to taste myself from inside you." I shift forward, unable to help the thrust of my hips, and her eyes widen.

"Keep sucking, sweet girl. Lick all my cock clean." Her small hand remains wrapped around the base of my cock, holding it in place. "We're almost home." I turn into the driveway and pull into the garage, but her lips remain steadfast around my cock.

"You can release me."

Her eyes shimmer with something akin to disappointment, so I'm quick to clarify.

"You've been a good girl. If you want a taste, jerk me off into your mouth."

Her grip tightens.

"Leave your mouth open. I want to see my cum coat you."

She nods, then opens her mouth, occasionally flicking her tongue over the bulging head of my now-solid cock.

"I've not done that before I met you," she whispers, and I choke. She's kidding, right? Jesus, she really was innocent when I met her, and now I've completely corrupted her. My lip twitches and my cock stirs, loving the fact she's only been with me.

Instead of questioning her further, the thought of her being only mine sends a territorial possessiveness flashing through me.

Each time she slides her hand up and down my length, I resist the urge to fuck her hand faster. Instead, I tangle a hand in her hair and drop the other down beside me.

"That's it, wrap your hand around me." Her fingers don't meet, and I delight in the fact that my cock is so big compared to her. No wonder she struggles to take me. Her small hand glides over my length. "Keep doing that. Fuck, it feels good, Sum."

Her chest heaves as she works my cock, the feeling so damn good, I want her to do it time and time again.

Leaning over her, I decide to push her boundaries a little more. She watches me beneath hooded eyes, her lashes batting gracefully as I deliver a slow stream of spittle over her fingers, lubing up my cock. Then I yank on her hair and grip her jaw, and she opens her mouth wide, allowing me to spit on her tongue. "Good girl." A moan leaves her, and that's all it takes for me to thrust my hips up, causing my slit to widen, and when my hot cum splashes into her open mouth, my jaw falls open at getting to witness the most incredible sight.

"Holy fuck. Holy fuck, Summer. Ahh. Holy fuck, sweetheart. Yes."

When my orgasm subsides, I fall lax against the seat.

"You're mine, sweet girl. My beautiful creation."

# EIGHTEEN

## SUMMER

AS SOON AS we're inside the mansion, I expected Mase to go back on his word, but instead, he acted on it. He spun me to face him, my back against the front door, and then his lips crashed down on mine. His tongue invaded my mouth, swiping, sucking, pulling the cum from me into him. Groaning, he ground his cock against my stomach, and his desire radiated from him.

Then he jolted, as if remembering himself, and when I expected him to let me leave alone, he shocked the hell out of me by following me up the stairs and into my bedroom. I watched in awe as he took my room in. I wonder if he sees it differently now in the light of day instead of in a cloak of darkness under the wrong assumptions and heightened tensions.

I'm sure a part of him hated the fact he was essentially standing in a teenage girl's bedroom, with makeup scattered across the dresser, photos of teenagers pinned up on my wall, along with a dream board of my future.

My bedroom is light shades of purple, lavish and grand,

everything a wealthy family would provide for their only daughter, but beneath it is a heap of darkness, hidden in secrets and lies, and Mase Campbell is completely unaware of it all.

The crystal furnishings are the best money can buy, and I'm sure Mase already knows this.

He steps toward me, then he snaps the photo of me and Travis at the park off the mirror.

"What are you doing?" I yelp, attempting to snag it from him, then he pockets it and raises an eyebrow at me. I glare at him, and he chuckles before turning away from me as if dismissing me.

He whistles low. "My father set you up good, huh?" He spins on his heels, scanning my bedroom. "You were daddy's princess," he snarks, ignoring me, and swoops his arm around the bedroom. There's a jealous edge to his voice, and I tilt my head. Does he think we played happy families here? Is that what he thinks this was? "Had all the fucking things you ever wanted." He clucks his tongue.

"Hardly," I snort back.

His steely glare turns toward me. "Doesn't look like it to me." He motions toward my walk-in closet, where dozens of fancy designer dresses hang on a rail, one after the other. See-through shoe boxes are stacked along one side of the wall, exposing the designer heels, all of them in various colors and some with price tags still intact. Purses are draped over crystal hooks as if on display. The contents of this closet would be someone's dream, but to me, it resembles a nightmare. These luxuries came with constraints to be the person he wanted me to be, down to the way I dressed—underwear and all.

I close my eyes at the memory of his father barking orders at the staff to dress me how he saw fit, hating the way it made me feel like an object, a possession, and ultimately, his transaction. He liked to dress me up and parade me around like a prized pony, and I hated every second of it. Still, I never had a choice. Not once. Not until recently, at least.

When I open my eyes, I recoil in the way Mase's mood has soured, and it's nothing short of bitter. This is the closed-down Mase, and the longer he stands in the room, the more the real him slips away.

I watch him closely as I deliver my next words. "I was his dress-up doll." My throat is scratchy with admitting my truth, but it does little to penetrate the stone walls he's constructed.

His jaw sharpens, then twitches before he pulls his gaze up to meet mine. "Yeah? How'd that work out for you?"

"He's dead, and I'm here with you as my guardian. So, I'd say pretty well, wouldn't you?"

Stunned is the only way to describe his expression, and I'm about to shock him further. With his eyes wide and his mouth agape, I unbutton my shirt and drop it to the floor, then unclip my bra, leaving my chest bare. I spin on the balls of my feet, unzip my skirt, and push it to the floor.

"All of it. I want to see you push your panties to the floor. Show me your slick pussy dripping with my cum." He groans, and I glance over my shoulder at him. His hand moves up and down his length over the top of his jeans, and I smile internally, doing as he asked.

"Are you going to give me my bath now?" I bite my bottom lip.

"Fuck yes," he growls, and I saunter into the bathroom.

# MASE

The water cascades over Summer's head as I use the showerhead to rinse the strawberry drink off her.

When she went into the bathroom, I was frozen to the spot, scared I wouldn't be able to keep my hands off her. Her ass was still welted from my spanking, and her thighs were coated with my cum. Every part of me wanted to take her again, but I need to be more than the man using her body for his own personal gain. I want to mean something to her, like she's quickly becoming something more to me.

When I finally entered the bathroom, she was already in the tub, with bubbles hiding her body. I was disappointed but partly relieved she'd taken the temptation away from me.

"We need to talk," I finally say as I finish rinsing her.

With her so exposed, a protective streak rifles through me.

"Hm, I figured." Her eyes meet mine, and they're full of uncertainty. Uncertainty I want to banish.

I shake my head. She thinks this is about us. It's not, not really.

"Are you aware of any cameras in the house?"

She stills, and who can blame her? She's probably realizing she was being filmed during private moments. I want to reassure her, but I also need her take on the situation.

"Did you know about them?"

Her face is pale, her chest rising beneath the bubbles.

"Summer?" My eyes ping-pong over her face, and she shudders despite the water being hot.

Then she shakes her head, snapping out of her daze. "Y-Yeah." Her eyes lock with mine. "I know about the cameras." The truth bleeds from her, and my eyebrows pull together as I contemplate if asking her the next question is a good idea. "Did you know there were some in your room too?"

She swallows hard, then licks her bottom lip while her stare remains locked on mine. "Yes."

"Do you know why?" My pulse races.

Her head rears back, and she blinks before a laugh gets caught in her throat. "Because your father was a sick bastard who wanted to control me."

Her words hit me square in the chest, cutting through my heart and twisting my insides. Tears pool in her eyes as she probably realizes that her honesty has also exposed her vulnerability. She turns her head away, but I catch her chin between my fingers. "Don't turn away from me, sweetheart. We deal with shit together, head-on from now on, right?" An arctic chill shoots up my spine, and ice fills my veins as I wait for her to reply, then I rest a palm on her cheek. "Di-did he touch you?" My heart thuds against my chest, but relief flows through me when she shakes her head, and all the tension that was there moments ago slips away.

"N-no, he didn't." Her words pour from her with nothing but sincerity, and the breath I hadn't realized I was holding releases.

Deciding to change the subject, I aim to lighten the mood. "Well, now we have something else in common."

She frowns. "What's that?" She shakes her head, making

her wet hair sashay. "Besides filthy, hot sex, I mean." Her smile hits me square in the chest. *Jesus, she's beautiful.*

Smirking, I feel like beating my fist on my chest like a primate, damn proud of her reference to our sex life. "We both hated the bastard."

When she beams up at me, the stars have aligned. "At least he brought me you."

A chuckle gathers in my chest, and I cling to the side of the tub to stop myself from crashing my lips against hers. As much as I tell myself not to get attached to another woman so soon, it's pretty hard not to when she's looking at me as if I'm her everything, and worse, I want to be.

# NINETEEN

**MASE**

"ARE you going to let me wash all of you?" I ask, referring to the fact I've only cleaned her hair. My cock throbs in my jeans at the thought of touching her bare skin, but I ignore it.

"P-Please."

My balls ache at her sweet words, and a spurt of pre-cum leaves my slit at the innocence behind her manners.

"Fuck, you've no idea how turned on I get by your innocence, Sum."

She chews on her bottom lip, ogling me. "I like it when you call me Sum." My lip twitches at her honesty. "And I want you to know. I haven't been with another guy, only you."

Jesus, I hope that's true, but after dealing with betrayal and lies for years, I genuinely don't know whether I can believe her. However, the thought of any other man touching her has me feeling murderous. My knuckles whiten as I grip the tub. "That better be true."

Her eyes bounce over my face. "It is. I swear it."

"So what the fuck were you doing in bed with another

guy?" I all but growl, showing how jealous of the little prick I am.

"Levi had thrown a drink over me. Trav took me upstairs. I changed out of my dress and ..."

"You got into bed with him?" I snap.

"If you'll let me finish." She rolls her eyes, and her bratty tone has my palm twitching. "I wasn't feeling well. Trav was looking after me."

I scoff at her ridiculous explanation. Either she's very fucking naïve or full of shit, but the idea of her getting into bed with someone else has me on edge.

Hoping she can see the fury in my eyes, I dip my hand into the water between her legs. "If I find out another man has touched this pussy, I'll skin them alive," I sneer, grazing the tip of my finger down her slit and over her hole before dipping it inside and cupping her pussy in my palm. Then I push in until she clings onto the tub with one hand and my forearm with the other. "You like me finger-fucking you, Sum?" I ask, pumping in and out of her tight channel.

"Yes."

"I'm pushing my cum deep inside your pussy, sweet girl. So fucking deep." I want to tell her so fucking deep I'll get her pregnant, but hell, I don't want to scare her with my insatiable need to keep her tied to me.

Her fingernails bite into my skin as I push in and out. "Y-yes, oh god, there, Mase."

With my free hand, I wash her back with the sponge down to the cleft of her ass. "Get on your knees, Sum. Let me finger-fuck your ass too."

She stiffens, and I nuzzle into her neck until she tilts her head to allow me more access and moves to her knees. Committing her scent to memory, I place tender kisses down her throat and over her collarbone while running the sponge up and down her back.

"I'll be gentle," I rasp, remembering how roughly I took

her there, and she hides her face as if hearing my thoughts. "You're the most beautiful woman I've ever seen, you know that?" I mean every damn word. Every. Single. One.

From her wavy blonde hair to the few freckles scattered over her nose, down to her pouty lips that sit like a bow constructed to perfection.

Her breath hitches as I work down her ass, and when her heavy breaths turn to pants, I slide one fingertip inside her asshole and past her muscled barrier. A strangled sound leaves her, and I revel in it. She's turned on, and now I make it my mission to make her come. With one hand thumbing over her clit and pumping a finger inside her pussy, I use my other hand to play with her ass, sliding my digit in and out of her tight hole.

"That's it, sweetheart. Come undone for me."

Her pussy clenches me, and the feeling is incredible. To have this power, this dominance over her is something else; she's mine to care for, mine to protect, my girl.

"Such a good girl." I place another kiss on her neck, then nip at her flesh, delighting in the knowledge I'm marking her. She combusts in the palm of my hand. Her head is thrown back, her moan of pleasure pure electric.

Her pussy clamps down around my finger, her ass tightens too, and her fingernails are bound to leave small crescent marks on my skin that I'll wear with pride.

I caused that reaction, that beautiful, magnificent reaction.

I did that.

Me.

As she slowly comes down from her orgasm, I slip my fingers out of her, and her body droops.

I'm torn between getting in the tub with her or getting her out. I opt for the latter. "Shall we get you out of here?"

She nods as if in a daze, and I can't help but smile at her stupefied state.

My tongue thickens at the water and suds cascading down

her tits and into the tub. Fuck me, she's incredible. "I don't like the thought of my cum being washed away." I shake my head. "I'll just make sure to fill you up again later. Come on." I grab a towel off the rail and hold it out for her. "Come on. You've had a shitty day. Let me take care of you."

# SUMMER

He's surprisingly delicate as he combs through my hair, each tender stroke of his fingertips sending a wave of anticipation through me. I sit cross-legged on the bed, and his solid chest radiates heat, making me feel completely secure in his arms.

All thoughts of being self-conscious around Mase have been obliterated, along with the thoughts of me selling my virginity to him having been replaced with affection and, dare I say it, almost loving care.

I always thought I would feel inadequate if I saw him again, putting him on a pedestal of being too good for me, too manly, but there's something endearing about him. Something vulnerable he doesn't like to expose, and I can't help but wonder if his father had a hand in his insecurities, or if it was someone else.

I've never paid attention to Jeff's tirades whenever he vaguely mentioned his blood son. According to him, he wasn't fit to receive the family name. Of course, I never believed a word the man uttered. The vitriol that left him on a daily basis had become like oil, sliding away with ease, but now I'm curious as to why he felt that way to begin with.

"Did you and your father have a falling out?"

"You could say that."

I tip my head to glance over my shoulder, and his lips spread into a huge smile I find myself mirroring.

"We never got along. He was an abusive bastard to my mom."

My stomach coils as he recounts his childhood.

"She tried to leave him so many times." He shakes his head. "One day, we tried fleeing, and she was in such a frantic state." He swallows, and I feel the emotion in his tone. "She panicked, and we hit the curb on a freeway. It caused a huge wreck, and it created a pileup. My mom and two others died at the scene."

I jolt in his embrace, my heart plummeting.

"Mase, I'm so sorry." I wrap my arms around his neck and cling to him.

"The necklace I wear, the ring on it, was my mother's. I never want to be without a part of her. She was my everything, and I'll never forgive my father for his ill treatment of us. He cheated on her so many times, and it broke her, Sum. I hated him for it."

My naked chest is against the fabric of his T-shirt, and the beat of his heart pounds against me so strongly it's like I've become a part of him too.

I never want to live another day without feeling him against me either. His strength, his dominance, and his control. I want to feel safe in his arms forever while he shows me the man I know he can be.

But that's not how my story is going to end; I know it already. My plan was decided a long time ago, before *Indulgence* was offered to me to get me the hell out of here, and now, there's no going back.

A sob leaves my throat, and I wish I could take it back. I wish I could be stronger for him. To be the person he needs me to be, to allow him to lean on me in this moment. But knowing what I know, the thought of never holding him again has my emotions bleeding out of me like a gaping wound I'm unable to mend.

The ring isn't a symbol of his love for an ex-lover, and while that brings me comfort, I hate the fact he's had to endure such pain.

"Hey. I'll keep you safe, Sum. I promise." He whispers soft promises into my hair and strokes my back. "Don't cry, sweet girl. I'm here for you." His words are meant to reassure me, but they only break my heart further. They're everything I want to hear and everything I shouldn't. Not while holding such a dark secret.

# TWENTY

**MASE**

SUMMER SPENT the night sobbing in my arms while I rocked her to sleep. Something tells me my confession wasn't the only thing that upset her, but I didn't want to cause her more pain by asking.

That's something I need to discuss with her, and soon. For some reason, I want to be open with her, but I want the same in return. It's something I never had with Tara, and as much as I refuse to put a label on whatever is happening between Summer and me, I know it's something significant.

She stirs in her sleep, and I itch to push the sheets off her and revel in the glory of her body, but she quickly rolls away from me, jumping out of bed and darting toward the bathroom.

When I reach the bathroom, I come to a standstill. She's bent over the toilet, throwing up, so I spring into action, kneeling on the floor to hold her hair away from her face. Terror-filled eyes meet mine before she heaves again and fills the bowl. Unsure what else to do, I stroke her back, up and down, like I remember my mom doing with me when I was a child.

"I'm here for you," I whisper.

She nods and vomits again, and when she's finally emptied her stomach, she turns to face me. "I'm sorry."

I chuckle to lighten the mood and get to my feet. "Don't be. Did you eat something? Probably the shitty cafeteria meals, right?"

"I'm not sure."

I scan over her face, and she scrunches her nose. "I had chicken salad yesterday. Maybe it was that?"

"You should take today off." In fact, that sounds like a pretty good idea. I can look after her while she's sick, then she won't be seeing that prick at her school. I wonder how long she can be off sick from a stomach bug?

She shakes her head. "No. I'll be fine once I've freshened up."

My jaw locks up, and I scan her face. She has some color coming back into her cheeks. "Are you going to be a brat?" I ask, and she blinks, then she jolts, as if realizing exactly what I mean. Which is, *are you going to contact the prick today, or do as I've told you and stay the hell away from him?*

She pushes past me and grabs the toothpaste and toothbrush. "I'll let you spank me if I am." Irking me with her response, she smirks.

Let me?

Her eyes meet mine in the mirror. "Can you go grab me my fresh uniform from the closet, please?"

"If you wear your hair braided today."

"Why braided?"

"More innocent." I shrug and decide to answer honestly. "Hopefully, less people want to fuck what's mine."

Her lips part, and I can't help but chuckle as I head to her closet. "Wear the white cotton panties too. Very fucking innocent."

"I thought men liked lace panties?" she shouts between brushing her teeth.

I scoff but know she can't hear me. When I enter her closet, I shake my head at the vast amount of clothes on the rails. My father really did try to buy her, so why the hell did she sell her virginity to me?

"G-strings too!" she yells.

"My ex-wife wore that shit. You are not."

I slide one of the drawers open and smile when I pick up the innocent cotton bra. Thank fuck my father didn't have a hand in purchasing her underwear. *Ew.* A shudder racks through me.

"You have an ex-wife?" Summer asks, and I turn to find she's poked her head through the doorway.

I clear my throat, unprepared for this discussion right now. "That conversation is for another time."

She narrows her eyes into unrelenting slits. "When?"

I chuckle. I'm sure she thinks I'm trying to get out of it, but honestly, I couldn't give less of a shit about Tara and our past. I consider myself lucky to have finalized my divorce. "How about after school I take you to dinner and you can ask whatever you want?"

Her eyebrows shoot up. Hmm, she wasn't expecting that response; I step into her space and wipe the toothpaste from the corner of her mouth with my thumb. "I don't want to keep anything from you, Summer, and I don't want you keeping anything from me either."

Something flickers over her face, but it's gone just as quickly. "Okay," she mumbles.

"Good girl. Now go get dressed for school. I'm taking you in today."

She rolls her eyes and spins to walk away, and her incredible ass sways with each step, each one a promise of a spanking.

# TWENTY-ONE

**SUMMER**

SCHOOL WENT AS WELL AS CAN BE expected, especially since I found myself being pulled from lessons to be given online classes in the library. According to our principal, he'd discussed yesterday with my guardian, and they agreed it was best for me to avoid classes until further notice.

When I tried messaging Travis, my texts bounced back, and when I tried to call him, his number came up as unavailable. A niggling feeling in the back of my mind tells me this is Mase's doing, and coming between my friendships is not something I'm willing to stand for.

Travis and I tell each other everything; he's been my rock, so Mase has no right to step between us. He needs to learn to trust me, because Travis and I never have, nor ever will have, anything sexual going on between us.

As soon as the bell rings, I pack up my bags and head out to the truck waiting in the same parking spot it dropped me off at this morning.

"Good day?" He smiles, and I scoot into the seat and slam the door shut behind me. Resting one hand on the gear shifter, he places the truck into reverse, and I squirm at the size of his hand. What the hell is it about guys with big hands?

I give my head a shake and focus on the road. "Are you kidding?" I watch him from the corner of my eye.

He rolls his lip into his mouth, a lip I'd love to suck on. *Jesus, Summer, get a grip.* "Take that as a no. Did you puke again? I told you to call me, and I'd pick you up."

"No. I didn't puke again." I cross my arms over my chest, and his eyes dart to my tits. "You got me moved out of class."

He pulls out of the parking spot. "Yeah."

Annoyance rumbles through me. "Yeah? Did you block Travis's number too?"

He turns his head. "I told you to cut contact with him. I switched your phone out, and now you only have the numbers in there that you need."

Who the hell does he think he is? He took my phone?

"You're to cut contact with *Travis.*" He sneers when he says his name.

"And I told you that wasn't going to happen."

"Pretty sure I spanked your ass, and you agreed."

My nostrils flare, and I shake my head. "That's not what happened, and you know it."

"Potatoe, potato." He shrugs.

Is he serious right now?

"Summer, look at it from my point of view. I come to my father's home, find the girl of my dreams in bed with a chump, half naked, and you expect me to be okay with your excuse of *he's my best friend. It's fine, nothing happened.*"

I soften beneath his words. When he puts it like that, the man does have a point, and *girl of his dreams*? Swoon.

"Nothing happened between me and Travis. It never has."

"And I believe you." He shifts in his seat. "But Sum, I'm not going to lie to you, I have trust issues." This is new information to me. "That ex-wife I mentioned ..." Yeah, the one who sends jealousy coursing through me at the thought of her existence. She had a part of him I will never have, and I hate her for it. My hands twist in my school skirt, and I remain silent. "She cheated on me a lot." Just hearing the word "cheated" on his lips makes me want to crawl into his lap to comfort him. I should high-five the bitch for doing me a favor, but with the disappointment in his tone, it makes me want to murder her, painfully.

But his words are also striking because it's not dissimilar to his mother's past relationship, where she was the victim just like he is. Only, I'm not sure he realizes it yet, and that's something he needs to come to terms with himself, so I don't mention it.

I scan over Mase and his gorgeous self. "She's insane."

He chuckles, and his lip lifts at the end. "Well, that may be so, but our divorce left me with a lot of issues."

Pulling into the parking lot of a diner, he turns the engine off before facing me. His fingers toy with the strands of hair that have broken away from the braid he insisted on me wearing.

"I don't want to hurt you, Sum. But I can't have you getting into bed with other guys. You're either all in or not at all, sweetheart."

I find myself nodding to his words, but deep inside, I know it's me who's going to hurt him with my secrets.

# TWENTY-TWO

## MASE

THE DINER IS JUST how I remember it, so much so, I swear it hasn't even been painted. The thought should turn my stomach, but the nostalgia from bringing Summer here has me smiling from ear to ear.

The last time I was here was with my best friends and fresh out of high school. It's where we planned our dream of building STORM Enterprises and everything in it.

I never could have imagined where it would lead us today, and I sure as hell never imagined sitting here in the exact same booth with a girl almost young enough to be my daughter, whom I've quickly become infatuated with.

Summer sucks on the straw of her milkshake, and my cock twitches at the reminder of her perfect lips suckling me in the truck the other day. It's without a doubt the most sexually vulnerable position I've ever been in before, and it's something I want to experience with her again and again.

The bell above the door chimes, and I grimace as another group of teenagers pushes into the diner.

There's already one group in football shirts becoming

louder by the minute, and Summer has taken it upon herself to slink into the corner away from their view. When I asked her what was wrong, she pointed out one of the guys from the office. The one who poured a drink over her head, the very same one I will be speaking to before he leaves here, but I need to pick my moment. I'm not going to make a scene in front of her. The last thing I want is to cause more waves, knowing how pissed she is that I switched her phone out. What she doesn't know is I'm having someone check through all her messages to be sure there's nothing to be wary of. Especially with Hugh's comment about me watching Travis around her. Maybe the little fucker is not the friend she thinks he is. Just another reason to keep them apart.

"Hey, Summer, why the hell are your messages bouncing back to my phone?" As if the devil himself summoned him to fuck with me. I snap my gaze up toward the punk she calls her best friend. Travis. Just the sound of his name has me gritting my teeth. Fucking Travis? Sounds like his parents were groupies and he got caught up in the middle of it.

Summer flushes bright red, and if that color was on her cheeks because of me, I would like it a whole lot more, but I find myself irritated by the fact she's been made to feel uncomfortable. My knuckles ache from the tightness of my balled fists, and I move them beneath the table to disguise my inability to control my simmering temper.

"I-I … I need to use the restroom," she blurts out, and I realize she's turned pale really quickly. She springs up from the booth and pushes past Travis before rushing off in the direction of the restroom, holding a hand to her mouth, and my eyes narrow. What the fuck?

"You're keeping her from me."

I slowly trail my gaze up toward the kid who is glaring down at me like I'm something he stepped in, a sneer on his preppy-boy lips. Turning my attention back to my meal, I pick up a fry, dunk it in the mayo, then take my time chewing it, not so much as giving the kid another glance.

"She's my best friend," he snaps, and I have to hand it to him; the kid has balls to stand up to me.

Still, I ignore him.

"Did you hear me? I said, she's my best friend." His tone has darkened, and I love the fact I'm pissing the little shit off.

"Not anymore," I grunt out with a sly smile.

A whoosh of air leaves his chest as if I've punched him. Then he scoffs and shifts from foot to foot. "Wow, you're just like him, aren't you?"

Languorously, I lift my gaze and nonchalantly raise my eyebrow, though my body is standing at attention.

"Your father. You're just like him. Like father, like son." Then he turns on his heel and heads toward the restroom, leaving me frozen at his words.

Am I just like him?

He's controlling.

Manipulative.

Abusive.

Cruel.

———

*Aged thirteen …*

*"I allow you to have the friends you have. Remember that, Mason."*

*I nod.*

*"Speak!" He slams his fist on the desk, making me jump.*

*"Yes, sir."*

*The sneer he throws in my direction makes me want to curl into the corner of the room. I've only been home from boarding school for an hour and he's already started pulling me apart.*

*He stands and straightens his tie.*

*"You'll be dressed accordingly and at the dinner table for seven*

*p.m. sharp. Do you understand me?" His stern voice leaves no room for argument.*

*I hate dressing in the crisp white shirts and ties that make me feel like I have a noose around my neck. "Yes, sir."*

*"Good. I'd like you to meet my new wife."*

*My eyebrows shoot up. I met one the last time I came home; what the hell happened to that one? When I went back to school and told the guys, they agreed my father has no loyalty whatsoever.*

*Something else I'm going to have when I grow up.*

*"I look forward to it," I reply robotically.*

*"She's a good woman. She's going to make a good mother to you."*

*A smile spreads over his face, and in this moment, I hate him more than ever.*

————

Present ...

There's no way in hell I'm anything like my father.

That's not what I want for Summer and our future, not at all. I need to do better, be better. Be the man I want to be.

My mind spins, and a shudder washes over me. A sudden need to reassure her and be the man she deserves over-whelms me, and I almost trip out of the booth as I move toward the restroom.

As soon as my hand is on the women's restroom door, I still at a sound coming from the men's. "Look, man, I just want to leave. I don't want any trouble." It's followed up by cruel laughter that has the hair on the back of my neck standing on end. What the fuck?

Instead of pushing open the women's, I head into the men's, and my eyes collide with Travis's terror-stricken ones in the restroom mirror. Four men surround him, but on second glance, I realize they're the same football guys from earlier, one of them being the prick who poured a drink over Summer.

Vengeance bubbles inside me.

"There a problem here?" I ask.

"I just want to leave. I don't want any trouble." Travis's eyes flit toward the door.

"Ahhh, the gay boy doesn't want any trouble," one of the kids mocks, and Travis flinches before his cheeks flame further. He darts his eyes away from me, making me feel like I've been punched in the gut at my misplaced jealousy.

How the fuck could I have been so stupid? So blind.

Embarrassment swims in Travis's eyes, and he struggles to hold his head high. The blush creeping up his cheeks turns deeper by the second, his ears reddening.

"You heard him; he wants to leave," I grit out, though every cell in my body is fighting for retribution at their remark and the way they've treated Summer. Not to mention the way I've treated him. I'm angry at myself, downright furious.

"Nah, I don't think he can leave just yet. He didn't get a view of my dick like he wants. I'm just going to piss right here." One of the guys steps up toward Travis, and he steps back until he hits the tiled wall. I watch the horror on his face when the one who spoke to him slowly begins to unzip his pants.

"Lewis, maybe that's enough." Levi attempts to pull this punk back by his arm, but he snatches it away, intent on following through with pissing on Travis.

Lewis turns his head in Levi's direction. "I don't think it is. Get your phone out. I want you to film it."

Levi's eyes meet mine, and his Adam's apple bobs while I leer back at him. *You do it, motherfucker, and you're dead.* My silent eyes drill into him.

"Don't worry about him. He can't do shit without getting

thrown in jail for touching us," Lewis states, with a smug smirk I'm about to wipe off his face.

"You sure about that?" I cross my arms over my chest.

"Absolutely." Lewis grins with a confidence he really shouldn't feel.

"This is too much, man," Levi whispers, shoving his phone deeper into his pocket. That move just saved his good looks.

Lewis shakes his head. "Pussy." Then he pulls his dick out, and the torment flooding Travis's face is enough to wrench me from my stare-off. With one hand on his head and the other on his shoulder, I drive him face-first into the tiled wall of the restroom.

"Should've fucking listened," I spit out, just before the sound of his nose cracking fills my veins with adrenaline, and blood sprays out over the white tiles.

One of his buddies takes a swing at me, and I duck before delivering a roundhouse kick to the third. I throw Lewis to the floor, where he rolls around howling in pain like a little bitch. The one who swung on me comes at me again, and I deliver a swift blow to his jaw that knocks him to the ground. Swiping the blood splatter on my jeans, I turn to face Levi. "You gonna be a problem anymore?"

His eyes bulge. "No, sir."

"Then you're not gonna breathe a word about this"—I tilt my head down at the scene of the three guys rolling around on the floor—"got me?"

"Yes, sir."

"Travis. Let's go, buddy."

Relief floods his face, and in that moment, I want to throw my arm over his shoulder and protect him from scum like this, from the world. Travis rushes toward me, his cheeks still bright red. He spins and glares down at Lewis.

"Piece of shit." Then he spits on him and follows me out the door.

# TWENTY-THREE



**SUMMER**

AS SOON AS we got home, Mase ran me a bath, brushed my teeth to get rid of the puke smell, and then washed and dried me.

What shocked me the most was the fact that he returned from the restroom with Travis, telling him he's coming home with us so he could make things right. Now, I'm in my sleep shorts and camisole snuggled up to Mase while Travis tells him about his predicament.

Mase sits and listens as Travis explains he's actually almost twenty, but his parents paid the school off to allow him to finish his final year after he spent a year at a camp designed to get his sexuality back on track. Yes, these fucked-up, cruel places exist, and all because Travis was discovered looking at gay porn.

"My mom and dad are going to throw me out if I come out as gay now."

Mase jolts and sits forward. "What?"

Travis nods. "It's not okay to be gay in our society."

Mase laughs, but it lacks humor. "Our fucking society?"

He shakes his head. "Your parents should want you happy above anything else. To be yourself."

"Like your dad wanted you happy?" he clips back, then darts his eyes away. "I'm sorry, that was uncalled for."

Mase shrugs. "I deserve it." Then he exhales. "Look, man, I know you don't realize it yet, but you can be anything you want to be."

"That's easy for you to say; you're straight." Travis sighs heavily. "At school, everyone fucks around."

Mase's muscles bunch tight.

"Apart from your good girl over there." Travis gives a curt nod in my direction, and I beam at Mase, who tightens his arm around me, pulling me closer, if that's even possible. "Like, how the hell do gay people experiment? I've never so much as glanced at another man's dick. It's pathetic."

Mase's eyebrows shoot up. "There's nobody at school you're into?"

"I'd get beat to hell if I inquired. The only action I've seen is on television or Summer's phone."

Mase's focus is on me again, and my neck heats under his scrutiny.

"It takes a lot more for people like me to be accepted, and I don't know how that's ever going to happen. Not when my own parents won't even accept me." His solemn voice causes a whimper to escape me.

How Travis's parents can't see him for the incredible guy he is, I don't understand. He's handsome, fit, clever, funny, empathetic, strong-minded, and stands up for what and who he believes in. He's a son and a person to be proud of, who just so happens to like men.

"God, I'm pathetic. I've never seen another man's dick in person, too fucking terrified of someone freaking out if I even attempt to look. How the hell am I ever going to experience life?" Trav says, but it's like he's talking to himself.

Mase's jaw sharpens. "You're not pathetic!" he snaps, then

shakes his head. "I'm sorry." He scrubs a hand over his head. "But you're not pathetic. Please don't say shit like that about yourself," he says, softer this time. "You need to learn to love yourself for who you are." His eyes are focused on Travis, but it's as if he's talking about himself.

"That's easy for you to say. I barely know who I am."

Mase nods at his words and sits back. "You're right. It is easy for me to say, but as soon as you finish school, you can lead your own life. I'm going to make damn sure you have the strength and support to be the person you want to be."

My heart soars on his words, and the part of me that fell for him during our one night together expands like a balloon.

"You have my support now, Travis. I'm sorry for the flack I've given you, but trust me when I say you have us." He squeezes me tighter against him, then glances down at my lips, and just that simple look sends tingles through my body.

"My parents hold my trust fund until I'm twenty-five. I'm not going to be doing anything without their say-so. Hence, being in school still. You've no idea how embarrassing that is."

"I'll loan you whatever money you need," Mase replies with a smile. "We're family now, Trav."

My pulse skyrockets, and my eyes pool with tears of appreciation.

I love this man.

Is that even possible so soon?

Travis's eyebrows shoot up, and he blinks slowly as if Mase's words are taking time to register. "Wh-what? Why?"

"You deserve to be happy, and Summer does too. You make her happy, and I'm grateful she has you in her life. I'm only sorry it's taken until now for me to realize it. It's my gift for both of you."

A choked sound comes from Travis, and he gulps. "Tha-that's amazing. But I don't think I can—"

Mase puts his hand up to stop him from continuing. "You can accept it, and you will."

Trav nods. "Thank you."

Mase smiles, then takes a swig of his beer. "So, what is it you want to do when you finally leave school, exactly?"

I sit forward with renewed energy and tell Mase Travis's plan. "Trav has a cool concept for the entertainment industry. There's this whole development downtown that needs fixing. It's boarded up, but it goes to auction soon."

Mase's eyes light up, and he lifts his chin in Travis's direction. "Send me the details."

Excitement pumps through me at the prospect of Travis's dream coming to life.

I just wish I was going to be around to witness it.

# TWENTY-FOUR

**MASE**

THE MOVIE CONTINUES PLAYING, and my eyes drift around the living room, unable to remember a time when we used this room during my childhood. My fingers play with the silky tendrils of Summer's wavy hair, and my cock twitches with each breath she takes. Her face is resting in my lap, and I'm unsure whether the move was strategic or not, but as her hot breath filters through the fabric of my gym shorts, I have a sudden need to feel her lips around the velvety flesh of my cock.

Travis has been asleep for the past half hour, so I decide to risk it. Let's face it, he isn't interested in my girl. Nope, if anything, he's more interested in me, and that's actually pretty fucking fine by me. I'm not in the least bit curious about the same sex, but the idea of someone watching me, someone wanting me for sex, has my cock stiffening with joy.

The whole delving into my fantasies is like a reawakening, something I've embraced with the time I've spent with Summer, and something I intend to continue exploring.

"Sum?" I nudge her. "I want you to suck me, Sum."

I shuffle my ass to tug my shorts down and pull my cock from its confines.

Summer lifts her head from my lap and quickly looks toward Trav. "He's asleep," I confirm.

As soon as her wet mouth encompasses me, I hiss between my teeth in pleasure. "Fuck, you feel so damn good."

She suckles on me at first, making my cock harder by the second. I dig my fingers into her hair, pushing her head up and down as I struggle to rein in the need to face-fuck her.

Something else Tara never allowed me to do.

"You look so damn beautiful stuffed full of me." She looks up at me from beneath her lashes, and satisfaction hits me in the way her mouth is stretched wide over my thickness. "Look at you stretching so perfectly for me." I groan with satisfaction. "Such a good girl for me."

A sharp intake of breath has my eyes snapping toward Trav. He sits there with wide eyes staring back in our direction, witnessing my girl taking me.

My balls pull up and my grip on Summer's hair tightens as Trav's and my gazes remain locked in a moment of indecisiveness. I should tell her to stop. Give her an out. Tell him to leave.

He should leave. Walk away from this moment we're sharing, but we both remain frozen.

Summer pops off my cock, and Trav's eyes grow wider, causing my cock to jump. Holy shit, he's looking at my cock. I glance down at his jeans, and a rush of exhilaration zips up my spine when I make out the obvious bulge. He's turned on. He wants to watch this; he wants to watch my thick cock being forced down Summer's throat.

Holy fuck, that's hot.

I wrap my hand around my thick cock and hit Summer on her chin with it. Then I spit, delivering her with a string of saliva that drips down her plush lips and onto her chest. *Fuck, that's hot.* "Suck, sweet girl," I grunt out. "Lick the head. Show Travis what a good girl you are for me."

Her eyes flare with arousal, and she slides off the sofa and kneels between my legs on the floor, allowing Trav the perfect view to witness the show we're about to put on.

And just like that, a switch has been flipped, and I welcome the feeling of power.

"Tip your head back and open your mouth first," I demand, my tone now full of dominance and darkness, just how I like.

I slide the straps of her camisole down enough to free her tits. Only I can see them from this position, and my mouth waters to feel her peaked nipples on my tongue.

She does as I ask, then I lean over her and yank her hair, tipping her head back farther.

"Like this, beautiful."

Her neck elongates, and I slowly deliver a steady stream of spittle into her open mouth, then another stream that runs down her chin and neck. All the while, I stroke my thick cock up and down.

"So, fucking beautiful on your knees for me, sweet girl. Beg to suck on my cock."

She struggles to swallow, and my cock jumps with antici-pation. "Pl-please."

"Please what? Say the words, Summer," I grind out.

My hand works faster, and Travis's heavy breathing ramps up my arousal.

"Please feed me your cock, Mase."

"Holy fuck." Travis's heavy pants fill the air, along with the fast stroking of my cock giving me the confidence I crave.

"Get your cock out, Trav. Let's see you come from my girl choking on her brother's thick cock."

A strangled sound leaves his throat, and when I glance up, he makes quick work of unbuttoning his jeans and freeing his cock from his boxers.

"Jesus, Trav. You hard?" I know he is, but I want him to admit it, admit how much this turns him on.

"Yes." His hand works up and down his length. "So fucking hard."

"You want me to choke her with it?"

His hooded eyes meet mine. "Yes. Choke her with it." His voice is dark and has an intensity to it that has me fisting my cock faster, my grip becoming painful.

"You want me to fill her hole with my thick cum?" I bite out, and my balls draw up.

"Holy fuck, yes. Do it," he heaves, the aggression in his tone evident.

"Please, I need it," Summer begs so beautifully, and I lean over her, delivering the first splash of my hot cum to her waiting tongue. It hits her cheek, her nose, then I aim it down her neck and over her bare tits. It feels like my supply of cum is never-ending, and hearing Travis experience his own peak only adds to my experience.

"Ahhh, fuck," Travis roars into the room, and I drop back against the couch, completely spent.

Summer swipes at her mouth, and I chuckle when she grimaces as her hand touches her cheek. "It's everywhere." She smiles back at me. "You're very messy, Mase. You need better aim."

"My aim was perfect." Grinning down at her lazily, I move to adjust her top and push her straps back in place. I take her chin in the palm of my hand. "You're the most beautiful woman I've ever set eyes on. I don't know how the hell I got so lucky to have caught you."

Emotion washes over her face, and she blinks away unshed tears.

"Pretty sure it was all thanks to an app where she sold her body. Against my wishes, I might add," Travis delivers while tucking his spent cock back into his jeans.

"You come?" I lift an eyebrow in his direction.

"Fuck yes. Hot as hell." He swallows thickly. "Thanks, man."

I nod at him, then move to my feet and lift Summer into my arms. "I'm going to spend the rest of the night appreciating this hot little body while thanking Oscar O'Connell for being a pure genius," I state, and Summer wraps her legs around my waist.

"Who?" Trav shouts as I head through the door.

"The Mafia!"

"The fucking what?" he screeches, making Summer and me laugh as I turn and head up the stairs.

"Do you think this Oscar guy can help with something else too?"

I pull back to peer into Summer's eyes. "Like what?"

She chews on her lip.

"Anything you need I can help you with, Sum. You'll never need anyone again, not while you have me."

"But I don't know how long I'll have you for." It's like she's trying to tell me something without uttering the words. I search her face, and something cold slithers down my spine, and I come to a stop.

I open my mouth to ask her, but she shakes her head, and her soft, salty lips brush over mine, seeking access. When her tongue prods at my mouth, I become completely consumed by this girl.

# TWENTY-FIVE

## SUMMER

TONIGHT WAS SIMPLY AMAZING, and the fact that Mase has welcomed Travis into our fold and accepted him feels like a dream. But the guilt eating away at me is rearing its ugly head, especially when the nausea rolling around my stomach threatens to erupt. Glancing at the clock, I see it's still the early hours of the morning. My sickness is coming at random times, making me believe there's no such thing as morning sickness. There can't be—or not in my case, at least. Instead, it's any-time-of-day sickness.

I peer over at Mase and take in his sleeping form, the way the sheet rests against his abs has my fingers twitching to lift it, and my mouth salivates to taste him again.

But when my focus latches onto the ring attached to the chain around his neck, my stomach lurches and vomit flames up my throat. I rush out of bed and into the bathroom, gently closing the bathroom door before dropping to the floor and heaving into the toilet. The burn comes after I expel the contents of my stomach, and I sob. "God, I hate this."

"Hey, it's okay." Mase strokes my back, and I freeze. "You finished?"

All I can do is dip my head, and he takes hold of my arm and gently helps me to my feet. Feeling his eyes on me, I avert my gaze, and he blows out a deep breath. Then, before I can think of my next move, he lifts me onto the counter, places toothpaste on my toothbrush, and slides it into my mouth. Tears fill my eyes. I don't even have memories of my mother brushing my teeth, and now I'm receiving the care from a man I so desperately want. Why does life have to be so cruel? To hand me someone who can bring me happiness, yet just as easily rip it away.

"I'm going to ask you something, Summer, and I want you to tell me the truth. Do you hear me?"

He stops brushing and points to the sink, where I proceed to spit the toothpaste before facing him.

His bright-green eyes shimmer; they're full of so many emotions: nervousness, concern and, above all else, longing. "Y-Yes. I hear you." My throat is scratchy, and I don't know if it's from the assault on my mouth last night or the sickness from my guilt.

"You pregnant?" His nostrils are flared, and the softness that was there moments ago is quickly being replaced by anger, making anxiety ripple through me.

His hands balled into fists rest on each side of me, caging me in on the counter. "Are you?"

"Y-Yes," I whimper.

A stuttered gasp leaves him, and a pained sound rumbles in his chest before he drops his head and shakes it. His body is taut, and unadulterated devastation radiates from him as he heaves in breaths.

I want to reach out and touch him, to give him comfort, but I sit there, frozen in place.

"The last woman who said she was pregnant to me was my wife, but it wasn't my baby."

His words tear through my heart and rip it to shreds, leaving it in useless tatters.

How could she do this to him? My beautifully broken man.

A tear slips down my face. "I swear I would never lie to you." I swipe away the wetness on my cheeks. Then with shaky hands, I grasp his face in mine and lift his head. "I swear it."

His gaze bounces over my face and settles on my eyes as if searching for the truth behind my words, so I allow him to see into my soul.

He licks his lips. "Is it mine?" he rasps.

My heart thuds. "Yes. I've only ever slept with you."

He gives a firm nod.

Then he steps back, releasing me from his aura, and my body cries out to feel him close again. For him to hold me and tell me everything is going to be okay. I want him to reassure me and take control of my escalating thoughts. When I said I needed the money for college, I wasn't lying, but I also omitted some truth, and the thought of losing him when I've only just found him is terrifying. He heads toward the door, and my heart sinks. Just before he walks through it, he says the very words I never wanted to hear.

"I need a DNA test, Summer."

# TWENTY-SIX

**MASE**

AFTER LEAVING THE BATHROOM, I went into a complete panic. The girl I had a one-night stand with, the one I paid for, the one I'm guardian over, is pregnant and telling me the baby is mine.

The first thing I do is call Reed. He is, after all, my attorney, not that he's any good. He called the doctor he has on retainer on my behalf, and within the hour, he was here taking Summer's blood.

"Can we talk?" Summer's sweet voice floats in the evening breeze. Tomorrow, I get to find out if I'm going to be a father or not.

Whether my dreams will become reality or I've only stepped into another nightmare.

Exhaling, I sit forward on the outdoor couch. "I really don't want to talk right now, Sum."

"Then let me look after you," she whispers, and I lift my head. She's wearing the same dress she wore the night she sold herself, and my cock throbs.

Is the dress strategic too? Does she think she can exploit

me by using me for sex? Is she manipulating me like Tara did?

I shake my head. As much as I want her, I won't allow her the control over me like I did my wife.

She blows out a deep breath. "I don't want sex, Mase. I just want to give you comfort." She gestures toward my groin, and my cock responds. "I know you're dealing with a lot right now." Slowly, I lift my eyes up toward her and blink. She's not once mentioned what she's going through or how she feels. Not once has she complained about being sick or pregnant. My sweet girl has accepted everything I've thrown at her, and here she is, offering me comfort.

Stretching my arms out along the back of the couch, I move to the side to make room for her, and she lowers herself beside me. Then I stare out into the gardens and allow her to pop open my jean button, slip down my zipper, and take out my semihard cock. I hiss through my teeth when her soft lips wrap around my cock and her tongue flicks over my slit, causing me to jolt.

Then as she sucks, I settle back against the cushions and take comfort from the girl I will not allow to break my heart.

I tenderly stroke my fingers through her hair. "I'm trusting you with my heart, Summer. Please don't fucking destroy it."

# TWENTY-SEVEN

**MASE**

SUMMER TOOK TODAY OFF SCHOOL, and she also spent the night alone in her room. I couldn't bring myself to join her despite wanting desperately to hold her and touch her stomach. But I knew I wouldn't be able to take it again. To learn the little family I desperately want is so out of reach.

My phone rings, and my stomach plummets with each ring.

One.

*I can't fucking do this.*

Two.

*Not again.*

A sound erupts from my chest that can only be described as an animalistic cry, and I slam my palms against my dresser.

"Mase?" I spin to face Travis. Surprised he's still here and I never realized. He steps forward and pulls me into his arms, holding me tightly against his solid chest as I cling to him for support. "You can trust her, man. I promise. She's a good girl, and she's absolutely terrified."

Pain rushes through my bloodstream, and I pull away

from him and stand taller. Swiping away the snot from the end of my nose and wiping my eyes, I press the button to redial the missed call.

Travis takes a seat on the edge of my bed, and I rest my ass beside him, grateful for his support in this moment.

"Th-this is Mason Campbell."

"Sir, we have the DNA results."

I swallow past the lump in my throat. "Okay."

"We can confirm we are ninety-nine-point-nine percent certain that the DNA proves you are the father of Summer Campbell's baby."

I end the call.

Elation grips my chest, so powerful it renders me speechless.

Holy. Fucking. Shit.

I eyeball my phone.

*Is this fucking real?*

"Are you okay?" Summer asks, and I lift my head to face her.

"I'm going to be a daddy." A smile creeps over my face, and I place my palm on her stomach. "Fuck, Sum. I'm going to be a daddy!"

She rests her hand over mine, and as I get lost in her blue eyes, guilt lances through me. With the bags under her eyes, I see the sadness and worry there, and suddenly, I want nothing more than to eradicate it all. To be the best partner and daddy for her and our baby, but first I need to reassure her.

"I'm here for you, Summer. I'm not going anywhere now, my sweet girl."

Tears pool in her eyes, making the blue in them darker than ever, and I lick my lips.

"I'm going to be your everything, because you're quickly becoming mine." My heart pounds as I lay my truth bare.

"And it's fucking terrifying, Sum, because I want this more than I've ever wanted anything before."

Her lips part, and a sharp breath of air leaves her. "Really?"

I nod and cradle her cheeks in my palms. "Damn right, sweetheart. You're mine." My mouth becomes dry and my hands tremble, preparing to open myself up to her further and silently begging her not to let me down. "And I'm yours, right? I'll guard your heart with my everything, Sum."

Please say yes.

"Always," she whispers.

That one word rights all the wrongs in my world.

# TWENTY-EIGHT

## MASE

"I'M SORRY, did you say twins?"

"Ye-yes, sir." The doctor nods frantically.

"Like, two of them?" My excitement is spilling over.

"Exactly."

My mouth falls open, and I gape at Summer. She chews into her bottom lip, but you can't miss the laugh she's fighting to hide as my eyes drop to her stomach.

"There's two in there?" God knows how; she's so small, there's barely a bump at all.

The doctor points to the screen again, where two small beans float around. "Definitely two."

"Can you tell the sex yet?" Summer asks, and the doctor shakes his head.

"They can't tell the sex until around four months, beautiful." I smile brightly at her. Of course I know all the facts about babies and pregnant women. I've witnessed this so many times but always from the outside looking in. I'm so fucking elated I'm almost lost for words.

"We're having twins," I say again.

"You are, Mr. Campbell, and they're perfectly healthy up to now. We will keep a close eye on babies and mom, but all is going well so far," he says, pulling the gloves from his hands and throwing them in the trash.

And they'll be staying that way if I have anything to do with it. Summer and our babies are my priorities.

"I just can't fucking believe it, a family of our own," I rasp. Summer entwines her fingers with mine, and I bring them to my lips, covering them in kisses along with a thousand promises to be the man she deserves, the one I want to be.

Myself.

# SUMMER

Taking another sip of the orange juice, I cast my gaze around the manicured park. The smell of our picnic fills the air and brings a smile to my lips.

*This is perfect.*

"My mom used to bring me here when I was a kid." Mase smiles wistfully. "I always imagined bringing my wife and kids here."

There's a lake with rowing boats, and Mase filled me in on the lengths his best friend Reed went to in order to get his family. He took his new family to the local park and hired rowing boats similar to the ones here and went overboard in order to save the dog he'd purchased that day to impress Gia and her son.

By the time he finished telling me the story, I was in a fit of giggles. It also made me realize how much his friendships mean to him, so when he suggested us trying to live in New Jersey before the babies come, I rapidly agreed. A fresh start.

The dark thought about my past looms in my stomach like a thick ball of dread, but I refuse to acknowledge it, not when everything is going so well. I deserve this; he deserves this. I refuse to let it cloud our day.

"It's a really pretty park." I smile while Mase stuffs another sandwich in his mouth. He woke early this morning to prepare a picnic for the park. Who knew he could be so sweet?

"My mom always made picnics for us."

"When the babies are older, we can bring them back here if you like?"

He stares off toward the lake. "I prefer for us to make new memories. All the ones here are diluted with bad ones."

I nod. "I get that."

"What about your mom? You don't talk about her at all."

I shudder and close my eyes, and when I open them, Mase is watching me closely.

"My mom was in this life for the money, and that's what she got." I shrug, hoping the conversation moves on. I've always had my suspicions about what happened to my mom and what part Jeff played in her death, but that's not something I want to really think about now.

"Sum, I want every part of you. Not just the ones you choose to share with everyone else." His words make my breathing stutter; they clutch at my torn heart and slowly begin piecing it back together. "When you're ready to tell me your secrets, sweet girl, I'm here for you." He links our hands and brings them to his lips.

His touch scorches my skin, delivering me with promises of a future I long to keep. Whatever it may cost.

# TWENTY-NINE



"ARE YOU GOING TO TELL HIM?" Trav asks from across the breakfast bar.

"No."

"Summer. What the hell are you thinking?"

"I need a way to get out of this, Trav. That's what I'm thinking." I slide my eyes down to my stomach and rest a hand there.

"You're going to break his fucking heart." His eyes drill into mine. "You know he loves you, right?"

A sickening feeling rushes through me, and my throat clogs. "Pl-please don't."

He entwines our hands together. "Maybe he can help?"

"He'll never forgive me if I tell him the truth," I whisper.

"Summer, you already said he hated his father."

"There's hate, Trav, and there's hate. What I've done is unforgivable."

"What's unforgiveable?" Mase asks, strolling into the kitchen, and dips his head to place a kiss on my head. He's completely shirtless and sweaty, and my body stirs with arousal. My gaze travels over his broad shoulders and the tattoos that run down his back as he opens the refrigerator. "Sum?" he queries, and my focus snaps up to his face.

"Huh?"

"I said, what's unforgivable?" He takes a swig from the water bottle. My shoulders bunch tight, and every cell in my body begins to panic.

"The baby names I suggested," Trav intervenes, and my body relaxes. "Dusty, Diamond, that kind of thing."

Mase wrinkles his nose. "The fuck? My kids are not going to be strippers or porn stars." I burst out laughing until I see the disgruntled look on Trav's face.

*Thank you*, I mouth toward him, but he shakes his head.

The doorbell cuts through the room, and Mase takes off toward the door, leaving me feeling more deflated and like a fraud than ever before.

# THIRTY

**MASE**

I SWING the door to the mansion open, and I'm stunned to find Reed standing on the doorstep. "What the?"

"You appeared severely distressed when I spoke to you last," he explains, pushing into the house.

"Hi." Gia nods and follows him inside, with a baby carrier housing little Jax.

"Dad, can I bring the soccer ball inside too?" Bryce chimes.

"Jesus, I hate fucking soccer so much," he mumbles, stepping past me. I'm not surprised by his comments; Reed gives us all a weekly rundown of how bad the team he coaches for his adopted son is. Last week, an elderly woman hit him in the face with her purse because he made her grandson cry. When I asked him what he did to deserve it, he said he told the kid he'd be better at something like chess. He even went as far as purchasing the kid a chess set in the hopes that it would encourage him to leave the team. According to Reed, this kid goes and collects his lunch from his grandmother midway through the game and sits in the middle of the soccer field to eat it, expecting the game to stop for him, or better yet, for players to play around him. So I can appreciate where my friend's misguided suggestion came from, he just needs to work on his execution.

I turn to see Bryce placing their family dog in a … "Is that a stroller?"

"It is. Apparently, the dog I purchased is indeed broken," Reed adds from over my shoulder as he wafts his hand in Bryce's direction.

A laugh rumbles from deep inside me. "What did you do to it?"

"He took her to the vet clinic, and they said that Bubbles is struggling to keep up with our demanding lifestyle," Bryce informs me, grinning from ear to ear. "Right, Dad?"

"Right." Reed nods.

"So, you bought her a stroller?" I quiz.

"She's almost …" Reed makes a slicing gesture across his throat as if to explain the dog is dying.

"Oh shit. Really?" I know how much Bubbles means to Bryce, and given the kid lost his biological father, I can appreciate why Reed is being cautious.

Another car pulls up behind their family SUV, and I make a mental note of the fact I'm going to need all this shit soon too, but I can't deny I'm buzzing about it. It's everything I've ever wanted, and Summer's the added bonus.

Shaw practically leaps out of his car, and his daughter, Eleanor, scrambles from the car seat in record time.

"Is Ree-Reed here? Bubblesss?" she squeals.

Shaw winces. "She means, Reed."

"I gathered." I smile down at her bouncing on the balls of her feet. Her cute little tutu is multicolored, and she has matching ribbons in her pigtails. "He's inside. Why don't you go find him?" I tell her, and she barges past me and into the house.

"Reee! I wove him."

I grin, imagining Eleanor tormenting Reed with her obsession with him. It drives him insane, but only adds to our entertainment.

The car door slams, and Shaw's wife, Emi, heads my way with their baby boy, Casper, in her arms.

Having my friends and their families here to meet Summer fills me with pride. This will be me soon with our little family too, and I can't fucking wait to get Summer back home to New Jersey to start our lives together.

———

Half an hour later, I'm sitting outside with my friends, nursing a beer while Summer entertains Gia and Emi inside. Bryce and Eleanor run around the garden with Bubbles following after them, looking like she's far from end-of-life care.

"So let me get this straight, there's no emergency?" Reed asks, and I scrub a hand over my head and shift on my feet.

"There was a little panic."

"Panic?" He rears back.

"You called me in the middle of the night, frantic." He leans closer to me. "I was fucking my wife at the time."

I grimace at the thought of him and Gia going at it. "Thanks for the visual," I quip. "I admit I was a little overwhelmed."

"Overwhelmed?" Reed repeats slowly, like a goddamn parrot.

"Yes, Reed, overwhelmed. I just found out my goddamn stepsister is pregnant, and she was telling me the baby was mine. Can you appreciate why I was overwhelmed?"

Shaw grins and leans back on the outdoor couch, watching our interaction with amusement in his eyes. It's probably the most entertainment he's had recently, especially with a brother-in-law like Luca Varros, a Mafia capo who happens to be certifiably insane. According to Shaw.

"Overwhelmed is having thirty kids scream your name all at once while you're trying to give them the logistics of a professional soccer game. Overwhelmed is having those thirty kids' parents give their insights into that game despite knowing fuck-all about the rules and regulations. Overwhelmed is—"

I hold my hand up and cut him off. "I get the point."

"Since when are there thirty kids in a soccer game?" Shaw asks.

Reed's attention slices to our friend, his stare filled with venom. "Since I became head coach."

Shaw scrunches up his nose. "Meh, Mase could bring in a bigger crowd than you, and how the hell did a kids' soccer game become labeled as professional? Isn't it classed as pee-wee or something?"

Reed's spine straightens. "I'm producing prospective professional soccer players. It's a big thing in Europe." He waves his hand around the garden.

Shaw and I burst into fits of laughter that have Reed scowling in our direction.

"Ree-Ree, I need you!" Eleanor squeals, making my ears ring with her high-pitched voice.

"Oh please, God no. Shaw?" Reed questions, with panic coating his face. The poor guy's chest is already heaving. How the hell a cute-as-fuck little three-year-old can have this effect on him, I'll never understand.

"Eleanor, stop!" Shaw's firm voice stops Eleanor in her tracks. "Go back inside to mamma." He points in the direction of the house.

Her bottom lip quivers, and I step forward and kneel to her level. "Eleanor, honey. Your mamma needs help with Bubbles. Can you go inside and take care of her? She's a little sick and needs to rest."

Shaw's eyes dart to Reed's, and he mouths, *Sick?*

"Okay, Mase." She nods and steels her shoulders, her bottom lip still quivering and making her look all the more adorable.

"That's a big girl. There's ice cream in the freezer. Tell your mamma."

"I will!" She runs off toward the mansion with an excited squeal, and you wouldn't know that seconds ago she was having a meltdown.

"Thank fuck. My child social battery has died." Reed drops down on the couch dramatically, then grabs his beer and proceeds to chug it, making my lip twitch.

Reed rolls his head toward me. "I can't stay here tonight; you realize that, don't you?"

I search his face. Why the hell would I want him to stay here?

"I booked us the house next door. It has been cleaned to my specification. They filled the refrigerator with my organic shit, and I don't have to endure Eleanor for the rest of the night," Reed says, uncaring that her father is right next to him.

"Now that we know you're okay, I'm going to book us a hotel near Disney." Shaw smiles broadly.

Reed shudders. "Better you than me."

"Well"—I shift in my chair—"I was going to ask you guys to help me with something."

They both sit forward, eyes narrowed, and I sit straighter, explaining my plan.

———

We've spent the last hour discussing what I have planned for Summer, and now I'm on to my next plan.

"So you know I went looking at potential property to expand STORM Enterprises?" I tell the guys.

"Not more work. Not yet," Reed grumbles.

I give him a swift kick. "Shut the fuck up and listen."

"Go on," Shaw says, eyeing me closely. The excitement is already sparking in his eyes; he always did love a challenge.

"Well, I didn't find anything. But Trav here"—I slap Trav's shoulder—"has the perfect business idea, along with a location." Shaw glances at the kid, and I can see what he's thinking. He's already dismissing him. Well, screw that. Everyone deserves a chance, and my protective streak has come out for him tenfold. Besides, this kid has potential in waves. "I've looked his plan over, and I'm telling you now, we're going to be interested." I squeeze Trav's shoulder with pride.

"Who else is going to work over here? Because I'm not moving to Los Angeles; I have a soccer club to run." Reed crosses his arms over his chest, and I swear he's pouting.

"What about Isaac?"

Reed takes notice when I mention his brother and sits up. "You'd give him a chance? A job?"

I shrug. "Sure. You said he's doing better."

The guy has had addiction problems for a long time, then he made a huge mistake that landed him in prison, but the guy has been through hell to prove himself. He just needs the chance. Maybe this could be it.

Reed stares back at me with a look of awe on his face. His Adam's apple slides down his throat before he clears it. "Thank you, man. That means a lot." I give him a firm nod.

"We need a couple of other guys. They need to be trustworthy," Shaw tacks on.

Reed nods. "I'm sure Owen knows someone."

"There's Todd too. Tate has been desperate to help him along," I add, referring to Tate's brother-in-law. Tate's wife, Ava, and her brother grew up in foster care. Tate didn't know it at the time, but when he had a one-night stand with her, she was actually in the care of his parents at a summer event they host for foster kids. I can't imagine how he felt knowing he slept with one of them. It wasn't until she became an intern at our company that they became reacquainted. Tate spent years pining after her —so much so, he tattooed his cock with her name.

"Well, I think it's a great idea. When you come home, why not arrange for Trav to come out and we can discuss it more?" Shaw suggests.

Hope sparks in Trav's eyes, and I smile back at him broadly; his excitement is contagious. "I'm going to see where Summer is," he announces, then heads inside with a broad smile on his face, and I imagine he's about to fill her in on my plan for his future.

Bubbles waddles past us toward the house, her tongue hanging precariously close to the floor, and Shaw turns to face Reed. "What's wrong with the dog exactly?" His tone is etched in concern.

"Bubbles is dying." Reed sighs.

Shaw pouts. "That's kind of sad. Eleanor will be devastated."

Reed rolls his eyes at Shaw's words. "The vet said she's exhausted and struggling to keep up." He sighs. "That's why her tongue is hanging out all the time."

I snort. "That and the shit Eleanor feeds her."

Shaw throws me a death glare. "I spoke to her about that. She hasn't done it since the day she pushed her down the slide."

"Dude, she was feeding her fucking fish from Oscar O'Connell's aquarium." I laugh as I remember the day Shaw was dragged along to a Mafia family function at the O'Connell's estate and Eleanor was caught feeding Oscar's fish to the dog. Turns out, Oscar loves those fish as much as his own kid. It almost ended in a bloodbath. Again.

"If we weren't stuck with the damn thing for weeks, we wouldn't have had to take her with us. It's like we have shared custody of the dog, but nobody bothered to ask if I wanted it in the first place." He moans like a petulant child.

"Well, excuse me for having to recover from being shot," Reed grumbles. "I was at death's fucking door."

"Pfft. I've been shot numerous times, and I don't take so long to recover," Shaw fires back, and Reed opens his mouth to respond. "Let me guess, you're allergic to bullets too, huh?" Shaw states. We all know how many allergies Reed claims to have.

Trav makes his way toward us, and Reed's eyebrows furrow. "Why the hell does he look like he wants to eat me?"

I take another drink of my beer and smile, refraining from saying, *He probably does.*

"Summer ordered pizzas," Trav declares, and his eyes drift over Reed before he drops down beside me.

"Hell yes. Summer's pussy is getting licked real good tonight." I smile, and everyone falls silent, making me acutely aware that I said my thoughts aloud.

Reed sits up to face me. "Holy shit. You're actually starting to live."

"Because I eat pussy?"

"Exactly." Reed points his beer bottle in my direction, but in a weird way, it makes sense. For years, I sat on the side-lines, wishing I could participate in my friends' banter, their worldly experiences. But I was trapped in a loveless, sexless marriage I was struggling to navigate, determined to conform. I never want that again.

"Is thirsty Thursday back on?" Shaw's eyes gleam with intrigue, referring to a bet my friends had about who could get the most blowjobs every Thursday in a row. "We can call it thirsty Thursday remastered," he jokes.

"I'm sure Tate will be thrilled to participate in a game that involves his sister sucking cock," Reed deadpans, referring to the fact that Tate's sister Laya, and Owen are married.

"You know. This shit with Summer has made me realize

something." I sit forward, and the guys hang off my every word. "There's no way in hell I'm ever getting married again," I breathe out with a heavy exhale.

A whimpering sound has my attention drawn to the side, and my stomach twists when Summer's devastated face comes into view. She clears her throat and wrings her hands in front of her. "I'm sorry to bother you, but the pizza has arrived." Then she turns and walks away, leaving the memory of her devastation etched in my brain.

"Sum?" I jump up from the couch, wanting nothing more but to pull her into my arms and tell her I'm sorry and I didn't mean it, but I can't find the words. Besides, I promised never to lie to her.

"Dick move," Trav grumbles and shoulder checks me on his way by.

Shaw slaps me on the back. "I always fuck up. Just got to learn how to grovel, man."

"Use your tongue and tell her you want more babies," Reed tacks on before rushing past Shaw to no doubt grab the first piece of pizza. The weird fucker insists on eating before anyone else touches the food, and he even uses a knife and fork to eat it.

# THIRTY-ONE

**SUMMER**

GIA AND EMI ARE AMAZING, their children are adorable, and Reed and Shaw are hilarious and welcoming. I can see why Mase sees them all as family.

"I can't believe you're having twins. That's such a blessing." Emi smiles in my direction as she takes another sip of her orange juice.

Gia scoffs. "That's hard work, that's what twins is." Then she grimaces when her gaze meets mine. "I'm sorry. I'm a realist."

I giggle. "It's okay. I know it's going to be hard."

"At least Mase is amazing with kids. He'll be really hands on," Emi adds to soften the blow.

The woman is so sweet and gentle; it's hard to believe she was a Mafia princess brought up around such cruelty.

Guilt stabs into me, piercing my soul, devouring me and spitting me out like trash. She's been through hell and has somehow managed to make it work after becoming pregnant after a one-night stand with a stranger. Whereas my one-night stand might have resulted in a pregnancy, but it won't have the same happy ending, as much as I want it to.

My betrayal, coupled with overhearing Mase tell his friends he'll never marry me, has my heart thumping in my chest and my stomach lurching.

"Are you okay, Summer? You're awfully pale," Gia asks, touching my forehead and placing me in the kitchen chair.

"Mom, can Bubbles sleep in my bed tonight?" Bryce asks.

When I discovered Reed adopted Gia's son and labeled him as his own, a newfound respect toward him overcame me. The man has taken over Gia's life and commandeered it. For a man who supposedly doesn't like children, you wouldn't have thought it.

Mase watches me closely from the living room, studying me as Gia places her hand on my forehead, then he springs up from his seat.

"What's wrong? Are you okay? Are the babies okay?"

"Mom, how do you get two babies inside one small stomach like that?" Bryce points in the direction of my stomach, and my eyes widen before they dart toward Gia.

"Ask your dad," Gia tells him, then winks back at me.

"Summer?" Mase's desperate voice cuts through the fog clouding my mind.

"Hmm?"

"What's wrong?"

"I just panicked about having twins. It's a lot." I lie far too easily and instantly hate myself for it. This house has slowly taken every part of me away from myself. I was fast becoming a person I didn't want to be, hence the *Indulgence* night, and only when Mase entered my life did I finally see myself as happy. It's just a shame it's all a façade.

Mase's shoulders relax, and his touch sends a flurry of warmth through me as he palms my face and tilts my head up to face him. "I've got you, sweet girl. Every step of the way."

Tears form in my eyes, but I blink them away, hiding the guilt and shame of my past actions. His eyes search mine, and he opens his mouth, but Eleanor's squeal of excitement cuts through the air and indirectly through the budding tension emanating from me in waves.

Bubbles is making a weird hacking sound, and Eleanor is bouncing on the balls of her feet beside her. "Bubbles found my pink hair clip, Mamma!" she declares, pointing at what appears to be dog puke.

"At least Bubbles hasn't died on us," Gia whispers under her breath.

"Come on." Mase lifts me into his arms, making me squeak, and I have no choice but to wrap my arms and legs around him like a koala. "We need to talk," he declares, and my stomach falls to the floor.

# THIRTY-TWO

## MASE

THE LOOK of sheer devastation on Summer's face when she overheard me tell the guys I wasn't getting married again is something that will haunt me forever and not something I intend on seeing again. It plays out in my mind like a bad movie. The way hurt flickered in her soft-blue eyes, and her face fell, then the shudder that racked her body was enough to stun me to the spot. What the hell did I do?

I want her more than I've wanted anything else in the world, besides our babies, of course.

But getting married again isn't something I can go through, despite every atom in my body screaming at me that this time is different.

I kick the door to my old room shut and slide Summer down my front until her feet touch the floor. Then, I back her up until she hits the wall and rest my arms above her head to cage her in, giving her no option but to listen to what I've got to say.

"I'm sorry." I kiss down her neck.

She swallows and turns her head to allow me access.

"I never meant for you to hear those words, Sum."

She shakes her head. "Doesn't matter. I understand."

Her solemn voice is full of resolution, and I fucking hate it. She deserves more than this.

I drop my arms and back up until my ass hits my bed, then I perch on the edge and scrub a hand over my head.

"When I married Tara …"

She flinches on her name, but I continue.

"I expected it to be for forever, Sum." My throat thickens. "I wanted to be the man my mom wanted my father to be. The man she deserved."

"Your father was a cruel, cheating prick," she spits out with fire in her eyes, and I love her for how defensive she is of me and my mom.

"He was"—I nod—"but I was determined to be anything but him. The complete opposite of him, in fact."

Her shoulders sag. "You are, Mase. You're so much more than him." The snarl lacing her words should be enough to convince me, but there's that familiar gnawing sensation inside me that tells me I'm not enough, and I want to be. I want to be the best version of myself for her and our children before I commit again.

"Our divorce fucked me up," I admit, and embarrassment curdles my stomach.

"She fucked you up," she snipes out, and she's not wrong; she did.

"I should have been stronger, Summer. I want to be stronger."

"I'm not, Tara, Mase," she implores.

My head snaps up, and I glare at her. "I know that. Fuck." I drag a hand over my head. "You think I don't know that? You're caring and compassionate, gentle, innocent. Trust me, I know you're everything she's not."

"But I'm not enough?" she whispers, and her words gut me.

She doesn't deserve to feel this way.

I jump up from the edge of the bed and take her in my arms.

"You're more than enough. It's me that's not enough, sweetheart. But I'm working on it." I tilt her head up to face me. "Just please stick with me. Don't—" Emotion lodges in my throat, and I struggle to swallow past the thick lump there. "Please don't give up on me, Sum. I want this." I rest my hand on her stomach, willing it to grow. "I want you more than you know. I just want to feel worthy of you all."

She clutches onto my shirt, her shoulders rack with sobs, and I loathe the sound, especially because I'm the one who made her feel that way.

Lifting her into my arms, I cradle her against my chest and position us on the bed with my back resting against the headboard.

"I wish I was worthy too." She says it so low I don't think I'm supposed to hear. I hold her tighter as she sniffles.

# THIRTY-THREE

**SUMMER**

UNABLE TO HELP MYSELF, I arch my back off the bed as Mase's thick tongue strokes through my folds in long, hard licks. He wrenches my legs apart, pinning me, and I love the bite of pain his grip leaves.

My heart races, and I grip his short hair, anchoring him to the spot to ensure he never stops exploring. Each flick of his tongue brings me closer to the edge, but it's his low growl of satisfaction that really pulls my arousal from me. He loves this. In this moment, my Saintly Sinner is immersed in utter gratification.

When his tongue sweeps over my clit, my pussy clenches, and he smiles against me. Then he retreats, and the sight before me is damn near perfection. His lips glisten with my arousal, his muscles are taut, and his expression is that of pure unadulterated bliss. He creeps up my body, dwarfing me and settling on his elbows above me. Our faces are so close his breath fans my cheeks, and when his soft lips meet mine, I open my mouth to accommodate him while my legs band around his waist to hold him in place.

His tongue delves deep into my mouth, toying with mine and playing with it tenderly, coaxing the pleasure from me while his cock finds my entrance, and he inches inside.

He pulls out and slides back in. In and out, and it's utter perfection.

This is lovemaking. This is what I've read about, heard about; this is everything.

He draws back, breathless, and the look in his eyes tells me everything I need to know.

He's falling in love with me.

His eyes search mine, no doubt mirroring my own.

Then he slams his lips against mine, swallowing down my moan of euphoria.

Our bodies move in time with one another, each thrust more meaningful than the last. The sound of our skin slapping fills the room, and he begins to lose control. "Fuck," he moans. "Fuck, Sum." The sound of his voice is almost unrecognizable, and I come, screaming with my head thrown back, then his body tightens, the telltale sign he's about to join me, and he holds himself deep. A feral sound leaves his lips when he presses them to my neck tenderly.

When he slips from me, I feel his loss instantly and sit up to watch him pull on his clothes. Is he leaving?

"W-What are you doing?"

He turns with a smile that stuns me. "I have a surprise for you."

My eyebrows shoot up. "You do?"

"Yep." His smile grows wider. "Get dressed, Sum." He taps my leg, and I blink several times. "Sweetheart, you're so stinking cute when you're shocked."

"I am not cute." I pout and push off the bed, then stare down at the mess sliding down my leg. "I need a shower."

"No, you don't." Mase shakes his head. "I want my girl covered in my cum today."

"Huh?"

"Summer, clothes." He points to the dress laid out on the chair, the same one I wore when we first met, and I wonder if that was picked on purpose. "On."

Instead of asking, I nod and move around the bedroom while Mase goes to the bathroom. "And sweetheart?"

"Yes?" I glance toward the door, and he sticks his head out.

"Put your hair in the braid." He winks.

What the hell does he have planned?

# THIRTY-FOUR

**SUMMER**

MASE HEADED DOWNSTAIRS five minutes ago, and as I head out the bedroom door, I hear muffled voices. What the hell is happening?

I come to a halt when I reach the landing.

Hundreds of pink and blue rose petals cover the white marble stairs, and my heart flutters.

My eyes follow the path and come to a standstill when I see Mase waiting for me at the bottom of the stairs with a look of pure admiration on his face. Slowly, he trails his gaze up from the ballerina pumps I'm wearing, to my face, and his assessment of me sends a flurry of excitement rushing through my veins. He smirks as if knowing, and I roll my eyes and move down the stairs.

When I reach the bottom step, he holds out his hand, and I blink away the tears threatening to spill.

"This is beautiful." I lift up on my tiptoes and press my lips against his.

"It's our baby shower." He grins proudly.

I pull back to stare into his eyes. Our baby shower? Can he be any more perfect?

"Come on, I have some more friends I want you to meet." He tilts his head toward the garden, and I follow his line of sight and gasp at the unisex balloon arch that leads into the kitchen.

"You like, huh?"

"I love." I smile back at him, and something flashes in his eyes, something that tells me he likes the sound of that. Though I don't think he's quite ready to hear it properly.

He guides me through the kitchen to outside, and the moment we step out, an array of congratulations are shouted from each and every direction.

Music begins to play, streamers and bubbles float through the air, and the small gathering of friends erupts into cheers of joy.

"Oh, wow. This is incredible." I blink back the wetness pooling in my eyes, and Mase drops a kiss on top of my head and pulls me against his firm chest.

I laugh with glee as Eleanor rushes toward me with a half-eaten cupcake in her little hand to show me what she's holding.

"I had to give her one. She wouldn't shut the fuck up about the damn cake," Reed grumbles, and points in the direction of a cake.

Butterflies flutter in my stomach at the sight of it. "It's beautiful." Even I hear the emotion in my voice. A white cake with a long, thick pink sash iced down one side trimmed in what appear to be diamanté, then the exact same is on the other side, only in blue to show the possibility of either sex. "Mase?" I turn to face him, and he beams down at me. A tear slips down my face.

"You like it, right?" He swipes the tear from my cheek, then cups my face in his hands. "I made sure it was dark chocolate."

Those butterflies take flight at his words. He remembered I like dark chocolate.

Reed breaks the moment between us when he marches past us to grab champagne from the table set up on the patio. He tips the drink back, emptying the glass, then reaches for another. *Oh, dear.*

Gia strides toward him and taps his arm. "No, you don't, fuckwit. You're on child duty tonight."

His mouth drops open. "I can't drink?"

"Nope."

"But you're breastfeeding. It's not like you can drink." He gestures toward the kids now running wild, chasing after the bubbles and balloons.

Gia crosses her arms over her chest. "Welcome to my world. Unless you want to say bye-bye to my breast milk, you need to entertain the kids so I can have a night off."

He leans closer to her, but we can still hear. "Gia, I don't think you realize how much Eleanor makes me need the alcohol." There's an edge to his tone that tells me he's unraveling.

He really is as antisocial as Mase explained.

She snorts. "Don't blame an innocent little girl for your lack of control, Reed, and if you make that little girl cry again, you're sleeping in the spare room."

He rears back as if she hit him, then slaps his chest.

"I'll be watching, and let's not forget how much you enjoy these." She glances down at her heavy chest, then sashays away from him toward the women.

My eyes widen, and Mase shifts from foot to foot.

"I guess he likes his milk, huh?" I smile.

"He's not the only fucking one." Mase grins down at me, then at my heaving tits, the promise in his eyes unmistakable. The dress sure as hell wasn't this tight on me when we first met.

My cheeks heat at the memory. "Come on, Sum. Let me introduce you to our family." And I swoon a little more.

# MASE

Summer has giggled, smiled, and joined in on every conversation.

After introducing her to Tate and his wife, Ava, I explained that they flew in for the day, and she couldn't believe the effort they put in to support us. I told her we're all one big family, and a smile filled her beautiful face, and her eyes gleamed with love, filling me with a sense of purpose, to make her smile like that every damn day.

"Ree-Reed, I need you!" Eleanor rushes toward Reed with another cupcake squished between her chubby fingers, the icing coating her mouth and chin and cheeks.

He holds a hand out in front of her, stopping her abruptly. "Stop! Do not come a step closer to me, Eleanor. You need to calm down, stop eating cupcakes and go wash your"—his lip curls and the disdain oozes from him—"dirty hands."

I bite into my bottom lip and rock back on my sneakers, loving the entertainment of a three-year-old obsessed with my best friend. Leaning against the wall, I take another swig of my beer and watch with a smile on my face. This is comedy gold.

Her face falls, then her bottom lip wobbles dramatically,

and Reed rolls his eyes. "Oh, dear God, no." My poor friend panics and glances around the garden, searching among the small crowd. Eleanor plonks her butt down on the grass, throws herself back on the ground, and slams her arms down beside her. When her face contorts into hysteria, I wince, knowing damn well this is bound to be another spectacular meltdown.

Reed strides forward, his face ashen. He leans over Eleanor and pokes her stomach. "Eleanor, get up."

She shakes her head and releases a rattled cry that makes her body shake.

"Eleanor, be a big girl and get up off the ground, please," he grits out. She shakes her head again. "There're ants on the ground, and they'll be getting in your tummy." He winces and snaps his head in Gia's direction. "Up, quick."

She turns to face him, her grumpy face making me chuckle, and shakes her little head again. Shaw has his work cut out with this kid. I wonder if ours will make us endure similar antics.

"If you get up, I'll get you more cake."

"Want that one." She throws a finger in the direction of the cake stand, and I glance over my shoulder to look at it. That thing cost me a small fortune—not that I care, I love the fact it's half pink and half blue—and I'm silently hoping we do in fact have one of each sex.

Reed licks his lips. "Yes, you can have some of that cake. But you have to hurry. Up, now." He pats her stomach again. "Quick, quick."

I shake my head at him, fucking amateur. When the hell is he going to realize you don't promise an infant more sugar.

The little terror springs up from the ground, all signs of devastation eradicated from her face. "Why don't you go and find Bubbles, huh? You like him, right." Reed tugs playfully on her ponytail.

"Cake," she snaps back.

"Jesus, you're such a pampered princess. You know that?" He groans, and I seriously think he doesn't realize she can hear him. I choke on a laugh when I imagine her repeating that to Shaw. He's going to be borrowing that gun that keeps shooting bullets into him, courtesy of its master, Luca, and deliver a swift bullet in our friend.

Reed's thunderous gaze locks on mine. *Help?* he mouths, and I grin wider when he nods down to Eleanor.

Pushing off the wall, I head over to my best friend to give him a reprieve. "Come on, toots, let's go find you a surprise." Her little face lights up, and her hand finds mine.

"You owe me." I smirk at Reed, who narrows his eyes.

Then I head round the corner to show Eleanor what that surprise is.

# THIRTY-FIVE



"I CAN'T BELIEVE he ordered a donkey for Eleanor. That's so sweet." Emi sighs and sits back against the couch.

"And the blue and pink ribbon around its neck, so cute," Ava tacks on.

My cheeks hurt from smiling so much. It's like I won the jackpot with Mase. How is this my life right now?

I sure as hell don't deserve it.

"You deserve to be happy, Summer, and trust me, Mase Campbell is going to make you happy." Gia pats my hand, and all the girls nod with smiles almost as wide as my own.

"She's right, you do," Travis adds, and I smile at my best friend.

*Thank you*, I mouth back to him, and he grins.

"Poor Reed looks like he'd rather be anywhere else," Emi comments, and we all look in his direction.

"Is he always so ..." Travis thinks for a moment. "Intense?"

"Yes." Gia smiles proudly, and we all nod. You can see the

love pouring from them just by a simple look, and it's so adorable.

"He got lumbered with leading the donkey round the grounds. I'm pretty sure Tate used entertaining Bryce as an excuse not to take his turn." Emi smiles, and I steal a glance at Tate; he's in a pop-up soccer net playing the goalkeeper while Bryce takes shots at him. Reed's eyes bore into him like lasers, and I smile at the anger radiating from him. He looks like he's seconds away from detonating. His face is getting redder by the second, his eyes are sharpening, and I can even see his chest heaving from where we sit. Definitely wound up.

"He looks …" Emi muses, then tilts her head from side to side. "A little angsty."

"He looks like he's about to blow a fucking stack," Ava tacks on, making us all giggle at her blunt words.

Gia pops another chip in her mouth nonchalantly, then sits back and crosses her legs, a smile playing on her lips like she's watching a movie. "Let's see how this plays out."

# MASE

My phone pings again.

Reed: You're up next, Mase.

Mase: It's my party.

Reed: And?

Mase: You said you'd help.

Reed: Help, not run the damn show.

I roll my eyes.

Reed: If I knew I was here as childcare, I'd
have hired a damn nanny.

Tate: Dramatic much?

Reed: You're not the one being lumbered
with this …

He sends a photo of the donkey with Eleanor sitting on its back, a toothy grin on her face and her lips and teeth coated in pink icing.

Shaw: Aw, that's my girl. She loves her uncle Ree-Reed.

Reed: Come and sort 'your girl' out. She wants you.

Shaw: Pretty sure she's shouting for Ree-Ree.

Reed: Fuck you! Where the hell are you anyway?

Shaw: Cinema room. Hot as fuck out there.

I glance up to see Reed turn an even deeper shade of red and shake my head on a chuckle.

Owen: Sorry I'm missing it guys. Romeo is still puking.

Poor kid has got the same stomach bug Owen's wife, Laya, just recovered from. There's no way in hell I want him risking bringing that over to the party.

Reed: Don't be sorry. You're the lucky one. This is literal hell.

Lucky? He knows damn well Laya has been suffering all week. Besides, this is the best damn party around. I made sure of it.

Mase: You're a dick.

Reed: You're not the one with a stinking,
short-ass horse grunting at him, and a
moaning child attached to you by a rein.

I can't help the snort that leaves me. This is classic.

Mase: It's a donkey, dumbass.

Reed: What the fuck ever. Can you come
take over?

Mase: No.

I grin to myself as he glances around the lawn again, pleading for help.

Reed: Tate! You either come and take your
turn or I'm abandoning the animals.

Shaw: Mase, there's more than one animal?

Reed: I can assure you there is and she's the
loudest.

Oh, hell no. I imagine Shaw flipping his shit at Reed's analogy. He's such a coldhearted bastard sometimes.

Tate: I'm doing my childcare part.

Reed: You're playing soccer with my son.

Tate: Exactly. You always moan about this,
and Bryce said I'm a better coach than
you, so ...

Reed: You don't know what you're doing.
You don't know a damn thing about soccer.

Tate: Bryce seems to think I do.

Tate: Apparently, I'm the best.

Tate bites his lip as Bryce takes another shot at him, and he quickly stuffs his phone into his pocket.

Reed pinches the bridge of his nose, then in an Oscar-worthy action, he drops his head back with a loud groan. "That's it! I'm fucking done!" he declares, throwing his arms up.

My chest vibrates with uncontrollable chuckles.

Oh, this is about to get good.

# THIRTY-SIX



"REE-REE. CAKE?"

Jesus, this kid has issues. So many fucking issues, I think she needs therapy. Already.

"Ree, cake!" She points again toward the cake. She's like a broken record.

My phone buzzes in my hand, and I stare down at the response from Tate.

> Tate: Exactly. You always moan about this, and Bryce said I'm a better coach than you, so …

Better coach? Who the hell is he kidding? My gaze slices over to Tate, and he holds his arms stretched out to catch the ball. I shake my head. He's holding them out incorrectly, for starters, and how the hell is he standing? Better coach, my ass. I need to get over there and undo his errors before there's no coming back from the crap he's telling Bryce.

I glance around the patio area and notice Ava has hold of her and Tate's son, Sonny. Typical, he left her with holding the baby while he opts to attempt to teach my son how to play soccer. I don't know how she deals with his lazy ass.

"Ree-Ree." I want to snap at her to shut up, but I exhale and will my patience to make an appearance. Or someone to take her and the donkey from me.

My fingers work quickly as I stab the keys to send another message.

Reed: You don't know what you're doing.

He has no clue, and I don't think he realizes the impact it will have on my son. He thinks this is a game.

Tate: Bryce seems to think I do.

Anger like no other flashes through me.

Tate: Apparently, I'm the best.

"Ree-Reed. Cake." For fuck's sake. "Cake!" she screeches, the tone so high-pitched my eardrums are bound to be damaged.

"Cake!"

"Yes! You're the best, Tate." Bryce jumps up and down with glee, pumping his fist in the air.

That's it. I'm done. D. O. N. E. Done.

"The greatest!" Bryce cheers.

Is he fucking kidding me right now?

I pinch the bridge of my nose, then drop my head back with an almighty groan. "That's it! I'm fucking done!" I throw my arms up in the air.

Eleanor giggles. Fucking giggles. "Cake, Ree."

Slowly, I turn to face the animal and the little girl with the cute pigtails and make a snap decision. Ignoring Eleanor and her ridiculous repetitiveness, I head toward the pool fence and tie the rein around the post. There, that'll do it.

I'm going to drag Shaw out here and demand he look after his child, then I'm going to show Tate how to play soccer because the poor man clearly has no clue.

I bet he's never read a soccer handbook in his life.

It's about time my friends step up and take control of their responsibilities. I snort and shake my head. They thought I was the clueless one. Idiots.

# MASE

Is he seriously tying the donkey to the pool post? I grimace, knowing damn well those things aren't the most stable. That's something I won't need to fix. Nope, we won't be here long enough to care. This place is going on the market the moment we step foot in New Jersey.

Bubbles makes a beeline for the donkey, and I wince and place my beer bottle on the table. The last thing we need is for the damn dog to spook the donkey.

She yaps and I frown, making my way over before things get out of hand. "Bubbles, no!" I shout toward the dog, but she yaps louder. The donkey rears back. *Oh, shit*. I slowly step forward with my arms out in front of me, trying my best not to scare the donkey as I inch toward it.

"Fuck!" Tate shouts and heads toward us, but his loud bellow doesn't help the situation because the donkey backs up, appearing more flustered than ever. Thankfully, Eleanor grins a toothy smile, completely unperturbed as Tate stands behind it. He gives me a nod, and I step forward, but in the blink of an eye, the donkey jerks back, making a grunting noise I didn't know they could make. It lashes out, kicking its back legs toward Tate.

"Holy! Fu—" Tate drops to the ground holding his groin, then stumbles backward.

My mouth falls open to warn him, but it's too late, as he falls into the cake stand, and the cake wobbles before collapsing on Tate as he hits the ground.

Ugh, fantastic!

"Ahhhh!" Eleanor lets out a wail rivaling a war cry, and the donkey pulls away, taking the pool post and fence with it. I have the foresight to dash out of the way as the net fencing is dragged open.

The women's screeches ring out in my ears, and I rush to grab the donkey. Who knew these things could run?

Shaw steps in front of it and grabs the rein, and the tension I was holding slips away.

The women erupt into cheers, and I roll my eyes. Not a single one of them has moved an inch.

"Cake!" Eleanor screeches, and Shaw lifts her from the donkey.

"I was only gone for five minutes," he declares, surveying the destruction while placing Eleanor on the ground. More like forty-five.

"Helll-p," Tate groans, and I spin to face him on the ground, cupping his balls. "Hurts." Oh shit, I think he's genuinely in pain. He writhes, appearing in agony.

Eleanor sits beside him, swiping the cake off his face and delivering it to her open mouth.

Then Bubbles waddles over and crouches over Tate's leg, and I watch on in horror as the dog begins to pee.

"Welcome to my fucking world," Reed says, standing over Tate with his hands on his hips and a hint of a smile on his face.

"Congratulations on the baby shower, man." Shaw slaps me on the back, and I laugh. When my eyes meet Summer's, I see the same sentiment firing right back at me.

This is happiness.

# THIRTY-SEVEN

## MASE

TATE WAS TAKEN to the emergency room. Reed brought his family home to the house next door, and Shaw managed to persuade Eleanor to leave with promises of Disneyland and more cake. I think Reed might be right; she has an addiction to sugary food.

If I were Shaw, after tonight's spectacle, I'd probably just give in too.

A team of cleaners is working through the house, and I'm conscious of the fact that Hugh has made himself scarce all night. Odd for a man who likes to know everything.

About twenty minutes ago, I sent Summer upstairs to take a bath, and I can't fucking wait to join her.

"Tonight was a huge success." Travis grins widely, wiping the kitchen counter.

"Thanks for your help." I nudge him. I'm excited about this kid's future as we step into expanding the STORM dynasty.

My phone pings with a message.

Reed: Why the hell is Bubbles shitting blue?

Tate: Eleanor was feeding her the icing.

I turn the phone to show Travis the messages, and he chuckles along with me.

Shaw: Oops.

Reed: I'll send you the vet bill.

Me: Why? Because you can't afford it? (Eye roll emoji.)

Tate: She might need a colonic irrigation.

Shaw: They do them for dogs?

Tate: I mean Reed has had plenty.

Reed: Funny!

Owen: Least the dog isn't shitting pink everywhere.

Reed: My dogs butthole looks like it belongs to a smurf.

I grimace at the thought of Reed inspecting the dog's butt.

Tate: I'm astounded you went there.

Reed: Trust me, so am I.

Reed: We had no clue what it was until Gia witnessed it for herself.

I shake my head with laughter.

Me: Did it have the cute glitter sprinkles on
top too?

Travis snorts.

Reed: When I think my life can't get any more
shocking something happens that reminds
me it can.

Owen: Bet the trauma got you a blow job
though?

Reed: Two actually. See, I'm in a full-fledged
relationship and still I'm winning at Thirsty
Thirty.

I roll my eyes. If they knew how much Summer liked sucking on my cock, he'd think otherwise. Pretty sure I'm winning.

The doorbell sounds, and I wince. The thought of Summer in the bath upstairs is calling to me. "Should I grab it for you?" Trav asks.

"No, man. You get on home; it's been a long day." He ducks his head and follows me to the front door.

"I really appreciate everything you're doing for me, Mase."

"I appreciate you taking care of Summer for me. You manned up when nobody else would, and I'll never forget that."

He shifts from foot to foot, and I get the distinct feeling he wants to tell me something, but the doorbell rings again, so I pull it open with a heavy huff.

My eyes widen as they latch onto a very shifty-looking Levi, and his gaze snaps to Travis's, then back to mine. "Can I speak with you?" He gestures toward Trav, and I narrow my eyes. *Not on my watch, fuckwit.*

Trav rolls his lip into his mouth before taking the door from me and gestures for Levi to step inside. "Sure."

I barely move back enough for him to close the door behind him, then cross my arms over my thick chest as I glare at the punk. His ears turn red under my scrutiny, and he swallows heavily.

"I, err. I just want you to know I made sure nobody will talk about the diner incident." He glances at me, then back at Trav. The need to protect him has me clenching my fists. "And my father has spoken to the school. He's going to make sure you can finish, if that's what you want." His hands tremble, and as if sensing me studying him, he stuffs them in his pockets. His gaze locks with Trav's, and there's a strange dull moment where I feel like I'm missing something. "I just need you to know something."

I watch with bated breath and a sharpened jaw as Trav struggles to hold his gaze. "Yeah?" he rasps.

Levi shuffles from one foot to the other. "I was never interested in Summer." His eyes flit to mine, then back to Trav who blinks rapidly and slowly, if that at all makes sense.

Oh, shit.

"I was jealous." He glances down at the floor, then back up at Trav. "Of Summer." His cheeks flush deeper, and his words are now barely a whisper. "Of the relationship you have. It's not Summer I'm into."

My heart skips a beat for them, and suddenly, I feel like an intruder in my own home.

"I'm going to leave you both to it." I gift them a nod and head upstairs.

"Mase?" Travis shouts, and with a hand on the rail, I turn. "Thank you."

"For what?"

He lifts a shoulder. "Helping me know I can be who I

want to be." His words have a meaning behind them he couldn't possibly know. Being here has allowed me to be who I want to be too.

I smile down at him. Something tells me we're going to be seeing a lot more of him.

"Welcome to the family, kid." I smirk, then chuckle at his shocked reaction.

Looks like this family is getting a whole lot bigger, and I couldn't be happier about it.

# THIRTY-EIGHT

**SUMMER**

THROUGHOUT THE NIGHT, Mase barely let go of me, only releasing me enough to pull the sheets over us and create our very own little sense of solace.

Last night his friends headed out, and Trav headed home, and now the house feels empty once again.

"Good morning, Miss." Hugh smiles warmly and steps into the kitchen.

Mase made me a slice of toast this morning before giving me strict instructions not to eat much more because we have breakfast plans.

"Morning," I mumble, averting my gaze from his intrusive one.

"Apparently, you have plans this morning." Hugh smiles in my direction, and the sight is so unfamiliar I find myself smiling back.

For some reason, I've always felt like he's seen me as a nuisance, but since Jeff passed away, he's been much less intense. Maybe his death was not just good for me but others around him too.

Maybe that's what I have to tell myself to survive.

"Mase is taking me out for breakfast," I say through munching on the toast.

Hugh watches me closely. "Any idea what time you'll be back?"

"No. Why?"

He lifts his shoulder. "I wondered if Mase would mind me finishing early today. I'll message and ask him."

Hugh never talks about his shifts with me or finishing early. Truth be told, I never took notice of his hours; he was just always here. "I don't see why not. You work a lot of hours, Hugh."

"Well, I have to find another job, don't I." He gapes, and his words slice through me like an accusation, all smiles banished as if they were never there at all. Odd.

"You ready, Sum?" Mase bounds into the room, rubbing his damp hair with a towel, and I turn on the kitchen stool to face him.

*Jesus, he's hot.*

The tattoos that creep up his neck make me want to lick the droplets of water from him.

With a chuckle, he shifts on his feet, then holds his hand out for me. "Come on, let's get out of here before you eat me." He tugs me toward him and nips at my ear playfully.

It's not until we head out the door, I wonder why Hugh didn't ask Mase about finishing early.

# THIRTY-NINE

**MASE**

SUMMER'S HAIR blows in the morning breeze as she sits between my open legs, resting against my solid chest. I breathe in her floral scent, basking in our embrace and willing today to last forever.

We've been up on the cliff all morning. Looking out to the national park, where there's nothing but trees and the sound of wildlife coupled with the steady stream of water from the nearby waterfall, while eating the breakfast picnic I packed for us.

Knowing Summer suffers with morning sickness, I made sure she ate before we left, to keep the traveling from upsetting her stomach, then we shared a platter of fresh fruit, pastries, and juice.

"What do you think we'll end up having, boys? Girls? Or one of each?"

Summer flinches, and it's a habit of hers I'm picking up on whenever I mention the babies.

My arms band around her, and I rest my hand on her stomach, letting her know I'm all in.

"I'm scared. That's all."

I'm scared too, I want to tell her, but I also want to be her strength. "Of something happening to the babies?"

"Of everything just disappearing. Every part of my happiness vanishing. Just like that." She snaps her fingers, and this time it's me that flinches; mainly because I've been there before. When every part of me was filled with joy only for it to be stolen so brutally.

"I'm not going to let that happen, Sum."

"What if there's something that already happened, something bad, but you couldn't stop it because it already happened?"

Her words send a surge of anxiety zipping through my body like gasoline igniting. Again, I get the feeling she's trying to tell me something, and as much as I want to push her to open up to me, I'm fucking terrified of her saying something that fucks it all up. I want to live in ignorant bliss; I want the happily ever after for once.

I want her and our babies, and most of all, I want them to want me just as much. My self-conscious, fucked-up flaws and all.

She clears her throat. "I'm hoping for one of each. Then hopefully I won't have to go through morning sickness again." She chuckles, but its weak, and the coward in me is grateful she breaks the tension that was settling over the morning.

"I can't wait for you to start showing," I rasp in her ear, and stroke her stomach. I'm not afraid to admit I've spent way too many hours watching videos of pregnant women. I know more than most about every aspect of pregnancy. I have numerous reasons to, and when my friends each discovered their partners were expecting, I became enthralled in the excitement of it all. Some might've called me envious, but it was never in a hate-filled way, always with longing and hope.

"I can't wait to go shopping for baby clothes, to buy a stroller for them, and little soft toys. I don't care what sex they are, as long as you're all okay."

She rests her hand over mine, and I entwine our fingers. "Me too."

"And trust me when I say, you best get used to being pregnant, Sum, because I intend on keeping you knocked up for at least the next ten years." I kiss her neck, and a shudder racks through her, making my cock twitch.

"You like that? You like the idea of me keeping you pregnant for me?" My hand roams over her stomach. "Making you all swollen, just for me?"

My cock thickens against her back.

"I want that," she breathes out. "I want that so bad, Mase." I'm unsure if she's talking about the pregnancy or if she's aroused and wants more, but in this moment, I'll take either.

"Lift your dress, Sum." I lick the top of her ear, then nuzzle into her neck and deliver soft wet kisses down and back up. "Show everyone your panties, my sweet girl." There's not another soul in sight, but that doesn't stop the adrenaline running through my veins at the thought of exposing us to the public. "Let the world see how wet your panties get for your brother."

Her chest heaves, and she uses her free hand to lift her dress to her waist.

"Good girl. Let the world see your pretty pussy dripping with your arousal." I nip at her neck, then follow it up with a quick lick to take away the sting. "You." *Nip.* "Dirty." *Lick.* "Little." *Nip.* "Slut."

She moans, and my tongue trails from the base of her neck to her jawline, and with our hands entwined, I reach down and hook two of my fingers into her cotton panties.

"They're all wet, Sum." My cock is rock hard as I touch the

damp fabric and push it to the side. "They're all wet and begging for my cum. Do you want me to stretch this little hole, Sum?"

Her head drops back against my chest, and she lets out a whimper.

"Ahh, Mase."

"Use your fingers too, Summer. Use your fingers to play with your little hole." I groan, and her finger rests on top of mine, but she allows me to guide her through her slick folds and into her tight hole. "You feel how tight you are, sweet girl?"

"Yes." We slide in and out of her pussy at a leisurely pace while my cock throbs to be let out and in on the action. "Please, Mase."

"Please what, sweetheart?" I mock, keeping my pace steady. Her finger pressing down on mine inside her causes arousal to surge through me.

"I want you to fuck me," she pants wantonly.

"Do you want me to stretch your cunt with my thick cock?"

"Yes."

"Do you want me to put a baby in here?" The palm on her stomach tightens, and although Summer is already pregnant, a thrill at the thought of continuing to breed her has electricity zapping through me.

"Yes. Please," she moans, and I know my girl has the same kink too. Could we be any more perfect for one another?

Unable to take the torment any longer, I remove our fingers. "Take your dress off, Sum. I want you to ride me."

I hold out my hand to help her up, and she stumbles to her feet, then I waste no time in lifting my T-shirt over my head and dropping it to the ground. Next, I pop open my jeans, lower my zipper, and pull my throbbing cock from my boxers—all while my eyes never leave Summer's. "Leave your panties on, sweetheart, I want them wet with my cum after."

The way her cheeks heat has me chuckling, but when her hand slides into mine for me to help her straddle me, all humor disappears.

# SUMMER

My panties are already soaked, but hearing Mase say he wants them wet with his cum has my clit pulsating with a desperate need to satiate, something only he can do.

He holds his thick cock up for me, and I push my panties to the side and slowly lower myself down onto his thickness. The air is knocked from my lungs the moment the head of his cock prods at my entrance with a promise of leaving his mark.

I'll feel this for days, and I want to. I want to feel Mase all over me as a reminder of our lovemaking, because contrary to what Mase says or believes, that's what this is.

This is more than a filthy hookup; we're building a future together. I just wish it wasn't built on the lies that haunt me.

I push the dark thoughts in my mind aside, and continue with the assault on my pussy, reveling in the bite of pain as I inch down.

"Fuck, you've no idea how much I want to destroy you right now," he grits out. His fingers bite into my skin, but I welcome the pain and the bruising that will follow, much like our first time together. "I want to fuck you so hard."

"Do it," I coax with a swirl of my hips.

He bites his lip, his muscles bunched tight, and I scan him up and down, greedily devouring every inch of his toned abs. "Don't want to hurt my babies."

I shake my head, and my braid brushes the top of my ass. "You won't. I checked. You won't hurt them."

One of his strong palms lands on my stomach, and I adore the possessiveness of his touch. The way his hungry stare equally penetrates me is an aphrodisiac to my soul.

"I love the fact I put my baby in here." He licks his lips, and I slide down his length, then hold myself still. "My innocent angel, growing my babies. So fucking beautiful, Summer."

He lifts to his elbows, leaning forward, and when his lips wrap around the tip of my pointed nipple, I throw my head back in ecstasy. "I'm going to milk your tits dry each time after you feed the babies."

"Please." I hold his head in place as he suckles, giving me no other option but to grind down on him over and over. "Please, Sinner," I moan.

His eyes darken, and he slams up inside me with such power I have no choice but to become his to use.

"That's it, take my cock. Fuck, yes," he spits out, like his action offended him. "Take it, little slut." I take everything he gives me, thrust after powerful thrust, until I feel the telltale jerk of his cock pulsating deep inside me. "Fuuuck," he growls.

Then, with his chest heaving and his cock still hard, he wraps a hand around me and holds my ass in place while the other props us upright. I continue bouncing in a steady rhythm on his cock while his tongue works over my nipple, flicking at the peak and bringing with it such pleasure my pussy clenches with each swipe.

"Yes. More. More, Mase. Suck harder."

His cum drips from me with each powerful movement. Pushing his cock deeper into my pussy, his hips power up, and he continues to suck so hard he's going to leave a mark, but I don't care; I will it to happen. I lift myself up and slam back down, meeting him with each movement. My pussy clenches around his thick length, and I replicate each groan of his pleasure with my own tortured moan.

"More. More," I chant with my impending orgasm.

"That's it, ride me. Ride that thick cock so I can fill you with my cum." His filthy words have my clit throbbing with an intensity I've become accustomed to with Mase.

"Oh god, Mase. More."

"Fuck, you look beautiful pregnant with my babies and begging." He thrusts up harder, sweat beading on his forehead, and I've no choice but to hold on tightly to him, and when he rolls his hips, I moan in delight, and my fingernails dig into his corded shoulders. "Fuck, yes. I'm going to fill you, then paint your pretty little lips." He slaps my ass hard, and with one final thrust, my pussy convulses, and I drop my head back, giving him access to my tits. When he bites my nipple with his lips, I soar, delighting in his stuttered breaths as he fills me with his warm cum.

# MASE

I thrust up again, my chest heaving and my balls spent, but I'm not finished with her. I want to make good on my word. Without giving her a chance to catch her breath, I pull her off my cock and push her panties back in position. My cum dripping from her pussy is not something I'm okay with, but the fabric of her panties being drenched and knowing she's sitting in my cum make it bearable.

She drops down onto her back, in the perfect position for me, so I kneel above her face, and her eyes widen. As I straddle her face, my cock is semihard and coated in our combined juices, my jeans and boxers around my ankles.

"Suck me clean, sweetheart," I rasp. "Lick our cum off my cock."

Hunger flares in her eyes, and when her tongue darts out of her mouth, my cock jumps. I hold my cock out to her, and she swipes over the dripping head, causing me to hiss in approval.

"Good girl," I praise, and she mewls.

My cock thickens, and I slowly inch inside her open mouth, loving the wetness and warmth of her. "I want to fuck your mouth so bad," I admit, glancing down at her. "I want to fuck it, and really hard." I swallow past the thickness in my throat. Admitting my dark, filthy thoughts is new to me, but Summer gives me the confidence to be my true self without feeling the shame I was accustomed to.

I withdraw from her mouth and jerk off over her. The thought of coming in her mouth or over her beautiful face has excitement sparking every dormant cell in my body to life. Marking her as mine for all to see, fuck yes. My hand moves quicker, my cock dripping pre-cum onto her lips, making a filthy mess that leaks down her chin.

"Use my face, Mase. Do what you want. Use me how you want."

My heart skips a beat, and my hand jerks at her words.

"Show me how filthy you can make me, marking me with your cum like your own personal slut."

The grip on my cock tightens to the point of pain, but I embrace it. "My little cum slut," I bite out, feeling absolutely fucking feral for her. Then I rise onto my knees and smack my cock against her lips. As her lips begin to part, I slam inside her mouth, forcing a gag, but I continue with my assault, surging into her throat.

I drop forward, resting my hands in the dirt, and with my knees resting on each side of her head, I lift, then slam back down, fucking her mouth like it's her pussy. "Fuck. That's it." *Thrust.* "Fuck, take it."

The sound of her gagging, the slickness of her drool, and the feeling of her teeth scraping as I slam inside her sends my arousal skyrocketing, spearing through me like lightning.

She clings to me like her life depends on it, her nails creating crescents in my thighs, and my quad muscles contract under each powerful thrust of me face-fucking her. "My little fucking slut to command," I spit out, and sweat drips into the dirt from my head. "Mine to fill." I pound into her. "Every fucking hole needs filled. Reminded it's mine."

Her gargled moan and the way her throat closes around

me pulls the cum from my slit in euphoric waves of ecstasy, spurt after spurt filling her hole and causing her to choke. I withdraw quickly then jerk my cock wildly over her face.

"Fucking beautiful," I groan and stare into her open mouth to see the cum painting her from the inside out.

# FORTY

**MASE**

WE REMAIN quiet on the drive home. I unraveled her hair from the braid I love so much so I could play with the golden strands while she rests her head in my lap, with her lips suckling me. It's as if she knew I needed comfort after my savage actions. My mind scrambled with turmoil as soon as I came down from my orgasm. I loved and loathed what I'd done, but Summer continuously reassured me it was what she wanted. But I knew by the way she spoke that I'd hurt her throat, and the last thing I want to do is hurt her.

The soft sounds she emits as she suckles brings with it a sense of solitude, and when I steal a peek, she smiles back up at me. With her lips stretched around my cock, she sucks so innocently while the turmoil plays out in my head like a movie. Only, it isn't, it's a fucking memory, yet another one that plagues me.

*Previously …*

*We went on a date tonight, and Tara flirted with every man in sight. I don't know if she even realizes she's doing it anymore because she no longer glances at me or attempts to catch my eye.*

*She just does it like I don't exist, like she doesn't care. Another way of humiliating me in front of my friends.*

*Owen asked me earlier if I told her about the divorce papers, but I didn't want to rock the boat. She's been better recently, not as angry or abusive, and I don't want to risk her mood changing where it becomes unbearable again.*

*"You've been quiet all night. What's wrong?" she asks, unclipping her diamond earring and placing it on the dresser along with the other. It's not lost on me that I don't recognize them. She might have purchased them for herself, but more than likely, someone else did.*

*Either way, I don't care.*

*"I saw you talking to Owen. You were fine until you spoke with him."*

*She's never liked my friends, not one of them. I'm pretty sure it's because they don't like her either. But our friendships are the only thing I'm not prepared to budge on. Besides, she knows I have to work with them to continue making our business a success and keep her in her luxuries.*

*"You should look at just selling your shares if your friends are making you miserable."*

*I spin to face her fully, and when she slowly peels her skimpy dress off her shoulders, my cock twitches to life. It's been a while since I saw her naked, saw any woman naked. My friends have encouraged me to join them at strip clubs, but I make an effort to stay away out of respect to my wife and the fact I'd probably come in my pants like a teenager just for seeing bare tits, it's been so long.*

*Her red G-string slides to the floor, and when she turns to face me, my gaze roams over her bare tits. They sit on her chest unmoving, an enhancement I never wanted her to have, but Tara insisted, so much so, she disappeared on me for weeks on end and returned with them done, along with an ass that looks nothing like the ass I knew her to have.*

*She said it made her feel better, and that's all I ever wanted, and like an idiot, her words had given me hope, hope she might just be a better person.*

*"Do you have a condom?"*

*This snaps me out of my daze, and I rummage in my jacket pocket for my wallet. "Get yourself hard, then. You can have me tonight."*

*She talks as if she's a reward, and I guess this is, but for what, I'm unsure. She lifts the bedsheets and slides beneath them.*

*I slowly undress, willing my cock to harden. Ever since she cheated on me, it's taken me longer and longer to get hard, and the more I think about it, the more difficult it becomes.*

*So, I've no choice but to do what I have to. My mind whirls, conjuring up images of the life I wish I had. A woman who appreciates me, someone of natural beauty, who wants me as much as I want them, not a calculated exchange in return for grandeur, making our love life seem sordid.*

*I pump my cock. The girl I'm with will beg me for my cock.*

*After another few pumps, I'm able to tear the condom open and slide it down my length. I climb onto the bed and position myself between her open legs.*

*"Condom, Mase." She taps my shoulder. "Are you wearing a condom?"*

*"Yes," I retort, pissed she's spoiling my moment. I want to tell her I will always wear a condom, that I don't trust her enough not to. I don't want her pregnant as much as she doesn't want to be because then I would be trapped, but I keep my mouth shut, knowing it will upset her.*

*"I don't want a baby, that's all," she mumbles as I slide inside her. How she's wet, I've no fucking clue. There's been no preparation on my part, but a part of me doesn't care.*

*She doesn't want a baby with me is all she means.*

*I close my eyes as I pull my cock out, then slide back in, hating the way this exchange is happening. The girl I'm fucking will plead for me to not just fill her with my cum, but come in her too. She'll fucking bathe in it.*

*My hand moves up toward her face with the intention of holding her in place for my lips to meet hers.*

*"Don't touch my face, Mason. I've done my skincare tonight. You know this. Jesus," she hisses. "You know I've been to the dermatologist this week. Did you forget already?"*

*I shake my head and try to get back in the moment.*

*"You always take too long to come," she shrieks. "I've never had this with any other guy." Her saying that out loud is like a blade, not only piercing me but also grinding as deeply as it possibly can, inflicting the most extreme pain possible. It's cruel and unjust.*

*My mind wanders. My girl would only ever want me, to fuck me all the time, to long for me like her life depended on it.*

*"Can you hurry up! I need to be up early tomorrow; I'm going out for lunch." Tara's whine spears through me, causing me to deflate, and I grind my teeth on a frustrated growl, pull my cock out, get off the bed, and head toward the bathroom.*

*She probably thinks I came. But I didn't. I can't. Not when she doesn't want me, and truthfully, I'm not sure I want her anymore either.*

*"Mason?" she calls out as I throw open the bathroom door.*

*"Yeah?" I drop the empty condom into the bin and glare down at my cock, not even a fucking twitch now.*

*"We're not getting a divorce if that's what you were discussing with Owen," she snipes, and I drop my forehead against the mirrored wall.*

What the hell are you doing, Mase? Your love for her has turned to loathing. She's destroying you from the inside out.

*"You don't deserve me; you know that, right? But nobody else would have you!" she bellows from the bedroom, and I flinch. I know… I don't deserve anyone at all.*

The memory sends a wave of panic through me, and my heart flutters with anxiety. My hands grip the steering wheel tighter.

Fuck, I hate this feeling of being so totally powerless.

But worst of all, I hate the fact that memories assault me at random times. Especially when we've had such a good day.

"I'm sorry," I say in a hushed tone as I glance down at Summer, and she searches my face. "If I hurt you, I mean."

She pulls my cock from her mouth, and I miss her instantly. She sits up, and I feel her scan my face as I look toward the road until she rests one hand on my cheek and the other on my shoulder, then I give myself over to her warmth.

"You." She kisses my cheek. "Mason." She places a kiss along my jawline. "Campbell." *Kiss.* "Could." *Kiss.* "Never." *Kiss.* "Hurt me."

My pulse quickens, and like a dam that's burst, a rush of love spreads through me like a wildfire.

"You're worthy," she whispers, and my breath hitches. Does she realize the impact of her words? The genuine smile on her face tells me she does, and Jesus, my chest swells.

Then she snaps me out of my thoughts when she lies back down and slides her lips around my cock, gifting me with the comfort she knows I crave.

How the hell can anyone be so in-tune with another? So perfect.

I think I somehow conjured up the perfect woman, and now that I have her, I'm terrified of losing her and everything she promises.

"I could watch you please me for an eternity," I groan, meaning every damn word. "But I'd rather experience it." Forcing away the memories that plague me and replacing them with the new, I thrust deeper into her throat.

Everything about tonight has been perfect. She's perfect, and there's not a damn thing in this world that could change that.

# FORTY-ONE


## SUMMER

THE MANSION FEELS empty when we return. It reminds me of a story my mom told me when I was little about an old lady who complained her house was too small. Then she filled it with animals during the winter, and when spring returned, she let the animals out and finally realized how big the house was all over again.

"I have some calls to make out back." Mase gestures toward the patio. I'm not sure why he always insists on making calls outside, but I do understand why he wouldn't want to be in his father's office. "Why don't you go pick a movie, and I'll be in shortly."

A movie sounds good. It'll also give me the perfect opportunity to wrap my lips around him. He smirks down at me as if reading my mind.

"Okay. Don't be long." I rise up on my tiptoes and place a tender kiss on his lips, then just as his tongue seeks entrance, I draw back with a smirk of my own.

"Fuck, Summer." He adjusts his cock, and I turn, smiling as I head out of the kitchen.

When I step into the foyer, my smile falls and a chill sweeps over me. I glance back over my shoulder, then take a detour toward Jeff's old office.

The thick wooden door creaks when I push it open, and I try battling the memories threatening to invade me like a horror show.

*"Here she is. The bride to be." Jeff's sinister smile encompasses his face, and I hate it, hate him.*

*Nerves dance in my stomach; I hate being in here. "Hugh told me you wanted to see me." I greet my stepfather and avoid looking at the other man in the room, knowing no good will come of acknowledging him. I already have nightmares about Jeff's intentions, and despite being thirteen now, they still haunt me every day since they celebrated our engagement two years ago.*

*"You're going to make such a perfect bride, Summer," the man says, his high-pitched voice full of wonder, giving away his excitement. "Why can't we do this as soon as she turns sixteen?" he asks Jeff. I jolt at his suggestion, and my blood rushes, causing me to feel dizzy, so I snap my hand out to grip onto the wooden desk.*

*"We'd have to go to court, and I already have the authorities watching me since her mother's death." My eyes fall closed as I try not to cry. I'm vulnerable and alone, so freaking alone, and I wish for nothing more than someone to rescue me.*

*They speak as if I'm not here at all. As if I'm completely unaware of their participation in my mother's demise. She might not have been loving, nor a parent to grieve over, but she was mine. She was all I had in this cruel world, and they took her from me. I open my eyes, with no more confidence than when I closed them.*

*"This way, it's done the right way." He taps his finger on the desk.*

*"She might not agree at eighteen," the man counters back.*

*Jeff's hand lashes out and grips my neck so hard my throat locks up and I begin to panic. Even the whimper I emit seems weak, powerless. He shakes me, and my entire body sways under his demand. "She will. Won't you?"*

*I try to nod. My lips are frozen, and my vision turns hazy.*

*"She's yours the moment she turns eighteen." He throws me to the floor like a ragdoll, and my hand moves to my throat. It stings, but his words sting more. "Then you can do with her what the hell you want." He talks about me as if I'm disposable, replaceable. Nothing.*

*Their loud chuckles bounce off the office walls, and my stomach rolls as they discuss their next meeting.*

*Little do they know, they've released something inside me, something terrifying. As I watch and listen to them discuss all the ways they're going to fuck someone until they can't breathe anymore, I remain motionless on the floor, not just taking in their words and twisting them to create my own thoughts. A plan forms in my young mind; I just need to be the right age to execute it.*

My body trembles as I move through the office, searching for my old phone. I try Jeff's desk drawers first, but they only have blank papers and pens inside, all traces of his misdeeds erased. Then I try over by his bar but come up empty. With my heart galloping in my chest, I scan the room until my focus comes to a standstill at a photo sitting proudly by itself.

I amble forward, an immense amount of guilt consuming me at the sonogram photo that's housed in a gold frame, taking pride of place on a lone shelf. Our babies. My hand automatically moves toward my stomach, and I inch closer. The moment I reach out to touch the perfect little beans in the photo, my focus is diverted to the phone jutting out from behind the photo frame.

"Thank God." My shoulders drop in relief, and I rush toward the door while powering the phone up. The quicker I get this over with, the better. I'm just about to pull the door wide open, but the sound of voices stops me in my tracks, and I close it enough to be able to peek through the gap.

"Look, you can stay in my old room," Mase says, and I glimpse through the small gap to witness him brush a hand through his hair. "You can find your way there, right?"

"I remember where it is. We used to fuck in there before you asked me to marry you," a woman's sultry voice purrs, and my breath hitches as I cling onto the wood to remain rooted in place. Asked him to marry her? This is his ex-wife. My gut twists and sickness rushes up my throat as insecurity grips me in its tight grasp.

"You could join me. For old times' sake."

*Don't do anything. Don't do anything,* I chant to myself while silently pleading with Mase to send her away.

My heart breaks a little as the woman steps forward, blocking my view of Mase's face, but her hand slides over his chest and down his leg toward his groin. I close my eyes, trying and failing to banish the image burned into my mind.

Finally springing to life, my phone beeps, and I close the door on instinct, worried the sound might have cut through their conversation.

As I switch my attention to my phone, an ominous feeling takes over me, and my blood turns to ice.

UNKNOWN: Tomorrow at noon.

UNKNOWN: Or I release the video to the police.

I can't let this destroy Mase, even if he's about to destroy me.

# FORTY-TWO

MASE

THE SUN BEAMS down at me as I step outside and glance down at the dozens of messages on my phone.

> Owen: Call me.

> Owen: You there?

> Owen: Mase!

> Owen: I'm tracking you now. Soon as you're back, call me.

> Owen: Call me. ASAP.

Oh, shit. I hope this isn't something to do with Reed again. Although, for all intents and purposes, his father-in-law is being tortured a slow death for his role in Gia's sickening childhood.

"I've been trying to call you. Where the fuck have you been?" Owen clips out when the call connects.

"Up on the mountain." He knows the story behind that mountain. I took him there once as a brother.

He audibly swallows. "Listen, Mase. We've got a problem. Multiple actually."

The doorbell sounds, and my eyes flit around the room for a sign of Hugh to answer it. *Where the fuck is he?*

"Hold on, there's someone at the door."

I stride through the kitchen toward the front door.

"Mase, I don't think it's a good idea," Owen states. "Really not a good idea, man." Confusion swirls inside me, and I glance down at my phone and swing open the door.

Tara stands before me with tears streaking her face. My first reaction is to check outside for what's caused her to cry.

But what the hell is she doing here? Anger boils inside me.

The last time I saw her like this, she'd had a spat with the young gardener; one I'm convinced she was fucking. He handed his notice in, but not before I witnessed his mother and Tara exchanging heated words.

There's nobody outside.

Just the two of us.

And Summer in the house.

I step outside, and she falls against my chest, clinging to my T-shirt for support, and her touch sends a vile sensation through me. Like a billion insects are trying to burrow under my skin. Slowly, I unpeel her hand from my T-shirt.

"What are you doing here, Tara?" I bite out. The anger in my voice is evident, and her eyes widen, and she scans me as if searching for the old Mase. The one she could walk all over, speak down to, and manipulate.

Something flashes across her face, then she clears her throat and shakes her head.

"I've got cancer!" she sobs, and I rear back, stunned. Of all the things she could say, I never expected it to be that. Never.

I might not like the woman; who am I kidding? I despise her, but cancer? I wouldn't wish that on her. Swallowing, I wait for the familiar feeling of guilt at letting her down, but it doesn't come. In its place is a steely determination, so I widen my stance.

"I'm sorry to hear that. But you shouldn't be here." My voice is devoid of emotion.

"Please. Can I come in? I have no one else." I find that hard to believe; she always had someone else. She spent enough time telling me so and enough time jumping from bed to bed. There was always someone, anyone but me.

"No," I grit out.

She gasps, and I want to roll my eyes at her dramatics. "Look, Tara. You can't be here. I'm sorry."

A strange wail leaves her, and I step back. "P-please. I don't want to stay at the hospital tonight. The last time I was there, I was pregnant."

"That was in New Jersey." I'm quick to correct.

"They put me on a ward where there're pregnant mothers, Mason. Have you any idea how that feels after losing our babies?"

I grit my teeth, hating the fact she refers to another man's child as my baby.

"I'm asking for one night, Mason. As the mother of your unborn children." I wince at her wording, and for the first time ever, I realize something. Not having children with Tara was a blessing. It saved any kids with her from having the childhood I had.

Without the abuse from her, I would never have had that one night with Summer, the night our babies were created. I wouldn't have had the secure, loving relationship I have now.

I wouldn't be happy.

"One night, then you're out. I'm sorry you're suffering, Tara, but I don't want to see you again."

Something flickers in her eyes, a sinister gleam that's quickly masked, and I'm already second-guessing my decision. But like a fool, I push open the door and allow her access to the mansion I equally hate as much as the woman stepping into it.

The moment she steps inside, all my energy is sucked from me. I've gone from sharing memorable moments with the woman I'm falling in love with, to being thrown back into the darkness with the one I once would have given everything to have love me back.

She totters around, circling me in her high heels, and the sound of them brings with it a rush of nausea. Dread lines my stomach. "Mase. I've started treatment and really don't want to be alone." She snivels and wipes at her nose.

I look her over. Her normally well put–together self is off. Something is off.

My phone blares through the foyer, vibrating in my hand, and I glance down at it to see Owen calling. He was trying to give me a heads-up of this bullshit. I silence it again.

"What kind of cancer?"

She wobbles on her high heels, and I step toward her, sniffing the air, knowing if she's been drinking, she's far worse, potentially violent, and I refuse to have that around Summer. "Huh?"

"What kind of cancer do you have?"

"Ovarian." She swallows, and her dark eyes meet mine. "I can't have children." Her glare is searing into me, tugging at the pain and torment that wraps around my heart like a cord, pulling tighter by the second. She knows this is my weakness. Does she also know I'm going to become a father? That I'm finally getting everything I ever wanted.

Her eyes skitter around the foyer. "The treatment is awful, Mase."

"I'm sorry," I respond grimly, and I am, but that doesn't mean I want her here, stepping into my life again when I'm trying so desperately to build my happiness.

"Can you hold me?" she sniffles, and I step back.

"No."

"No?" Her tone turns harsh before she brushes at her eyes, and her jaw sharpens. "There was once a time when you'd hold me whenever I asked."

"We're not married anymore, Tara," I bite out. "And I told you, after tonight, I don't want to see you again."

"B-But I still need you," she sobs, and this time tears cascade down her face, and I want to tell her there was a time when I needed her too. Needed her not to cheat, lie, or become an abusive, cruel bitch.

"You can stay the one night, but then I want you gone. No bullshit."

She steps forward, and I somehow manage not to recoil this time. I don't want her to see my weakness, because she sees it as a game, and as a master manipulator, she's incredible at it.

"Look, you can stay in my old room," I breathe out, my chest heavy as she steps closer. "You can find your way there, right?"

In other words, fuck off out of my space while I find Summer and try to explain.

"I remember where it is. We used to fuck in there before you asked me to marry you." Her hand finds my groin, and fire burns behind my eyes as she gives my limp cock a sharp squeeze. "You could join me. For old times' sake." She smiles, her tears all dried up.

Her mouth drops open, and a sound from my father's office has her eyes darting there before they quickly land back on me.

*Just what the fuck is Hugh doing in the office again?*

My phone vibrates in my pocket, and annoyance rumbles through me.

I grip Tara's wrist in mine, pressing down hard in warning, and her eyes widen at the brutality of my touch. I lower my head until we're on the same level. "Listen, and listen really fucking carefully, Tara."

She whimpers.

"You don't get to touch me anymore. You don't get to come into my life, flirting with me," I seethe. "Because I'm not fucking interested. You can stay tonight because you're clearly distressed, but then you need to find somewhere else to stay." I release her and throw her hand to the side; she quickly pulls it up against her chest and rubs at it. I ignore the guilt rushing through me at the way I handled her; never in my life have I treated a woman so poorly.

"Follow me!" I bark out and start up the stairs. "I'm showing you to the room in case you forget your way." *And to make sure you don't accidentally on purpose bump into Summer.*

The moment I open my bedroom door, I feel like something's wrong. There's a coldness in the air, the hairs on my body stand upright, and when I turn my head over my shoulder to face her, the look in her deranged eyes tells me all I need to know.

I'm fucked.

A sinister smile spreads over her face, and a sharp prick in my neck has me wincing before the room tilts and my footing wavers.

*What the actual fuck?*

All I can think about as my head hits the floor is Summer is in danger, and our babies too.

# FORTY-THREE



A THUD SOUNDS from down the hall, followed by a loud cackle that causes my stomach to plummet. I close my eyes at the prospect of what that sound might mean.

As much as Mase has reassured me he and his wife are over, I know they have a lot of history. History I cannot compete with. How can I possibly? She's the woman he fell in love with as a teenager, childhood sweethearts. He married her and dreamed of creating a life together, a family unit. Me, on the other hand, I'm the woman from a one-night stand, one thrust upon him, forcing him to do the right thing.

The two clearly don't compare, nor could they ever.

I glance down at my phone. My pulse pounding as I read the words.

UNKNOWN: Tomorrow. Come alone.

Turning back to my bed, I stuff Mase's T-shirt into my backpack, then grab my purse, throw my bag onto my shoulder, and open my bedroom door.

I slink through the door, but loud laughter brings my feet to a halt, and like someone has doused me in cold water, I freeze at the sound of a bed squeaking coming from Mase's room.

My heart plummets, and it's painful, so freaking painful.

Please, no.

My mouth is suddenly dry, my throat clogged with prickly emotion, and I pray the tears forming in my eyes not to fall. Not yet.

Because he wouldn't do this to me.

He wouldn't do this to me and our babies.

He gave me his heart.

I inch toward his bedroom door, and the only thing I can hear is the steady thud of my heart thumping against my chest, beating so loud I feel like it's vibrating through me, causing my pulse to skitter with a furious rush of anxiety.

He wouldn't.

"Yes, Mase!" the woman screeches, and I wince, telling myself not to open the door, to leave, but something inside me tells me to do this. To force this torment on myself, to create this reminder that my happiness is just an illusion. "More!"

Sickness rolls in my stomach, bubbling and burning, threatening to expel at any second.

Please.

My throat burns, my eyes well with tears, and I clutch at my heart when a dull ache catches my breath.

Oh, God, what's happening?

Please no, Mase.

I push open the door and peek inside. Mase has his jeans and boxers around his ankles, and it takes everything inside me to stifle the sob clawing up my throat.

Tara grinds down on him, throwing her head back in glee, and when he slowly pushes up into her, she lets out a joyous moan. My lungs seize as every part of me crumbles at what's happening before my very eyes. He grips her wrists and pulls her toward him until she falls, her lips brushing over his, and I snick the door shut, careful not to make a sound. It's only when my feet find the way to the neighboring house that I let my emotions out.

I pound on the front door, and when Gia opens it, I fall into her welcoming arms.

"Can you help me?" I cry out in desperation.

She clutches me to her chest. "Always. Come on, let's get you inside, sweetheart." Her term of endearment makes my heart twist; a bitter reminder of the sweet words whispered to me from Mase.

A bitter betrayal.

# FORTY-FOUR

## MASE

TARA GRINDS down on my limp cock like it's a fucking pogo stick as I try and fail to regain control. What the hell is happening to me?

My vision is hazy, my head is cloudy, and each move I take to push her off makes her screech a noise that rings in my ears like a siren.

I feel like I'm fading away as I battle against her, but I refuse to give up the fight. This bitch is not going to do what she thinks she is.

"Do you need me to pretend I'm her?" She slaps my face, and I'm stunned before I shake her hand off me. She knows about Summer. This isn't good. I attempt to push her off me, but she only cackles louder. "I have some little blue pills I can shove down your throat and get your cock hard. Then I'll get all the evidence I need of you fucking me." Her eyes are alight with insanity.

Jesus fucking Christ. I lived with her, and at one point in my miserable life, I actually thought I loved her.

I lift my hips in an attempt to throw her off, but all it does is have her bitching up a storm. It's like she's only pretending to enjoy this, and I know Tara better than anyone; she's not enjoying it. Maybe if she enjoyed me, we might have lasted a bit longer. Who am I kidding? We were never meant to be. We never should have been.

"Tarrra," I croak out, my tongue thick somehow and my words slurred. "Stoppp."

She lifts her palm and slaps me again, but I don't feel it. Every muscle in my back coils as I raise my head from the pillow in an attempt to move, my body feeling so unbelievably heavy. Then she hits me again, and I fall back against the mattress, feeling utterly useless.

"Jesus. Just stay down, you dumb fuck!" she hisses.

She grabs something off the dresser, and I turn my head to see what she's reaching for, then a shooting pain splintering through me is followed up by everything going black.

# FORTY-FIVE

## OWEN

"COME ON. ANSWER THE FUCKING PHONE." I scowl at my phone screen as ringing from the call to Mase blares back at me. "Fucking pick up," I grit, my body vibrating with tension.

When the call goes to voicemail, I move on to Reed, knowing he's close by.

His phone continuously rings out too, and I'm torn between trying him again or Gia.

Something flashes in my mind, and before I know what I'm doing, I'm calling someone I swore I would never ask for help from again. More because the pompous prick loves to hold it against me than anything else.

"Owen. To what do I owe this pleasure," he drawls, with an almost mocking tone.

"I need your help."

"Of course you do. That's why you're calling after all, is it not?"

I pinch the bridge of my nose. "Yes. You know it is."

"Then stop wasting my time and tell me what it is that you want."

"Are you still in LA?"

"I am, for"—I imagine him glancing at his watch—"the next twelve minutes, we're currently six-thousand feet high."

They're in a helicopter. That's great; this could work. Hope blooms in my chest.

"I need you to make a slight detour."

"I don't do home visits," he snarls, and I roll my eyes.

"Who the fuck you speaking to?" a deep voice booms from inside the chopper.

"Can you lower your tone? I'm on a business call," Oscar snipes back.

"Who the fuck is it?"

I should have just called his don in the first place. I listen in as their conversation plays out.

"It's, Owen."

"STORM guy?"

I want to balk at his reference to me, but in all honesty, I'm grateful he remembers who I am.

"Yes. It appears we're going to be slightly late getting home."

"Sky is gonna bitch."

"Well, perhaps tell your wife you're the don of the O'Connell family, not the lacky."

"The what?"

"Lacky." He tsks. "Forget it. Tell her you'll be approximately forty minutes late."

"You hear that, Owen? I'm giving you forty minutes of my valuable time."

I swallow. "I heard. Oh, and Oscar?"

"Yes."

"I hope you have an axe handy. You're going to fucking need it," I quip, knowing he once took his brother's ex's head off with the tool.

"Ugh," he groans, and a sly smile spreads out on my face. It's about time Tara got what she deserved.

# FORTY-SIX

**MASE**

FOG FILLS MY MIND, and something warm trickles down the side of my face. The moment I smell metallic, I realize the bitch hit me with something and I'm bleeding.

Something digs into my wrists, and I attempt to move my hands, but they're cable-tied to the headboard. "The fuck?" I groan, tugging on my restraints.

"Indeed." A deep voice captures my attention when the bedroom door is flung open to reveal Oscar O'Connell. He straightens his sleeves and adjusts his cufflinks as if he has all the time in the fucking world.

The next thing I know, his older brother, Bren, barges past him. The man is a mountain of a man and the family don. He exudes power just by the sheer size of him. Stepping toward the bed, he grips Tara by her throat, lifting her off me like a ragdoll, then throws her to the floor, causing her to shriek in pain. "Fucking cunt," he spits as his venomous gaze remains locked on her, pinning her in position. "Missing my kid's school play for this bullshit," he growls.

Oscar's head spins to face him, and he crooks an eyebrow. "What's he playing?"

"A tree," Bren responds, his focus unwavering.

"How … riveting," Oscar muses dryly.

What the hell is this? House Husbands of LA?

"C-Can you help?" I tug on the cable ties again, drawing Oscar's attention back to mine. "She tied me up."

Oscar blinks, then gives his head a shake before removing a switchblade from his pocket. "What is it you do for the company again?"

I search his face, my vision still blurry, but I'm struggling to tell if he's joking or not.

"How hard did she hit your head?"

He slices through the ties, and my arms drop like heavy weights. I attempt to sit up, but wooziness overwhelms me, so I drop back onto the mattress.

"Are you always this … slow?" Oscar eyes me skeptically. Is he for real right now?

"She drugged me. Hit me with something." I press my fingers against the side of my head and wince. *That fucking hurts.* Then I glance at the floor and see the marble candle stand coated in blood. Jesus Christ, was she trying to bash my skull in? Wow, she really didn't care for me at all.

"You drug him, little bitch?" Bren growls, then lifts Tara by her hair, causing her to release an agonizing scream.

"She was hoping to fuck you and blackmail you. If I were you, I'd make sure your girl is well aware of the predicament you've been placed in." Oscar speaks as if he's reading from a script. I've heard rumors of his quirkiness, but I've never truly encountered him.

I somehow manage to sit up. "You own *Indulgence.*"

"Ah, yes, I hear you have a complaint, but as I explained to Owen, you need to be seeking answers a little closer to home." He glances toward Tara, and I narrow my eyes before his attention lands back on me. "Don't even attempt a lawsuit; I'll see you all in the ground sooner. Besides, Owen owes me after this one." He tilts his head toward Tara.

I don't give a shit about a lawsuit or the fact that Summer wasn't twenty-one, as she should have been. "Okay," I groan, dragging a hand over my head, and attempt to stand. "Thank you," I rasp.

"You should pull up your jeans and underwear," Oscar asserts. "It appears your girl found you in quite the position." His attention travels up and down my body with a sneer, and the moment his words register, they send a pool of dread into my stomach, infiltrating my bloodstream, and my legs feel heavier than ever.

"Need Summer." My voice is hoarse as panic floods me.

"She's currently with your friend, Reed." Oscar nods. But how can he truly understand? She probably thinks I cheated. Hell, I feel like I have. It's like there're insects crawling over my skin. Tara's perfume lingers on me, and my skin feels scorched from her touch.

"I'll take the bitch to Luca's. He has a basement to play with pieces of shit like this." Bren's hand tightens on Tara, and all I can do is nod, no longer giving a shit about Tara or her screams of injustice. The only thing I can think about is holding Summer and never letting her go.

# FORTY-SEVEN

**MASE**

I ABANDON my truck in the hedge and throw open the door. I really shouldn't have driven over here. It takes a lot of concentration to remain standing, so I stumble over my feet in a rush and head toward the front door. Reed is waiting for me with his arms crossed over his chest and a twist of his lips as he wrinkles his nose.

"Have you been drinking?" he clips out.

"S-She drugged me." I swipe at the sweat running down my face, and he grimaces as his eyes follow the action.

"S-Summer," I pant out.

Reed shakes his head. "I don't think that's a good idea, Mase." His pointed stare lances through my chest, pulling on the one organ that's keeping me upright. My best friend is keeping her from me. "She's pregnant and upset. You don't want to cause her anymore hurt." Oh, Jesus, what the hell do they think I've done? What did she see? Does she think I …?

I blanch, and Reed takes a step back, giving me the perfect opportunity to use what little strength I have to push inside the rental home.

"Mase!" Reed bites out, following behind me. "I told you; now's not a good time!" His sharpness sets my teeth on edge, and the lines on his forehead deepen.

I swipe at my face. The sweat is literally pouring off me as I come down from whatever shit she injected me with. "You don't understand." Sharking my head, I glance around the foyer frantically. Where the hell is she?

"She drugged me." I turn back to Reed, hoping he can see the truth in my eyes. Then I press my palm against the pain in my chest. "Tara drugged me and tried to rape me. Have you any idea how that feels? Every fucking inch of me is crawling with her filth." I push my hands over my skin, the need to claw at it consuming me. "I just want Summer. I need her." Wetness swims in my eyes, and I need my friend to understand, to see the turmoil in my eyes as my lip wobbles uncontrollably. My entire body no longer feels like my own. She touched me when she had no fucking right to. When I belong to Summer, the one woman who loves me, darkness and all. Tara tried to destroy that. Hell, she probably has. "She fucking tried to … I don't know if she …" I can't say it. "I need my girl, right now." I swipe at the snot dripping from my nose.

Reed steps forward, his face ashen. "Mase. I think she thinks …" His words hang in the air, and my legs buckle because I know what she thinks. I've thought it a million times myself in the past. I've felt that crippling feeling of betrayal, the worthlessness and shame. I've felt it in my soul as my heart laid tattered by the one person I trusted to keep it safe, and I'd never do that to her. Never. My knees hit the floor as pure devastation pulverizes me.

"I love her," I choke out. "She gave me her heart, Reed, and I swore to protect it." I thump my fist to my chest. "I didn't do this." I can barely see my best friend through my tears. "I swear I didn't." I shake my head. "Please help me."

# SUMMER

Frozen, I watch in horror through the spindles of the staircase as Mase recounts his experience. Vomit threatens to make an appearance as he tries to explain what that bitch did to him.

Did to us.

When his sobs echo through the foyer, a shudder takes over my body, and a low whimper startles me, then I realize it came from me.

He needs me.

I need him.

I need to make this right.

Fury coupled with a fierce need to comfort and protect the man I love has my feet hitting the marble staircase and racing toward him. When he lifts his face to meet mine, I fall to the floor at his knees, at the power of the absolute devastation on his face greeting me.

He looks distraught, sick, his face etched in torment yet drained of blood, and with every fiber of my being, I vow vengeance for him. For me and our babies.

I softly cradle his face in the palms of my hands, much like he has done with me time and time again.

"You've always kept my heart safe, Mase. I believe you," I

whisper against his soft lips. His shoulders relax, but he retreats, making me jerk back, and regret rifles through me. Have I lost him? I search his eyes for an answer.

"Don-don't kiss me, Summer. Not … not yet." He shakes his head furiously. "She tried …" She tried to kiss him. I nod and get to my feet, then hold my hands out for him. The uncertainty in his eyes makes me want to crumble to the floor, but I want to be his strength like he is mine.

"Shall we get you showered?" I suggest, hoping he takes the lifeline.

Taking my hands, he stands to full height, his hold on me so tight, as if he's terrified I'm going to change my mind and release him. "Yeah. Is that okay?" He flits his eyes toward Reed, and his Adam's apple slides down his throat.

"Sure, man." Reed gifts him with a firm nod, then I take my time guiding him up the stairs and into the spare bedroom.

The silence between us is odd, comfortable, yet full of something tangible. I head into the bathroom and switch on the shower, and Mase drags his feet behind me. I get the feeling he's scared of letting me out of his sight.

He jolts and rushes over to the sink, where he dumps toothpaste on a toothbrush before scrubbing frantically at his teeth. Then I realize, with blood crusted on his skin, he's been hit with something, and fury burns inside me, forcing me to breathe out through my nose in order to control it.

By the time he's finished, he's panting wildly, and I tug on his arm. "Shall we get you out of these clothes?" I suggest, hoping he doesn't hear the anger consuming me.

He turns to face me, scanning my face. "I want you to burn them."

"Consider it done." My lips twitch, knowing it's no hardship. I'll happily burn them, along with her, but not until after I'm finished with her. She's going to pay for hurting what's mine.

He lifts his T-shirt over his head, and I pop open his jeans, then he kicks off his shoes and toes off his socks before I drag his jeans to the floor. I tuck my fingers into the waistband of his boxers, and he sucks in a sharp breath. Freezing, I lick my lips. What if this is too much for him? "Do you want me to stop?"

"Fuck no. I want her touch gone." He says it with so much conviction, I know he needs this; any doubt is banished from my mind.

I nod and lower his boxers. He steps out of them and kicks them to the side, then watches me closely until I'm naked and leading him into the shower.

# MASE

My head is still cloudy, and my body feels weak, but at least my fingers are entwined with Summer's, and I never want to let go.

She's my strength on a stormy day, our babies are the light in my darkest, and together, we're indestructible. There's not one part of me that wants to let her go.

She squirts some shower gel onto a washcloth and washes me all over, starting at my face and moving tenderly down my neck, avoiding the lump forming on the side of my head. Then she washes my shoulders and chest, around my waist, and steadily works down my thighs. She scrubs at my legs, followed by my feet, then back up. Tapping my ass, she motions with her finger for me to spin around, and I huff at needing to release her hand, and she giggles.

When she repeats the process of washing me, she stops at my waist and looks up beneath her wet lashes at me from the shower floor. Jesus, she's stunning.

"Do you want me to wash?" She points to my cock that's standing tall, and in all honesty, I'm unsure if it's the drugs or Summer's doing, but I'll go with the latter, knowing the effect she has on me.

"I want her gone from me, Summer. Every fucking memory erased." The words come out sharp, but I mean them to. I feel fucking furious about what Tara has done—enraged doesn't quite cut it. If I could shoot her dead right now, I would.

She could have destroyed my relationship with Summer. Hell, she almost did, and my babies would have had an absent father. The one thing I want most in the world, a loving family, destroyed. Not to mention, the violation of the act. She knew damn well I wasn't interested, hence having to drug me to take what she wanted.

I curl my fist around my cock, then point it toward Summer. "Wash me, then lick me clean, Sum."

She licks her lips.

"Make me yours again, sweet girl."

Her pupils flare with arousal, and when she takes my cock from me and washes down my length, I tip my head back, relishing the feel of her soft hand sliding up and down me. She pays extra attention to the head, then massages my balls, giving me no choice but to shift on my feet and widen my stance, allowing her access.

My body coils when her finger swipes over my asshole, never having felt anything foreign there before.

"Shh, it's meant to be good. I don't know if she touched you here, and I want my man back to being mine."

"Fuck, Sum." My chest puffs with pride, loving the way she claims me. Having never had anyone feel that strongly about me before has me eager to comply. I should tell her Tara never touched me there, that she wouldn't, we discussed boundaries early on in our relationship, and while I was eager to try everything and anything, she was the complete opposite, preferring to keep our interactions vanilla, as she called it.

So I let her run with it instead of questioning it. I embrace the feel of her hand sliding up and down my shaft while her finger toys with the entrance to my ass. The feeling is different, but in a good way. I find myself parting my legs farther, and when the tip of her finger breaches my hole, a hiss of air leaves me.

"Holy fuck, Sum." I grip my cock again and stare down at her to tap it against her cheek. "Suck me, Sum. I need you to suck me," I pant out between ragged breaths.

Removing her finger, she uses her hands to steady herself on my thighs, and I miss the feeling of it there instantly.

She opens her mouth, and I use my free hand to press down on her lip while guiding my cock inside with the other. I watch in rapture as she gags on me, but the determination on her face has me almost ready to combust. Fuck, she's beautiful on her knees and choking around my thickness like the good girl I know her to be.

The moment I hit the back of her throat, panic flashes through her eyes.

"Shhh, you're doing so good, Sum. So good, making me feel better."

The panic quickly subsides when I speak, and my heart swells at the equal effect I have on her as she has on me.

"We're meant to be. You and me," I croon, and slowly slide out of her mouth, then back in until she gags. "You take me so well."

Drool slips from the corner of her mouth, and it only adds to my heightened state of arousal.

Then she slides her hand over my balls, cupping them while using her finger to push at the entrance of my ass again.

My head drops back against the tiles, and I stare up at the ceiling. "Fuck, Sum, that feels good."

When I glimpse down again, it's to see her trying to smile around my length. I thrust harder into her mouth, my fingers now holding her head in place as my hips work quicker, in deep punishing thrusts. The finger near my ass slips inside, and I slam into her mouth in response. "Holy fuck, Sum," I pant. "Fuck," I grunt, and my hips work quicker, in time with her finger now pumping in and out of me. When she crooks it ever-so-slightly, pressing over another untouched spot, it causes lights to flash before my eyes. A choked breath leaves me, and my cock swells, the sensation overwhelming and causing unrelenting waves of heat to sweep through me. I stumble forward so quickly I snap out a hand against the shower glass to steady us.

Cum spurts in rapid waves of euphoria, spurt after spurt hitting the back of Summer's throat, causing her to choke and splutter, but my palm tightens on her head, holding her in place and forcing her to take every drop while I use her mouth on my command. "Fuck, yes," I groan in absolute bliss.

Slowly, my orgasm dissipates, and I'm left motionless.

"Come on, big man, let's get you to bed." Summer grins, tapping my chest as she stands to her full five-two against my six-three. A stark power imbalance that until now I've loved every second of, but being stripped bare of my power has left me feeling more vulnerable than ever before.

I blink. "You're not leaving, right?"

"Never." She smiles back at me, and that's one of the last things I remember, barring the sheet being pulled around us while she snuggles against my chest.

# FORTY-EIGHT



MY HAND SEARCHES the bed to pull Summer closer, but she's not there. Eyes darting open, I sit up, my head pounding as I try to focus.

Where the fuck is she?

It takes a few minutes before I register where I am and what the hell happened to lead me here, but when I do, sickness rushes through me. "Fuck," I groan, palming my face.

Where the hell is Summer? She's the only person who will make me feel better right now.

A memory of Summer serving me on her knees in the shower last night comes rushing back to me, and I delight in it. I swing my legs over the side of the bed and glance down at my rock-hard cock. Remembering the way she slid her finger into my ass has me smirking, and I head toward the bathroom, but when I swing open the door and there's no Summer inside, worry gnaws at me.

"Get a fucking grip, Mase. She's probably having breakfast," I grumble to myself, but still, the thought of her leaving me here when she said she wouldn't, riles me.

I grab a towel from the bathroom, wrap it around my waist, then head out of the bedroom in search of my girl.

Loud voices can be heard from the kitchen, and when I enter, all heads turn toward me, but not a single one of them is Summer.

Reed scans me, his face still the same haunted pale he wore yesterday. Shaw grimaces, and Owen's flash of concern has my spine straightening.

Roaming my gaze around my congregated friends, it latches onto Travis. He grimaces, then quickly looks away, but my eyes remain trained on him. He's here for a reason; the little fucker knows something.

"Don't look in my direction," Reed declares while staring Travis down. Then he lifts his hand and uses the other to point at his ring finger. "Happily. Married." He punctuates each word, and Travis's lips turn up at the edge before he shakes his head.

"Where is she?" I rasp, my heart pounding against my chest.

Owen drags a finger over his lip. "There's been a development."

I rear back, and it causes me to stumble. Clearly, the effects of the drugs still have a hold on me.

"You best sit down." As he points to the chair at the kitchen table, I shake my head. He crosses his arms over his chest. "Sit! Otherwise, I'm not telling you a damn thing," he growls, and I move quickly, dropping into the chair with a heavy huff and blurred vision; I don't know whether it's from rage or the aftereffects of the drugs.

My pulse rushes at the concern in their eyes, then my gaze latches on to Gia's, and she looks away, but I don't miss the tears shimmering in her eyes. I swallow hard. "Where is she?"

"I'm waiting on an exact location," Owen tacks on. "She has secrets, Mase." The confirmation of my thoughts has the sound of my heartbeat ringing out in my ears.

I drag a hand over my head. "I know that." My chest feels like it's closing in on me.

"I hacked her phone," Owen confirms, and I nod. I knew he would; I wanted him to. When I first discovered Summer was pregnant, I was convinced she was lying to me. Why wouldn't I when I'd almost become susceptible to women's lies?

"She did the *Indulgence* job to get money for college." Again, I nod at his words. She told me as much, and I don't blame her for not wanting to create a future on my father's dime. Owen looks at me pointedly. "What she didn't tell you is that she's being blackmailed."

I flinch, because what the fuck?

Raw anger surges through me. "By who?"

"Why would someone blackmail her?" Shaw scoffs, and I sneer in his direction.

"It appears she was being blackmailed because your father promised her hand in marriage to a business associate of his. He signed a lucrative contract. I'm guessing she's paying him off." Owen stares at me as fury ravishes through me.

"Who?"

"Gareth."

That sleazy old bastard. The thought of him touching her has bile rising in my throat.

My poor girl was selling herself to get away from this life she desperately hated. She must have been terrified of her future. My stomach twists at the thought of the pain and anguish she must have endured. How utterly alone she would have felt.

The fact that my father set these wheels in motion doesn't surprise me. He was fucked up and would do anything to profit at someone else's expense. If he weren't dead already, I'd happily torture the old bastard. But I'll take that wrath and hatred out on his good friend Gareth. This isn't the Mafia with arranged marriages in exchange for business agreements, but they can sure as hell help us end people like him.

"There's more." Owen glances around the room. "Oscar looked into this Gareth guy. It appears he and your father were into some fucked-up shit." The look on his face says it all as it twists in disgust. "They raped women, Mase. Then Gareth would dispose of them."

My jaw drops open.

"He killed them?" Shaw asks.

"Yeah, and your father would encourage him to do it." Owen eyes me, as if waiting for a reaction.

My heart falls to my feet, and I wonder what Summer was aware of—definitely more than me. Was her mother a victim? "I don't know what Summer knew or saw," I breathe out, and hurt coils around my heart. She's in real fucking danger.

"I think it's a high possibility they had something to do with Summer's mother's death, and probably why they had cameras throughout the mansion." Owen's face twists. "Oscar's looking into the footage now."

Holy shit.

That's fucked up.

"There's also not a complete trail on the phone," Owen says.

I grit my teeth. "What does that even mean?"

"They deleted the messages?" Shaw asks.

Owen shakes his head. "There're not a lot of messages of interest and not a single one of them from Gareth. I'm surmising there was a middleman, someone she knew and spoke with on a regular basis, but their name remains listed as unknown. I'm also struggling to track it."

Slowly, pieces of the puzzle start slotting together. Someone must've known what was happening in the house.

Owen's phone pings, and when he lifts his head, his eyes bore into mine.

"Hugh knows something!" I snipe out before he has a

chance to speak. Realization sits heavily in my stomach. The bastard has to know something; he quite literally knows everything.

"He does," Owen confirms.

Reed appears with a bundle of clothes in his hands, and it's not lost on me how I'm so discombobulated I wasn't even aware he'd collected them. I drop my towel, and I spring up from my chair, trying my best to ignore the way my body sways with the movement and begin dressing.

"Oh, fuck." Travis's eyes widen, and I throw him a death glare.

"Let's go." Owen nods toward me, then withdraws his gun from his back and checks the clip before tucking it into the waistband of his jeans.

"We gonna need that?" I motion toward the gun, and we head toward the door.

"I expect so," Owen grumbles.

The sun hits me in the face, causing my head to throb as we step outside and head toward his SUV. "You got another?"

Owen stops in his tracks, and when I turn my head over my shoulder, a sinister grin encompasses his face. "Obviously."

"Good, because I want in with whatever is about to go down."

I jump into the car, and the moment Owen is settled behind the wheel, I narrow my eyes.

"Now, tell me what the fuck is going on."

# FORTY-NINE

**MASE**

OWEN EXPLAINED that Hugh does indeed know something. In fact, the old bastard knows everything. So much so, he currently has my girl holed up at an abandoned apartment building on the other side of town.

Travis tipped the guys off this morning when he came to the mansion to alert me to the fact that Summer had him take her to the bank this morning to withdraw a huge lump sum before having him drop her off in town. Turns out, Travis knew about the blackmail all along.

Owen collected Travis from the mansion and drove him over to Reed's rental, where they were waiting for news of her location before they planned to wake me, or so he told me. I wouldn't be surprised if the fucker hadn't planned on collecting Summer himself and having her back in bed with me before I even woke.

"Was gonna make sure she was back with you before you woke. Then just have whoever was involved delivered to Luca's basement for you to deal with," Owen states, confirming my suspicions, and I sneer back at him. My muscles are coiled rigid and my fists clenched with adrenaline. I want these fuckers dead, Tara included. I want to start my new life with no threats made against us and our little family, and there's only one way to ensure it.

We turn into a sketchy parking lot next to the derelict apartments, and I scan the area all the way up to the third floor. "You sure he's up there?"

Owen assesses the building opposite, and I realize he has someone watching the apartment. "Absolutely," he confirms, then leans into the back seat and pulls a duffel bag onto his lap and unzips it. "Take your pick."

An arsenal of weapons has my eyes lighting up like the Fourth of July. "Fucking, yes." I grin back at my friend.

"Use the silencers."

I nod and screw the silencer on my Glock. "What's the plan?"

"He's not working alone." He glowers at me, and I swallow past the knot forming in my throat. My girl is in serious danger. "Appears he has a son living in there." He hoists his thumb over his shoulder toward the building. I know he has a kid, but I never thought any more of it. Now I'm kicking myself. All the warning signs have been there, and I've not pushed further to delve into any of them. "Bunch of thugs who need dealing with," Owen states. By dealing with, he means taking out, and I'm only too happy to oblige, desperate to burn off some of my raging anger and frustration. Not to mention, my growing concern for Summer and our babies. Rolling my neck to ease the tension, I quickly tuck that thought aside, knowing I need to keep my head in the game. "We have backup." Owen is quick to tack on as if preempting my spiraling thoughts.

My throat is dry, and a strange sound leaves me when I'm unable to construct the right words.

He gives my shoulders a tight squeeze. "We've got this, man; we'll get them out of there unharmed." The confidence in his tone has me nodding robotically.

I just hope he's right.

# SUMMER

Carrying a sports bag full of cash up six flights of stairs while pregnant is not a good idea. By the time I reach the door to the apartment, I'm exhausted, breathless, and, quite frankly, riddled with panic.

There're some very scary people living in this building. Each and every person I've encountered has eyed me like fresh meat, and I'm conscious of the fact I need to be able to get out of here before Mase wakes and starts asking questions I'm unprepared to answer.

I swipe my sticky palm down my jeans and rap on the door a couple of times, trying my best to ignore the guy who appeared to be following me up the stairs at a steady pace.

The moment Hugh swings the door open, I want to hug him just from seeing familiarity, but I know deep in my bones he's not a good guy, nor does he have my best interests at heart.

He's not who he portrays to be. Not only has he encouraged me to sell my body on an app I've never heard of, but he's been blackmailing me in order to get money.

The man has been relentless and claimed every tactic in the book to extort money from me, despite the fact I've proved I have none, so he came up with a way for me to get it.

He cranes his neck outside of the door, then nods in the direction of the odd guy who followed me up the stairs. My legs tremble when I realize I'm outnumbered and most definitely underestimated just who Hugh is and what he's capable of.

"Get in here," Hugh demands, and just the cruel, sharp tone of his voice sends alarm bells thrashing through me. Every cell in my body is telling me to turn and run, but realistically, how the hell am I meant to get out of this? Especially when I clock another guy walking up the stairs giving the original one a chin lift and smug smile.

Hugh's hand snaps out and grips my arm in a punishing vise, making me whimper.

It's not the first time Hugh has handled me this way. Over the years, he's always been cold and hard with me, his patience thin and kindness even thinner.

My stepfather couldn't have cared less. The only input he had was how I appeared to the outside world; a pretty girl in his care who just so happened to be worth some cash the moment I turned of age.

He practically drags me into the room, then slams the door behind us, causing me to jump.

I assess the room, only too relieved to see it's fairly well kept, if a little worn. It's basically a small apartment with a skylight and neatly kept furniture, but a little on the older side.

"Is it all in there?" He motions toward the bag, and I drop it to the floor, pleased to be releasing the heavy weight. I stroke over the mark it left behind on my hand.

"Of course."

Hugh's eyes light up, and a smile creeps over his face. "Andrew, come in here." A man steps out from another room, and I take a step back, my back almost flush to the wall beside the door.

The guy, Andrew, is a little older than me, maybe earlier twenties, and scans up and down my body, making me feel dirty. When he drags his eyes back up, his greedy eyes rest on my chest, and I have a sudden need to wrap my arms around my stomach to protect me and the babies from his view.

I can make out his resemblance to Hugh. The sharp nose, lean physique, and distinctive gray eyes, and for the first time, I realize Hugh must have relatives after all.

"She's hot as fuck in real time." His laugh is sinister, and the more I scowl, the more excited he appears to become; he's practically bouncing on the balls of his feet. This guy is not all there, not at all, and the idea of being in this room with him is creeping me out.

I want to go home.

He wears slacks and a shirt buttoned up to his neck, looking geeky, but he's giving off a crazed vibe. Then he pushes his glasses up from the tip of his nose and licks his lips without taking his eyes off me. The movement makes him appear like a predator, and I am most definitely his unwilling prey. "I can see why he wants her. She's even better in real life." He gloats to Hugh but stares at me, seemingly uncaring of how uncomfortable I appear. Who's he referring to?

When he takes a step toward me, I attempt to shrink back but find myself unable to, so I close my eyes and will myself to remain calm.

I feel his hot breath on my ear, and the scent of his musky cologne turns my stomach.

Then he threads his fingers in my hair, and I snap my eyes open. "Plea-please don't."

His lips part, and I grimace. "I just want a little taste."

My stomach falls, and I step up on my tiptoes, attempting to shy away from him.

He tilts his head to the side. Those gray eyes of his are like laser beams, firing straight through me. "Just a little fucking taste."

I whimper, and he rolls his lip into his mouth as if swallowing my cry.

He twirls a lock of my hair around his finger. "I've been watching you. Watching you grow and undress." As he licks his lips, his rancid breath has me recoiling. "I've witnessed you naked, Summer." He grinds his hard length against me, and I bite the inside of my cheek to stop myself from crying out. Something tells me he would like the sound, and that terrifies me. He runs his fingers down my arms, and I flinch, hating being in his proximity. Then he brushes his nose against my cheek, and I have an overwhelming urge to push him away, but I remain frozen to the spot, unable to move a muscle. It's almost like my body is shutting down on me. "I've watched you have sex, sweet girl," he rasps. The use of Mase's endearment on his lips causes me to whimper, and his eyes flare in delight.

Oh, Jesus, the sick bastard is getting off on my fear.

My mind whirls as I scramble to make sense of his words.

"I like watching you," he says, and I make the connection.

As if in slow motion, everything slips into place for me. The cameras around the mansion, the changes of the rules on the app that got Mase so aggravated, the flash drive I'm being blackmailed with. He's been watching me; they both have.

"Leave her alone. If it means that much to you, you can have her when we've finished with her."

My body somehow becomes almost impossibly more tense than ever. Finished with me?

"Those babies inside her will be worth a small fortune, and you said you can hack into anything? Surely, someone would be willing to pay for them?"

My heart stutters.

They want my babies. My hand trembles over my stomach, but Hugh looks completely composed, as always, and that only worries me more. How can he say such things?

These men, along with the ones outside, aren't going to let me leave here, and with no way of letting Mase or Travis know where I am, how the hell am I going to get us out of this?

Pure horror grips me, and my legs almost give way. I'm only too pleased to have the foresight to slap my hands against the wall to steady my body as it slumps to the floor in complete terror.

Please help me.

# FIFTY

MASE

THE MOMENT we step out of the SUV, a man opens the downstairs entrance and heads toward us. He puts his hand in his jacket, but before he has a chance to make another move, Owen pops a bullet in his head.

"Like that, is it?" I smirk at him.

"Kill on sight." The firmness of his words sends a ripple of anxiety through me, another confirmation of the severe danger my family is in.

Owen opens the downstairs door and steps inside, and I follow with my Glock in hand and ready to go.

There're six flights of stairs ahead of us, and Owen signals for me to cover him as he quietly heads up the staircase. The moment he is halfway up the first flight, a shadow looms on the flight above him. Without a second thought, I fire my weapon, and he tumbles down the stairs, the sound causing a barrage of footsteps from above us. Owen nods at me, and we surge up the stairs, and I'm only too grateful for my gym sessions, every single one of them.

Bullets are fired in all directions, and when Owen jolts back against the wall with his T-shirt soaked in blood, I mentally kick myself for not being quick enough to respond against the assailant, but manage to get a bullet in him before he takes advantage of Owen's predicament. "You okay?" I ask, eyeing his bloody shoulder.

His lip twitches. "Go get your girl. I'm right behind you." He tips his head toward the stairs, and I don't have to be told twice. Now it's him having my back as I stride up the stairs two at a time. My heart pounds harder with each step I take, knowing I'm getting closer to Summer but potentially putting her more in danger. Hugh and his scumbags are no doubt aware of our presence by now.

I duck and deliver a bullet to the bastard's neck at the top of the stairs, then jump out of the way as he rolls headfirst down them like a sack of potatoes.

My chest heaves, and I scowl at the door in front of me, but Owen's hand on my chest makes me pause. He holds up his hand with his palm spread out and counts down on his fingers.

Five.

My rapid breaths fill the smoke-filled space.

Four.

I lick my lips, praying Summer and my babies are unharmed.

Three.

Just the thought of someone touching her sends a wild fury through me.

Two.

Every cell comes alive with the need for retribution.

One.

I kick the door in and aim my gun.

Hugh's face falls. One hand is full of money, and I quickly realize he's currently not a threat. I step inside and spin on my sneakers when I witness some punk getting up close and very fucking personal with my girl.

The red haze I've been fighting to keep in check is back at full capacity, and I quickly pop two bullets in the back of both his kneecaps, causing him to drop to the floor. I rush forward and take Summer's tear-streaked face in the palms of my hands, and just like that, my fury is heightened. I'm going to make these fuckers pay. Every fucking inch of them will pay in blood.

I'm vaguely aware that Owen is now in the room, apprehending Hugh as I scan my beautiful girl for signs of injury, and I'm relieved not to find anything obvious.

"Ma-Mase. I need to tell you something."

I shake my head. "Not now, Sum. We need to get you out of here." When I glance over my shoulder, Owen is wrapping cable ties around Hugh's wrists.

"Pl-please." Her sweetness has always been my weakness, and I find myself nodding. "They were blackmailing me."

I choke on a sardonic laugh; does she really think I wasn't aware by now?

She shakes her head. "I drugged him."

I still, and I'm pretty damn sure Owen has too. My eyes bounce over her face. "I'm sorry." Her bottom lip wobbles, then she shakes her blonde locks. "I'm not sorry he's dead. I'm sorry if I hurt you in the process."

My eyebrows pinch together. "What the hell are you talking about, Summer?"

She whimpers, and I stroke her arms in a soothing motion.

"Shh, it's okay, sweetheart."

Her entire body rises as if she's about to have a panic attack, and my first thoughts are the babies need checked over ASAP.

"I drugged your father. Hugh had the evidence on a flash drive; he was blackmailing me for the money. He and him"—

she points to the scum on the floor—"they set the app up so I could get the money, the rest I was using for college. I'm sorry."

My eyebrows shoot up, and I stare at her dumbfounded.

"I drugged him because he was horrible, Mase. H-He made my life miserable… He was going to sell me." She's becoming hysterical, and as her words settle inside me, I become acutely aware that my girl has sure as shit been harboring a secret. A big fucking secret.

From the corner of my eye, I watch Owen smirk in my direction with a look that says *You've got your hands full there.* And yet something akin to pride expands in my chest. There's not a damn doubt in my mind that my father deserved to die. He was a sadistic prick, who I hated, but instead of tackling him head-on, I ran, creating my own life but never fully dealing with him. His cruelty led Summer to take matters into her own hands. The thoughts of what she could've been exposed to turn my stomach, and I'm only thankful she had the courage to do it.

"They were going to—" I can't let her say the words. I know what they were going to do: sell her to Gareth for him to use and dispose of her.

My lips smash against hers. My brave, beautiful girl.

Out of the corner of my eye, I see another figure emerge from another room, Gareth. "She was meant to be mine!" he roars, and I turn just in time to cover her as he releases a shower of bullets in our direction; each one causes my body to jolt.

One.

The fear flashes on her face.

Two.

My muscles tense to take the hits as pain hits me.

Three.

As I suck in a sharp breath, I realize something profound.

Four.

I want to marry her.

Five.

I never got to tell her I love her.

She opens her mouth to scream, and a tear slips down her beautiful face as it twists in tortured silence.

# FIFTY-ONE

**SUMMER**

IT ALL HAPPENS SO FAST I barely have time to register the action. A quick succession of bullets being fired makes me wince. Mase shields me, bracing both arms on either side of my head, and his body jolts repeatedly. I feel the impact down to my bones. His mouth falls open, and the brightness in his eyes dulls, and in this moment, I feel like my entire world is being ripped apart, crumbling at my feet until it's nothing more than ash.

A shrill scream leaves me, causing my ears to ring, and in slow motion, glass shatters from above and a rope of some sort drops into the room. Guns fire, but my focus remains locked on the man before me. The man I love more than I love myself.

Every tender moment shared is floating away, becoming a memory instead of a promise.

Each touch we ever encountered washed away in the pool of tears falling down my face at the agony in his. The dreams we had of our babies together, creating the perfect family we both so desperately longed for.

A strangled cry escapes my lips, and his attention slides toward my stomach. Our dreams, our little family, drifts away in the blink of his eyes as the light behind them becomes extinguished. A gurgling sound comes from his throat, and I desperately cling to him until his weight hauls me down, and we slump to the floor with his warmth coating me like a cloak of pain.

# FIFTY-TWO

**SUMMER**

MY BODY RACKS with tortured guilt and torment, and my hands fist the hospital sheet into a ball with each agonizing sob.

It's my fault.

It's all my fault.

If I hadn't insisted on Mase listening to me at that very moment, it never would have given Gareth the opportunity to emerge from the bedroom. Granted, I wasn't aware he was there, but still, it's all my fault.

Five bullets sliced through his back, each one requiring removal. They placed him in a medically induced coma, and now, slowly, they're trying to bring him to, but he's yet to wake.

I'm just grateful he's off most of the machines, even if waiting is torture.

Each day is like a new hell. Hoping and praying for progress but finding none.

I've refused hospital treatment. Refused to leave his bedside. It's been nine days, and the pain of him simply lying there, bleeding out in my arms, doesn't get any easier. The guilt doesn't lessen.

When he wakes, he'll hate me.

I know he will.

I murdered his father in cold blood. Hell, I did it with a smile on my face, thinking I was ending my torture. Now this is my penance, to see the man I love fighting for his life.

"Summer? Why don't we grab something to eat, hun? The babies need some nourishment. Mase is going to be asking about you all as soon as he wakes up."

I want to tell her Mase won't be asking about me when he wakes. That he'll want the babies, but he won't want me. Why would he? Nobody else ever has. I killed his father; I'm probably going to prison.

"Summer?"

As I sob harder, Ava moves around the bed.

"Listen, sweetie."

I lift my head to face her.

"He's fighting right now to come back to you, and he expects you to take good care of your babies for him, because he can't." She stares at me pointedly, then pushes a plate with a sandwich toward me. "Now, make sure his babies are healthy, like he wants them. Don't disappoint him."

Ava's taken on the role of caring for me. Possibly due to closeness in age, she feels like an older sister, one I'm eternally grateful for.

Her words hit me, and as much as I'm not hungry, I lift the sandwich to my mouth, grimacing at the scent of the cheese.

"Eat every fucking mouthful." The raspy growl emits from Mase's throat, and I turn to face him. A low, strangled whine causes me to choke, and when he lifts his hand to rest his palm against my cheek, I cry tears of joy. Streams of tears flood my face while I full-on shake, and a team of doctors rushes into the room. "Eat," he repeats. "I need my girl healthy." His words fill me with hope. "You're mine, Sum," he mumbles, and his words settle the raging storm inside me. "I need you and my babies." A ghost of a smile plays on his lips, and I'm forced to move from his side and watch the doctors assess him.

As my ass finds the chair in the corner of the room, I lift the plate toward my mouth and start eating the sandwich, determined to make Mase proud.

"Shall I get you checked in to be looked over now?" Ava asks with a soft smile.

I lift up on my seat to watch over her shoulder, and Mase is staring back at me with narrowed eyes. "I think that's a good idea," I whisper, and she gifts me with a wink that has my chest warming with comfort.

Maybe everything is going to be okay after all.

# FIFTY-THREE

## MASE

IT'S BEEN six weeks of grueling rehabilitation and a further two weeks of Summer not letting me leave her side, but finally today, I'm taking a visit to Luca Varros's estate. The man is a sadist and has an entire basement equipped to meet his and his sadist associate's needs, but thankfully, our business links with him coupled with Shaw being his brother-in-law have benefited us on more than one occasion now.

I roll my head to ease the tension building in my neck, then push out my chest and pull the door to the basement open. With each step I take down the concrete steps, it feels like I'm coming to the conclusion of my past, closing a door on it so I can move freely into my future.

My father is gone, along with his ill treatment of me and my mother; the sick bastards linked to his depraved needs are slowly being uncovered and will be dealt with.

Hugh and Andrew are about to realize their fate, then I'll put Tara out of her misery. They'll all be gone.

One by one.

When I reach the bottom of the stairs, Finn O'Connell is

leaning against the counter wearing a leather jacket and has a toothpick hanging from his mouth. As I approach, he gives me a chin lift, so I step forward and grasp the man's hand in mine. He entered the apartment building abseiling through the skylight and placed multiple bullets into Gareth's head without a second thought to protect Owen and my girl. He then administered medical care to me tirelessly while waiting for the emergency services to arrive and take over. I owe him my life without a doubt, and one day I hope to repay him. "You good?" he grumbles when our handshakes turn into a shoulder check.

I smile back at him broadly. "Never better."

He slaps me on my back, and I clench my teeth at the impact. Right above my fucking wound, the prick, but instead of showing pain, I widen my smile, hoping I masked it quick enough.

"Pleased to hear it. Make them pay, then live your life. Twins are hard fucking work." His grin mirrors my own. I can only imagine what his home life is like. Feral, I imagine, like him. Owen has told us stories of the O'Connell families, each of them as wild as the next.

Oscar pulls away from the wall, the man is always in the shadows, the older brother of Finn and much more put together, the IT genius.

"I've unearthed evidence of Andrew's and Hugh's connections to Tara. They were offering her a lump sum to seduce you in order to divert your attention from Summer. Ultimately, they wanted her vulnerable for the taking, and your *ex-wife* was more than happy to oblige." Was she ever really sick? I open my mouth to ask the question on the tip of my tongue. "There was never any cancer; she deceived you," he sneers, and awareness prickles along my skin. She lied about having cancer? Is nothing off the table for her? Was there ever any positive qualities about her? Anything at all?

"We located your father's laptop, along with several flash

drives of interest. We've extracted the information we require from him and will use it as we deem appropriate." He's referring to Andrew; Oscar discovered he was the one to hack into his system to place Summer as an *Indulgence* girl. The fact he even managed to get past Oscar's firewalls is baffling, but something Oscar insisted on investigating further. "He's yours to do with as you wish. Please dispose of him appropriately."

Owen snorts. "Obviously."

Oscar glares in his direction before heading up the stairs and out of the basement without a backward glance. The man is pretty squeamish, which is rather odd, considering he was brought up in the Mafia.

"Mase. Mason, I need you to help me." Tara shakes the chains she's bound with, and I finally turn to give her my attention. The bitch almost destroyed me. She used my kindness to manipulate me, and she belittled me, lied, cheated, attempted to break me and Summer up, determined to ruin my chance of a happy ever after, all for her own twisted satisfaction and of course, money.

She's slumped on the grimy floor, her hair disheveled, her skin pale and free of makeup in comparison to her normally well put–together self, but the tears that streak her face look good on her. It's the only thing that does. After spending years of being a front-row witness to her crocodile tears, seeing the real thing sends a rush of adrenaline through me.

"Payback's a bitch, Tara," I bite out.

I step toward the table housing the instruments. Scalpels, barbed wire, nails, a drill, every item you could imagine inflicting pain with is on this table or hanging from the wall above it. But my gut twists at the thought of putting her through unnecessary pain. After all, I once loved this woman enough to endure the pain she sent my way, so with that thought in mind, I opt for the familiar weight of the Glock.

The basement door opens, and my spine snaps straight

when light footsteps come down the stairs, so I turn quickly. "What the hell are you doing here?" I snap at the sight of Summer breezing into the room in a yellow sundress that emphasizes the small bump of her pregnant stomach.

"Me?" She points at her chest. "What are you doing here without me?" She taps her ballerina shoe on the cement floor and places a hand on her hip. A hip I clung to last night when I fucked her into oblivion. I fucked her so good, I hoped it would leave her in a state of bedrest while I snuck out to take care of business. "I told you I wanted to see this through to the end, Mason."

"Mase, please," Tara blubbers, and I pinch the bridge of my nose. The stupid bitch does not know when to give it a rest.

Summer spins around so fast her hair whips me in the face. "Do not speak to my man, you home-wrecking bitch!" she screams, pointing toward Tara.

Owen releases a strangled sound, and when I turn to face him, he's biting his fist in a lame attempt to smother his laugh. I glare in his direction, but his shoulders bunch up and down, and I give up looking at him for support and shake my head.

"If you think I'm going to let you end her life without my input, you can think again," Summer screeches, and I rub at my temple. I know she wanted to be a part of this, but there was no way in hell I was going to allow it. She's pregnant, for Christ's sake, and she's been through enough trauma to last a lifetime, and I don't want to add any more to it. "Oh, no you don't, Mason Campbell." She waggles her finger at me. "I'm not a broken little doll you need to protect. Did you forget I killed your father?" She crosses her arms over her chest and lifts her chin with pride.

A strange choking sound comes from Tara, but we all ignore her. Especially when I have my girl in front of me going all badass on me.

I step forward. "Sweetheart, I just—"

"She tried to destroy us, Mason. Tried to destroy you." Her tone softens, and when she rests her hand on the swell of her stomach, my body sags in defeat as I soften at her whim. "I once told you I wanted every part of you. Not just the ones you show others, now it's your turn to have every part of me too."

Holy shit, how the hell do I argue with that?

As if realizing her triumph, she smiles at me. My hand tangles in the back of her hair, and I haul her toward me. "You're my little psychopath. You know that?"

I lean down as she presses up on the tips of her toes and brushes her lips against mine. Then she snatches the gun from my hand and skips off toward Tara. "Thank you," she singsongs.

Owen lifts his eyebrows, and mouths, *Really?*

"Shut the fuck up," I hiss. Maybe I should stop the mother of my babies from taking vengeance, but she needs to do this; she needs closure and revenge too. This is her way of protecting me. She needs to do this not just for her but for me too.

Tara stumbles to her feet as Summer approaches, but Summer moves quicker, delivering a nose-cracking punch that makes Tara fall on her ass with a heavy thud. "Did I say you could get up? No! Now stay the hell down and listen up, bitch." Summer begins pacing, and I'm really starting to second-guess my decisions. "You hurt what belongs to me. You hurt him, manipulated him, and drugged him. You were going to steal his family from him, when you've done that time and time again. You touched what doesn't belong to you. You sick bitch."

My stomach rolls at the mention of Tara's past actions. The way she's used and abused my good nature while holding the promise of a family over me.

"He wanted—" Tara's words are cut short by the sharp slap of Summer's hand hitting her cheek.

"Shut up. It's our turn now, our turn to tell you that evil will not destroy us. Evil will rot in hell; it will not see the light of day again. Do you understand me? We're going to flourish, and you, and them"—she waves the gun in the direction of a gagged Andrew and Hugh—"you're going to be pig food."

*Pig food?* Owen mouths, with jest dancing in his eyes.

I shrug with a smirk, loving seeing this side of her. I knew she was strong and determined but this part of her, the mother bear, the protector, who is standing up for me, putting her life on the line for me, it's all-consuming, and I couldn't love her any more for it.

"Say goodbye, motherfucker."

She lifts the gun and presses it against Tara's head. The sound vibrates off the wall, and the weight of Tara's body hitting the floor fills the room.

Snivels can be heard coming from Andrew as he pulls against the restraints he's hanging from.

Summer delivers the gun back to my hand, then does something I do to her regularly, palming my face. "Make it hurt," she whispers against my lips before placing a soft kiss on them. Then she practically bounces back up the stairs like she didn't just blow my ex-wife's brains out.

"You're so fucking screwed." Owen grins smugly.

He's right, I am. But I couldn't be happier.

# FIFTY-FOUR

## MASE

WHEN THE BASEMENT door opens again, I drop my head back and stare at the ceiling. I try not to inhale the stench that is down here making it difficult to breathe. The thoughts of Summer joining us again makes me want to wrap my hands around her slender throat and throttle her while I fuck her. Although, given her current predicament, that's currently off the table.

The heavy sound of shoes hitting the stone stairs has me lifting my head to face the entrance.

Luca Varros stands in all his glory, and I swallow the ball of dread rising in my throat. The man screams danger, and the darkness inside him isn't just of a sexual nature. Nope, the man's soul is coated in the blood of his enemies.

The small baby attached to the front of his chest makes him appear a little more human, and yet I find myself attempting to mask the grimace of him bringing an infant into this hellhole.

The little guy attached to his father kicks his feet out while making soft cooing noises, and the sight is strangely adorable.

He has a mop of thick dark hair and even darker eyes, with drool seeping from his gleeful lips. A cute little guy, even if his father looks like a complete sadist.

Oscar's following behind him, his eyes flaring with panic. "Luca. I'm simply saying the child will end up traumatized. You can't take a baby in there. The first few years of their life are fundamental in their development."

Luca's gaze slices toward Oscar. "Nonsense. It's my son's legacy, of course I can." His face is deadpan, and he stares back at Oscar head-on as if taunting him.

"A legacy of blood and fear. How inapt," he clips back.

"Unlike you O'Connells, I have a reputation to protect, and when my sons supersede me, they will not shrivel under simple torture techniques." His lip curls, like he tasted something disgusting.

"Pass me the axe. I think taking the bitch's head off and displaying it in the staff quarters will be a good deterrent for the maid's continuous advances on me." He holds out his hand toward Owen, and I watch on in horror, unable to fathom if he's being serious or not.

Oscar's eyes dart around the room before he blanches. "You son of a bitch," he snaps, and I remember the story Owen told me of Oscar beheading his brother's ex. Then he throws his arm out. "Fine. Suit your fucking self and traumatize the next generation." He heads back up the stairs. "I'll send the rest of the kids down, shall I? Children's tea party?" he singsongs in a tone that I don't think he uses that often, if at all.

Luca's nostrils flare, and he tilts his head up toward the stairs. "O'Connell, don't you dare!" he bellows, and the deep sound echoes off the stone walls. "My wife will have my balls in a vise if the children see down here. This little guy won't remember a damn thing, will you, Julian?" he whispers, patting the baby's stomach, then follows Oscar back up the stairs. The moment the door is closed again, I breathe a sigh of relief.

"Did that just fucking happen?" I ask Owen, and he bursts into a fit of laughter.

"It sure fucking did. I don't know what I'm more surprised at, Oscar handing Luca his ass or the fact Luca is terrified of his wife."

"Your friends are fucked up," I tell him.

"I know." Tilting his head toward me, he smiles broadly. "Now, what do you want to use on this fucker?" He kicks a foot out at Andrew.

"Definitely the axe." I grin back.

# FIFTY-FIVE

**MASE**

AFTER SPENDING hours torturing Andrew and Hugh, we finally put the fuckers down. There's only so much chopping off limbs after burning off their skin with a blowtorch you can do without them no longer feeling it. Luca suggested dragging it out for days, weeks even, allowing them to recuperate and inflict the pain on them all over again, but there's no way I was going to do that. I wanted it over with.

I've a new life to lead, and I intend to start living it.

So as I push through the basement door after slitting their throats and putting them out of their misery, I smile at the way things have turned out.

The weight on my shoulders has dissipated, my head finally free of the torment we've endured. Now it's time to go home to the woman I'm going to spend the rest of my life with and slip between her silky thighs and remind her of just how strong we are together.

———

I purchased the mansion we're living in three weeks ago, and we're slowly making it our home, back in New Jersey away from the dark memories that no longer haunt us but fill us with pride as survivors.

We're safe here, surrounded by our chosen family instead of those forced upon us. Our life and fresh start are with them by our side, and the fact they've embraced Summer so affectionally, like a younger sister, couldn't make me any happier.

My cock is rock hard as I step out of the bathroom and take in the sight before me. Who the hell am I kidding? It's been rock hard since the little display of being a badass she put on in the basement for me. I almost shot my load in the shower but stopped myself; the need to fill her pussy until it overflows with my possession is at the forefront of my mind.

Summer's ass wiggles in the air, and I want nothing more than to mark it. She's on all fours on the edge of the bed, and my mouth waters to taste her. "Fuck, Sum. My cock is dripping for you." I have no choice but to fist it, releasing a steady stream of pre-cum down the head and over my palm, giving me the perfect lubrication.

She's braided her hair just how I like it—innocent looking, but I know otherwise. She's a force to be reckoned with, a spitfire, a woman who is prepared to do anything for her man, for me, including killing another woman, and my cock couldn't be happier about it.

I step up behind her and press a hand into the center of her spine, forcing her to bend so her face is flat on the mattress. Then I bend over her and lick from the top of her spine all the way down and over her asshole, and she reaches out to grip onto the sheets when I push the tip of my tongue into her hole and suck while eating her ass. I slide two fingers into her sopping pussy. "Dirty girl likes having her ass eaten, don't you?"

"Yes. Oh, god, Mase," she pants, and I flick my tongue over her taut skin.

"Ride my face, Sum. Push back and fuck your ass against my face, sweet girl. Show me how much you like it." My fingers plunge in and out of her pussy, and when she pushes back against me, I groan in ecstasy.

"Lick me, Mase," she breathes out. "Lick it."

"Oh, fuck, Sum." I suction my lips over her ass and grip her ass cheek, then roughly deliver a smack to it for emphasis. She continues rocking herself against my face in erotic splendor.

She comes hard. Her pussy convulses around my fingers, and I use the moment to withdraw them, causing her to whine at the loss. I rise onto my knees and position my cock at her entrance. Then I thrust forward, slamming inside her so hard she shifts up the bed, but I quickly grip her hips to hold her, pounding in and out of my woman at a crazed speed.

"Take it, Sum. Take all this cum."

"Yesss," she screeches, and my slit widens, delivering her with the flood of my cum.

"Fucking perfect, Summer," I grunt and thrust forward again, allowing her to milk my cock. "So truly perfect."

# SUMMER

I lie on his chest as he toys with the strands of my braided hair, and I breathe him in.

"Did you just sniff me?" He chuckles, and his chest vibrates with his laughter.

"I love the smell of you." I smile against him. It's a reminder he's here and we're in this together, that he's my protector and savior too.

"Love, huh?" I feel his smile as he speaks, and I nod while the words hang comfortably in the air. Neither of us acknowledges it any further, but we also don't feel the need to. I draw circles on his bare chest with the tip of my finger.

"Are you sure you don't want to find out the sex?" I ask again for the thousandth time.

"Not if you don't," he says. I tilt my head to face him, and his eyes are hooded as he watches me, then his cock stirs to life inside of me.

"You're ready to go again?"

"Always." He grins, and I straddle his hips before rotating mine and bringing his cock back to life. Feeling him thicken inside me is an aphrodisiac. Knowing I have the power over him when it's him who normally holds all the power is something that gets me hot and bothered. It's like he can't get enough of me, and I bask in it.

His thick palm rests on the swell of my stomach.

"Can you suck my nipples while I ride you?" I rasp with each steady sway of my hips.

"Fuck yes," he grunts, and thrusts up inside me as if he's unable to help himself.

When he sits up and tilts his head, I lift my tit to his open mouth. "So good," I moan and throw my head back in pleasure.

"I can't wait for your milk to come in, Summer."

"Yes." I swivel my hips, then lift onto my knees and drop back down. "I want you to lick them, clean me up."

"Fuck yes, I'm going to keep my milky girl clean."

"Holy fuck, Mase." My pussy grips him tightly, our filthy words building the overloading sensations bubbling inside us.

"That's it, beautiful. Milk my cock while I milk your tit."

I freefall.

Closing my eyes, I surrender to the feeling of his consumption.

His love.

Knowing that my life and my children's lives will never know loneliness and fear again. Only security and sanctuary in a loving home.

A beautiful life with a lifetime of his promises.

# EPILOGUE

**SUMMER**

**SIX MONTHS LATER ...**

ENJOYING THE DAY IN BED, I stretch like a cat, a smile on my face. When the door bursts open, I don't even need to raise my head to know it's Mase delivering our little bundles to my side because it's become somewhat of a morning routine.

He wakes with the babies, changes them, then brings them in to be fed. They're five weeks old now, and Mase is constantly on the go with them while I recover from childbirth.

Tatum Finn Campbell was born first, weighing six pounds two ounces, followed by his sister, Avery Gianna Campbell, weighing four pounds six ounces. Their names are a nod to our little family and the people we treasure. Both are healthy, with a small flurry of blond hair on their little heads that make me believe they will take after me. Their bright ocean-colored eyes are the perfect combination of mine and their daddy's.

"They're ready to feed, Momma," Mase declares, walking around the bed, and I delight in the stretch of his T-shirt over his chest.

*Jesus, he looks hot with a baby cradled in each arm.*

I sit up and place a pillow on each side of me, then hold out my arms for Mase to rest the babies down against them.

Straight away, my gaze latches onto their little outfits, both in white rompers; Tatum's reads "Marry" in blue, and Avery's reads "Me" in pink.

My breath hitches, and I turn my teary gaze away from the twins to compose myself, only to witness Mase lowering to his knees, his eyes shimmering much like my own.

"You're my world, holding my world, Summer Campbell. I promise to love you for an eternity. I promise to keep your heart safe in this life and the next. I love you, sweet girl. Will you do me the honor of becoming my wife?"

This man, the very same who declared he would never marry again, is on bended knee, promising me the world without realizing he already has it.

He holds the ring out from his necklace, his mom's ring, and my eyes sting at the significance behind it.

"Yes," I rasp, and emotion clogs my throat.

His hand wraps around my neck, and he pulls me in for a kiss.

A promise of our new beginning.

# OSCAR

My eyes flick over the screen showing the contents of the flash drive belonging to Andrew Bassington, the illegitimate son of Hugh Bassington. He had a talent for hacking; I'll credit him that. However, the people he was dealing with were so out of his league he truly had no idea of the enormity of what he unraveled. Or he has and was enjoying viewing the countless videos of innocent women being abused, raped, and tortured until they were fortunate enough to die of the mistreatment, and sometimes, even then the abuse didn't stop.

My finger twitches over the keyboard; do I do this? Open the door to the apocalypse, knowing the gravity of my actions.

But when the screen changes to the bright eyes of a small boy cowering in terror, I know it's the right move to make.

These human traffickers are about to be discovered, and it will rock the Unholy Savages MC to the very core.

Pre-order:
UNHOLY SAVAGES MC KILLA Book 1.

# MORE?

Would you like to read more of Mase and Summer?
Click on the link below to read some Saintly Sinner and
Innocent Angel messages.

Saintly Sinner and Innocent Angel extra messages.

# ACKNOWLEDGMENTS

**Tee the lady that started it all for me. Thank you for an eternity.**

*I must start with where it all began, TL Swan. When I started reading your books, I never realized I was in a place I needed pulling out of. Your stories brought me back to myself.*

*With your constant support and the network created as 'Cygnet Inkers' I was able to create something I never realized was possible, I genuinely thought I'd had my day. You made me realize tomorrow is just the beginning.*

## SPECIAL MENTION

**To Jo, thank you for being my go-to, for allowing me to randomly drop 'extra' ideas your way and not once do you complain.**

**Thank you for pushing yourself as well as me, in a quest to help me achieve. Knowing I have you behind me, and you're willing to learn anything in order to assist me means the world.**

Jaclyn, I cannot tell you what your friendship and support means to me, but I'll try, having someone in author world can be lonely and you can constantly doubt yourself but having you in my corner always willing to build me up and make me stronger has me extremely grateful for the connection we've built. I'm proud to call you my friend, thank you!

Lilibet, you're amazing! I know you don't believe it, but I believe it enough for the both of us. Thank you for everything you do, you truly help me become a stronger writer and in a world where we're full of self-doubt that is immeasurable. Thank you.

Terra, Debbie and Ann your friendship and support this year has meant so much to me, your messages and check-ins help keep me sane in my crazy BJ head and I wouldn't want it another way.

Terra, I hope you're prepared for what's to come in my next world. Something tells me the messages are going to be wild y'all.

**My Incredible ARC and Street Teams.**

Thank you to my incredible teams. Every post, share, every comment, message you send and video created. I appreciate you.

I'm so thankful to have you on board.

A special shout out to Elsa who always goes above and beyond with her videos.

**My Reckless Readers!**

I absolutely love our reader group and all of you in it. I feel incredibly privileged to have the support you bring my way. Thank you for every post and interaction.

**To my world.**

Boys you are growing up so fast, smashing your own goals while supporting mine. I'm proud of the young men you're becoming. Love you.

**To my hubby, the J in my BJ.**

Johnny, let me know who your favourite is now. Ha ha.

Thank you for helping build our dreams and being a part of living it.

Without you I wouldn't be BJ Alpha. Love you trillions!

**And finally…**

Thank you to each and every reader.

Your support encourages me to write the next and I cannot wait to share with you what's to come.

Love Always

BJ Alpha. X

# ABOUT THE AUTHOR

BJ Alpha lives in the UK with her hubby, two teenage sons and three fur babies.

She loves to write and read about hot, alpha males and feisty females.

Follow me on my social media pages:
Facebook: BJ Alpha
My readers group: BJ's Reckless Readers
Instagram: BJ Alpha

# ALSO BY BJ ALPHA


**SECRETS AND LIES SERIES**

CAL Book 1

CON Book 2

FINN Book 3

BREN Book 4

OSCAR Book 5

CON'S WEDDING NOVELLA

O'CONNELL'S FOREVER


**BORN SERIES**

BORN RECKLESS


**THE BRUTAL DUET**

HIDDEN IN BRUTAL DEVOTION

LOVE IN BRUTAL DEVOTION

**THE BRUTAL DUET PART TWO**

BRUTAL SECRETS

BRUTAL LIES


**STORM ENTERPRISES**

SHAW Book 1

TATE Book 2

OWEN Book 3

REED Book 4

**VEILED IN SERIES**

VEILED IN HATE

**CARRERA FAMILY**

STONE

AZRAEL


**MAFIA DADDIES**

DADDY'S ADDICTION Book 1

POSSESSION Book 2

DECEPTION Book 3

DOMINATION Book 4

UNTAMED Book 5


**UNHOLY SAVAGES MC**

KILLA Book 1

www.ingramcontent.com/pod-product-compliance
Lightning Source LLC
Chambersburg PA
CBHW070747190726
48292CB00002B/441